KAY BOYLE

was born in St Paul, Minnesota, in 1902. She attended the Cincinnati Conservatory of Music and the Ohio Mechanics Institute where she studied architecture. Her first marriage to a Frenchman took her to Europe where she remained for twenty years. Much of that time was spent in Paris where she knew Robert McAlmon, Djuna Barnes, Nancy Cunard, Gertrude Stein, Ernest Walsh, Sylvia Beach, Ezra Pound and James Joyce. Her experiences are recorded in *Being Geniuses Together, 1920-1930* (1968), which she wrote with Robert McAlmon. Kay Boyle returned to America in 1941 and soon afterwards separated from her second husband, Laurence Vail. She then married Joseph von Franckenstein, an Austrian Baron who joined the US Armed Forces in 1943. During the McCarthy era he, then a Foreign Service officer stationed in Germany, was subjected to a Loyalty-Security Hearing—Kay Boyle was one of the charges against him. Although both were cleared of all charges, Kay Boyle was temporarily blacklisted as a writer and her husband lost his Foreign Service job, but was reinstated nine years later.

Kay Boyle has had a distinguished academic career, with posts at numerous American universities, including fellowships at Wesleyan University, Connecticut (1963) and the Radcliffe Institute for Independent Study (1965). She was Professor of English at San Francisco State University from 1963-79, and has received several honorary degrees and been Writer-in-Residence at two universities.

She has written, edited and translated over thirty books including novels, short stories, essays, poetry, and children's books. Her first collection of short stories was published in 1929. Her first novel, *Plagued by the Nightingale* (1931) is published by Virago who also publishes *Year Before Last* (1932) and *My Next Bride* (1934). Kay Boyle was awarded Guggenheim Fellowships in 1934 and 1961 and won O. Henry Awards for the best short story 'Wedding Day' in 1935 and for 'Defeat' in 1941. In the 1960s Kay Boyle was imprisoned for protesting against the Vietnam War. More recently she has been involved in American Civil Rights and anti-war movements and in Amnesty International. She is a member of the American Academy of Arts and Letters. Kay Boyle's most recent works are a collection of essays, *Words That Must Somehow Be Said* (1985) and a collection of new poetry, *This Is Not A Letter* (1985). She has six children and lives in Oakland, California.

YEAR BEFORE LAST

KAY BOYLE

With a New Afterword by
DORIS GRUMBACH

Penguin Books—Virago Press

PENGUIN BOOKS
Viking Penguin Inc., 40 West 23rd Street,
New York, New York 10010, U.S.A.
Penguin Books Ltd, Harmondsworth,
Middlesex, England
Penguin Books Australia Ltd, Ringwood,
Victoria, Australia
Penguin Books Canada Limited, 2801 John Street,
Markham, Ontario, Canada L3R 1B4
Penguin Books (N.Z.) Ltd, 182–190 Wairau Road,
Auckland 10, New Zealand

First published in Great Britain by Faber & Faber Limited 1932
This edition first published in Great Britain by
Virago Press Ltd 1986
Published in Penguin Books 1986

Printed in the United States of America by
R. R. Donnelley & Sons Company, Harrisonburg, Virginia
Set in Meridien

THIS BOOK

IS DEDICATED TO

EMANUEL CARNEVALI

AUTHOR'S NOTE

The characters in this novel are entirely fictitious and have no reference whatsoever to real people, living or dead.

PART I

CHAPTER I

The château he brought her to had been built by a French shoeman at the high mouth of the valley. In the hallway stood Monsieur Simon's own likeness, life-size, in bronze, with one of Ezra's overcoats over his shoulders, and a beret. When they came into the house it was the first thing Hannah saw in the candlelight: the French shoeman's bronze wart on his cheek and the hair water-waved over his head. The bastard, said Martin. We found his papers put away in a drawer, and you know they were after him because he made nothing but paper soles to shoe the French army. You great big patriot you, he said. Martin held his nose. Do you know what he does now? The ghost of him flushes the cabinay-wishbox at any hour of night or day.

The bitch, Mirette, sat down at their heels, waiting, and the other dogs sniffed in the corners of the house, whining through their noses because the place was strange to them. Martin said: It's rotten, the servants cleared out this morning because my cheques hadn't come and left the kitchen in a mess. Would you like a bath?

In the kitchen there were the dishes, some with ends of butter and some with ribbons of cheese-rind on them, and Martin said that to wash them all would mean lighting the stove with the pine-cones and those smooth little eggs of coal. Hannah started in to make the fire in the stove and Martin stood behind her saying it's nice the way the hair grows in the back of your neck. There was a wing of roast left that she put into the water with bread to stew for the dogs, and the three of them stood on the tiles in the kitchen waiting and watching her with their tails waving slowly back and forth in the heat. When she had served it out to them they began slopping it up greedily, and Martin ran around them with a little rag mopping off the floor where the rivers of soup ran out of their mouths. Whenever he came too near, they thrashed their wide tails and growled at him in mock distrust. Do you think they will be devoted to me, said Martin, and bring me my letters every morning?

He was searching about all over the house for clean cloths with which to wipe the dishes, and everywhere he went Hannah could hear his voice talking to her. I am going to read aloud to you while you work, he would say in one room. And I bought you a whole gallon of Chypres this morning, you can simply drown in it. I was going to buy lobster and Pouilly but I had the lousiest bill from the garage. We can always go down to a place called—he was coming downstairs again—called Gorges-des-Loups. Hannah laughed at the way he said it. You'll like it, he said. Cold as ice and the real pink trout, you know.

Have they really had enough, said Martin. Me a family man, what? The funny blue tits under Mirwotte's belly, he said, and he began to wipe the dishes. In the back of their minds, waiting there, were Dilly and Eve. Hannah was uneasy because neither of them could bring themselves to say their names.

I've got Ezra piled this high and all the pages marked, Martin was saying. I used to sit up there on the terrace and scream them aloud to. . . .

He could not speak her name, and Hannah said it for him.

Why did Eve go away, she said. She could see the silky water in the dishpan gathering in suds about her wrists. Martin put down the dish he had been drying, set it carefully on the table.

We liked each other, said Hannah, looking at the water. Eve always seemed to like me very much.

Yes, you were nice as Dilly's wife, said Martin. Or you might do as mine. I'm not so sure about that. But she doesn't like you this way. I can't wait, I told her. Maybe I'll be dead to-morrow or the day after, I told her. And off she went with this idea.

Did she call me a lot of pretty names? said Hannah.

It doesn't matter if she did, he said.

Suddenly the cabinet flushed of itself on the other floor and Martin laughed out loud. Oh, the white people, the white folk, he cried. How I'd like to pinch their little bottoms!

Martin, said Hannah. I'm so glad the servants have gone, and the money not come, because now you must see, now you must know how it is with me.

What a way to go on, said Martin. Will you please say it in this ear, and in this ear, and in this ear.

They sat down together and put their feet in the oven, and Martin said:

I must have been dying, and that was what was happening to me. I was dying, for everything was drying and withering up in me, and whether you came or whether you didn't come didn't matter until you said you were coming. I know that whatever death was in me was only in moments and now I am no longer in despair. The only relief is to be with you and who can say it does not matter as long as we two simply start out together on something, and not too serious about it either. Any interests in common as common as, what? I want the concern with something else again.

Martin jumped up and went into the bathroom, and Hannah could hear the geyser explode and the water running out into the bath. She was becoming lost to herself in a magic of weariness and hunger, listening to the water running and to her own heart going slower and deeper in her body. Martin was back in the kitchen, close to her again, talking and taking himself to pieces bit by bit in his mind.

In Paris I bought five suits and a chamois cape and I lived at the Claridge like I had money, he said. I ate soup and bread and soup and bread in a café for months, yes, for months it was one winter, and sometimes the Claridge people got sorry and let me come and look at the four other suits they were keeping for me and the nice pigskin bags until I could pay the bill. And then Eve came along.

Here the story halted, both of them seeing the arrival of the Scotch aunt. They saw Eve the provider, paying the Claridge, paying the café for soup and bread, proudly and in irritation saying to him: What are you fussing about, or what are you so fussy about, or you're always worrying and fussing about something or other, will this keep you still?

With her head down on the kitchen table in the heat, Hannah could hear the Scotch voice with an echo in it because Eve was deaf. She lay thinking of this, and then the cold blue nose of Mirette came seeking in under her hand. It was always Mirette who would come and bring her the news of what had taken place. In the north when the hens would lay an egg, it would be Mirette who would come running into her with this news, excited and eager, with her long dry teats swinging under her belly. Hannah lifted her head from the table and turned to Martin's voice, and she saw that all the dogs had edged nearer the stove. After them, a long spreading line of water was coming across the kitchen tiles.

That's the bath, said Martin. Come all the way downstairs to fetch you.

He leaped sideways out over the water that lay in a thin widening chain against the wall.

I hear an army, Martin was saying from a long way off. It's one of those lovely baths that comes right up to the ears.

Eve's yellow rags for her face and slivers of soap were left all over the bathroom, the cream she put on her nails and a bath towel striped with rouge. A tube of half-used toothpaste left on the washstand by the bath. Hannah saw it clearly that night when Martin came in and sat in his bath-robe squeezing the sponge out over her head. He sat there sopping it full of water until it was big as a cabbage, and wringing it out thin in his hands.

We must make some promises to each other, he said. We must promise each other never to die and go away, he said. The taste of the soap and water was running into Hannah's mouth. Martin rubbed her face dry with a towel and stuck a point of it in to clean out her ears. Allegiance, he said, to the glory, the pomp, the persistance which drags things out of seeds, bulbs, mould, mildew, and makes them flower. Your neck, he said, is black.

On the warm January morning which followed, Hannah awoke and the first thing she saw in the room all around Martin's bed were the pictures Eve had been painting on the Riviera all winter. She lay looking up at them on the walls where they hung, hard, solid and humorous. They were what Hannah had expected Eve to be after she had read of her flogging Lloyd George with gusto. The strong bleak hills that might have been Ireland, the ditches turned with a strong unshaken hand, the paint rolled off the brush as magnificently as turf heaping the canvas in these few squares that hung around Martin's bed.

Hannah turned her head to the sweet curve of Martin sleeping beside her. Behind him in the window, the sky was as clear as a well, and the milk of the clouds flowed steadily out of the strong teats of the southern wind. The room was tiled in terra cotta like the kitchen, and there was a fireplace in it as wide as the whole house, and in the window the milk of January drained down over the warm flowering trees.

She wanted to lie this way, drenched and drowned in it, with the room conniving, but there was Eve as good as in bed with them. Hannah closed her eyes to the canvasses on the wall, thinking that these moments of coming awake with Martin were a few flowers of edelweiss given to her fresh and colourless with the same cool fierce intention to never fade. But there was Eve as well, between them there on their first morning together: the woman who could go to prison for a thing, who could close her mouth to food and water, and who could bite the torture instruments by which they tried to feed hunger-strikers in British jails. And stand it, the food pumped into her lungs, with anger and not remorse. That was at a time too when she was doing it when there was attached to it no tradition of honour. She was a brave woman, thought Hannah, and where is she now?

She lay thinking of Eve, and how when they let her out of prison she bought a red wig and burned British churches. Eve had been very dexterous at getting in and getting out of small windows. She was tough as a bean. And with all this pride in her, Hannah knew she could be demanding of everyone who passed her in the street an admiration for her hard British face. The room where Eve had slept on the other side of the château, was charmed by a little pink lamp that burned all night so that Eve would not be afraid. Sitting up all over Eve's bed was a grand collection of bisque dolls in satin dresses. She had been half-killed for suffrage for women, but she was irritated to sit out in a café with a woman alone, or to walk into a restaurant even with another woman. But she had led a single, virgin life. Because of her suspicions of what men might be after, she had never given in.

One night in Paris she had stood up from her table on the sidewalk, laughing and calling out to Dilly and Hannah who were walking by.

Come and meet my nephew, she was calling out.

She was sitting very happy with Martin having a drink on the sidewalk. Hannah and Dilly sat down, and this was the first time they had met Martin, and he was dark and excitable and tipsy from wine. He was wearing his chamois cape over his shoulders, and his eyes were filled with love. Hannah sat and watched him at the table, and she was thinking that she had never seen such beauty and that her own youth and life had dried in her and withered away.

Eve was deaf, and she had turned her eyes away from their voices and sat there smiling, as if suspecting something were in the wind. Smiling with her eyes centred tight and bitter behind her glasses. Surely, it must have been written on my own face, thought Hannah, that nothing at all mattered after then. In a little while Dilly left the table and Hannah watched him walking out tall and angular to the urinal in the street. She and Martin picked up their glasses at the same moment, and while they were drinking their eyes crossed and Martin said:

Who is Dilly?

Dilly is my husband, said Hannah.

Martin's hand was lying near her on the table, and every pore of his skin was curious and erect with life.

Everything I have been saying, said Martin, is true even though drink leaves me no simple mind, and sometimes I think it leaves little pride either. For the sake of knowing how the honesties of people lie I destroy things that might have charm to them. Whether it is pride or chastity or any of those qualities which in themselves ask homage.

Homage, said Eve suddenly through her nose.

Homage! He gets it from every pair of beautiful eyes he meets! All along, said Eve, looking at Hannah, for all of your sweet shy ways, young woman, all along I suspected you had a bit of the other thing in you that would give your dull husband a pain in the heart one of these days.

She was piling up moment after moment of neglect: chairs Dilly had not pulled out for her, cakes Hannah had passed first to other ladies at tea, cognacs no delicately bred English girl would take in public.

What the hell are you talking about? said Martin to her. His nose had suddenly turned white and thin and the beauty had fled from him. Eve sat laughing in her bosom.

Blarney! she said. BLARNEY! She sat screaming it at him. Blarney. BLARNEY. Her earrings leapt and quivered in agitation, and suddenly aware of them shaking in the lobes of her ears, she leaned sharply forward and with a flick of her fingers snapped one of Hannah's green earhoops under the table.

There, she said. Just there lies the entire difference between us. My earrings are of jade. She shook her head sideways at Hannah, wagging her fine earrings and exposing her snug little ears. JADE, she said. D'ye understand that? None of this cheap frip-frap. You would wear painted celluloid, wouldn't you? The cheapness of it! God knows, she said, God knows what Martin is doing sitting here with this sort of run that's so alien to him!

She was smiling very sweetly, directly and sweetly at Hannah, with only the quivering of her short upper lip betraying her.

Martin with the likes of you! she said.

Martin sat looking at her, as cold and white as if he had died.

What in hell is eating you? he said.

CHAPTER II

In the autumn the leaves fall, and people who are ill feel their courage and strength shed from them. All those days in Paris, this thought must have lain heavy on Eve's mind. She must see Hannah and Dilly off to Le Havre together again, and herself gone south with Martin, and then her Scotch heart would thaw again to them all.

She was careful, thought Hannah as she lay beside Martin, never to leave us alone together. When I went back to Le Havre I had nothing at all left of Martin except a little blue flower made out of glass.

She thought of the place near Le Havre that was known to her as well as her own hands: every ditch and slope, and where the earth was sandy and where it ripened into loam. She thought of all that there would be to do that spring for it, where to put in the peas this year, and where the radishes, and where the long blossoming eels of beets. It was all these things talked out and understood between herself and Dilly that had been keeping her with him so long. The bed she had bought cheap and scoured of bed-bugs, and the china lamp and a chest on four legs that the worms were at.

She thought of the snow beginning to fall on that last morning as she went up the little street between the old houses, and the pump in the square frozen tight and covered with a thick curly glacier of ice. In this place there was never any change in the winter, and the cold coming day after day was a forlorn thing closing the roads off into solid rancid corners of the country. When it broke, there was the hard impersonal wooing of the animals to be begun again, for it was only the dogs who could come into the house all year and keep themselves established.

Dilly had gone off for two weeks to Lyons to find an electrical machine for his company. Every morning when he was gone she would get up in the cold as usual to make the fires, and when she would see herself in the glass, her long thin face and her eyes burning out of her head, she would say out aloud: This isn't the way you get tuberculosis. The black would stay in her hands, lie persistently in her fingers, determined to remain there forever, and she would say to every mirror: Dilly, Dilly, Dilly, Dilly, Dilly, Dilly, Dilly, I don't want to die.

Every night she had a feeling that she would never see Dilly in this place again, in spite of his cards saying he would be back in four days, or five days, and the picture of the rivers at Lyons running in two directions on the other side. And on the last evening there was a telegram from Martin, in the south, saying:

I cannot be any longer without you. Or why should I make out any longer without you. The day after to-morrow or the next day I may be dead.

On the last morning she went up the Montivilliers road to the post office where there was a fire in the stove. The three dogs followed her in and sat down sighing near the fire, already impatient with the time she was going to take. She sent away two telegrams and went out into the cold again with the dogs shouldering at her knees. She went off to say good-bye to the butcher and to the lady whose face she could remember so clearly like a little wren's. She said she was going south for the worst months. In them even there was suspicion in their faces. You'll get rid of that cough, they said. Yes, that's why. That's why I'm going, she said looking away from them. Outside the dogs were racing back and forth in the street, taking quick nips out of the drifts of snow. She thought of them on the Promenade des Anglais, maybe. It's going to be too swell for us, she was thinking.

The clarity of that night which streamed past the windows of the train was never repeated. It was so beautiful that there was no need for sleep, but Paris on the January morning which followed was a thing to be defeated, to be stepped on and despised. The pavements streamed with rains as foul as if the sewers had disgorged them, and the streets were to be walked over in disdain with a bellyful of hot coffee and pride. It was the dogs' terrible despair that kept up her arrogance. She hadn't a kind word for them because of their cringing ways in the city, and she chided them for trailing their tails after them in disgrace.

Here is your capital, she said to them as if they were responsible for it.

After lunch she walked them up the Champs Elysées in the little pieces of sun that had begun to appear. It was then she began to see in the eyes of other people that her short fur coat went up in wings on her shoulders and came in too tight at the waist. She took the dogs to their Arc de Triomphe, and they cowered under it as if she had beaten them sore. The city was no success whatever for them, and they were grateful to get into the train at night and lie as quiet as badgers under the seat.

When it was day again they all saw what had happened to the country. It had begun to go smooth with idleness, so unlike the north, with no crops prepared, but with warm currents of tufted grass and deep islands of shrubs, and even a few little olive trees. There were many fancy little trees, twisted as if they had been taken out of glass jars with a fork, and everywhere the soft flowing country broken, tossed-up, dammed and bursting over rocks, rushing up in high peeling waves.

And then the awful, the arid waste began to set in. The mountains were as bare as bones knuckling the sky, and the sky cracking in two like a shell with the heat. The only thing Hannah knew of the south was from reading of it on bill-posters on the cold walls of Le Havre, that there was a battle of flowers and of leaves a yard wide and strong as silk. But here it was as if they had gone beyond all vegetation, into the heart of a crater, into the dry burning centre that had been stripped clean by fire. To be the first people here, there would have been some meaning to it: here with the dogs, building a wall out of the stones that lay there bleaker than skulls.

Suddenly the man travelling across from Hannah in the wooden wagon began talking to her as if he had taken a drink; speaking to her of the difference in the country where they were, a fellow with no money going back to his people who still called the place Neetsa, as if they had never given in to the French. He was going back to work in the south again after Dijon, and as they went deeper and deeper into his country he took off his scarf from around his neck, and his vest off, and changed his wool socks for cotton ones, sitting for a little while in the heat of the wooden car with his feet bare and his toes uncurling in the sun. He was suddenly drunk in the boxed heat of the wagon, talking to her about the French Senate and saying that among themselves they were like enemies for the war there was in their spirits, one from the south, and another from Sotteville, maybe, with those different temperatures in them to make up the heat for a nation. Auvergnats: at their hands he must have suffered, thought Hannah, trying as he would have to cheat them in his bastard-Italian way. Maybe he had been done in by them, and exploited; anyway he had lived poorly when he worked for a company of them in Dijon, and now he was going back to the wealth of the south.

He satisfied it to himself by saying that the human things that he had in him were too good for the north. He had a black conceited face, but in spite of his small suspicious eyes he insisted that the north had failed him because he had gone there with his southern nonchalance and gaiety, and the north had no time for these human things.

Out of the window he saw Cannes, and he stood up as if the sacrament were passing. Great stalks of flowering marble and the false deep sea. Hannah put her hands over the worn edges of her pockets, thinking that if she could step off with leather boxes after her she would be a pride to Martin. There was no place for her to put away the woollen gloves that were too warm to wear in the heat, so she left them stuck down in the corner of the wagon and walked off the train.

Whether Eve would be there too or not, she didn't know, but in a minute she saw Martin's face coming down the platform smiling among all the other faces under his hat. What? he said. You and the dogs looking awfully—he took her arm—serious. They didn't know if they were to kiss each other or if they were to shake hands. She was thinking she did not know him in the least. What? he said. We'll have cocktails up here. His skin was so beautiful.

Martin, she said. How are you? His lashes were as thick as tar turned up to his brows.

Like a million, he said. Look at me. I've gained three kilos. I'm awfully smart.

They went over the hot square from the station, and Mirette squatted down to water the cobbles and the two other dogs nosed back and forth at the lamp-posts and lifted their legs.

We'll go home after and bath and dress, said Martin.

Martin, you're beautiful, said Hannah.

They sat staring at each other over the table in the café. Martin put down his glass.

I'm fine, he said. I've got another five years to live.

The dogs had turned suddenly to summer, beginning to snap lazily under the table at the flies.

CHAPTER III

Martin had been born in Cuba of Irish people, his father having been a coffee planter there. This could explain a part of him to Hannah, his black hair and his rich black eyes, but for the most of him there was no explanation. The two faces that were set inside one frame on his chimney-piece were his people behind him. But they were never the authors of his grace or vehemence. His mother's face was an Irishwoman's, with a hand-made lace collar-piece coming up high under the lobes of her ears. Hannah could see the whalebonings in it that encased her, and the hard little wreath of fair hair set on her brow. Her head was inclined, as if fondly, upon her husband's shoulder, but her eyes looked out of the picture winsomely aware of the man taking their picture. The husband had long silky dark moustaches and a high pure brow like Martin's with soft hair falling two ways upon his forehead. These were Martin's people who were dead.

Suddenly Martin woke up and looked at her as though she were a stranger.

It's me, said Hannah.

I don't believe it, said Martin. In a minute, if I'm not careful, he said, I'm going to cry.

Ah, don't, said Hannah. She was kissing him into life again. I'm going to get you some breakfast, she said.

You can't leave me, said Martin. He looked at her. My God, he said, I forgot to give you any supper last night. I forgot, didn't I? he said. I had two cocktails and then I forgot all about it.

It didn't matter, said Hannah.

Wait, said Martin. The cheques will come to-day and we'll have a celebration. We'll have langouste, and birds on toast, and three kinds of wine.

Now I'll get you some breakfast, said Hannah.

There's usually a can of milk and a bottle of cream, said Martin, somewhere outside the door.

Hannah went out alone through the tall black rooms, down the hall and the wide stairs of the château. Cigarette stubs and cold ashes in the chimneys; the odorous cold rooms shuttered away from the sun. The light struck her eyes like the side of a hand as she stepped out into the garden. Everything here grew in a dry wild confusion, and a pail of papers and refuse was standing by the gate.

The mail was in the box and the milkcan was empty. A bill for five hundred francs was thrust in under the lid. She sat down, wondering, in the miraculous warm sunlight. All about her was the confusion of the plants and mosses, and the sight of this in her own cold bitter world would have set her anger aflame. But here she sat at peace with the wondrous tide of warmth breaking over her. Here something shiftless may become of me, she thought. Where it is harder you do not give in. If they stole or cheated me here, it wouldn't bring out the gooseflesh on me. It would leave me warm and wondering if it mattered at all. Where it is black as iceland, you take the six months of midnight and the small pea-green sun, what there is of it, but if that came here it would break their hearts. They would be deceived by a God in whom their faith had flowered.

Here she saw the three dogs nosing out of the doorway of the château, blinking and smiling at her in the brilliant light. She thought of how the dogs used to shinny uneasily along the edge of winter, sniffing in the garden at the old rat-holes to fill in the time. They were uneasy and restless in the first cold early darkness, pacing along it and turning listlessly after smells. Coming in finally up the steps to the fire, to sit down beside it and work at pulling the burrs out of each other's coats.

Here if the winter came it would betray them all. She saw the water lying like an idle snake coiled in the warm stone fountain, and she thought of the springs that bubbled up in the streets in the north in the summer. But in winter, now in January, they lay spitting and snarling, to be got at with an axe. Hacked and chopped at, the same water that in springtime ran out over the buckets, slap, slap into the house like a bare foot on the floor.

My love, said Martin out the window. Look at her. Sitting on her backside in the middle of the garden.

He wore a yellow silk dressing-gown, and standing in the sun with the shutters thrown back he began to sing.

That's beautiful, said Hannah when he had finished. I've never heard anything quite so beautiful.

I know, said Martin. He gave a little dance. Are the envelopes with the cheques in them in the mailbox? he said.

I'll bring you the letters, said Hannah. There's an enormous looking bill in the milkcan.

How silly, said Martin. Hold up the letters so I can see. Of course! he cried out. They're there!

I want to kiss you, said Hannah. So many people write to you!

I'm a great editor, said Martin. I'm a rich man. I'm a wealthy young aviator who got gassed in the war.

Did it hurt you when they gassed you, Martin? said Hannah.

No, said Martin. What do you mean? It gave me a pension. Now we can go to Cannes and buy everything we like.

In the market place there was so much that they had their arms filled with it: salads and carrots, and bouquets of white turnips, and birds with sprays of feather on their brows. Even there in the fresh market place in the afternoon the high sweet smell of ripe game was already clinging to their feathers. Here everything was in season at the same moment: grape fruit and honey—melon and peaches running with juices that anywhere else come once in the year.

Here too in a shop were boxes with American labels on them: corn on the ear and tins of baked beans. Martin pointed to them with his stick, three and four at a time to the salesman. And out of the great silence hollowed in Hannah for the sound of English, from the deafness of years turned French in the cold, came the young salesman's voice saying righto, or right you are, sir. That singing servile speech made her blood flow in comfort in her body, and she touched Martin here and there on his sleeve or his shoulder, touching the rough cloth of his coat to know that he was real.

The bill in this place was so much that Hannah went over the numbers again with the salesman. She was thinking in shame that the price of it was more than Dilly was paid in a week's time. Coming home seven times over on a bicycle at night on the foul road from Le Havre into the country. Here what they spent in jars of stuffed olives and in bacon sliced thin was what Dilly got up in the cold for one morning after another for a week of work.

They drank their pernods by the harbour on a glass terrace that was filled with *Carmen* sung strongly from some foreign city. Whatever she did with Martin was carved separate and clear. The air was as perishable as glass, and the sky was another colour. Whatever words he spoke made her thoughts spring up like wild winds in her. She could feel the dark cool wings of love rushing through her heart.

Without Martin, she thought, I could not sustain it. Without Martin, the air has no flavour. Without Martin, who is an honest curse on all the nostalgias of ambition, who is a loud word of joy, who is my love with doe's eyes. She sat drinking the strong drink down and watching him as he talked, harking to his voice in a happiness as speechless as her mouth. Dilly and Eve were somewhere else in sorrow. There was no place for them. Dilly and the question of him she put behind the pernod, behind the café glass where he stood in the north looking into the warm café and buttoning his coat up against the weather. What must she feel for this poor man, for this Frenchman left to his own country, for Dilly whose wife, whose wife had gone deeper, farther, into the rich, hot south? My God, Dilly, now you're rid of her! What a bitch you had three years in your blood! What a weak thing her fidelity was if it came to this at last.

She sat close to Martin, with the pink wax angel he had bought spreading its tinsel wings in her hand. She looked into the angel's eyes, and the pernod slowly caressed her. Dilly and Eve were somewhere else, and she had no thought for them. She sat looking at her wax doll as purely as though she had ascended serene and blameless to this heaven.

Martin, she whispered, I am drunk with heaven.

And Dilly's face outside in the north looked in at them. Well, have it then, Dilly! Have it if you must: a well of pity, a sink of pity, a bog of pity, a slime of it! Poor Dilly deserted by his lean young mouth-upon-mouth, tongue-upon-teeth, poor Dilly, poor fellow, how to explain that his wife—Suddenly Hannah pressed her nails sharply into Martin's palm.

From his father, Martin had learned that the taste of coffee is better found in the dry bean of it. If you break the hard shell with your teeth you find the real flavour as rich and oily as its smell. When they came out of the café, they embraced under a budding medlar tree in the gardens, and Hannah said: I forgot the coffee. The night had come down all about them, black and beautiful, and lights were shining out in the streets.

The first shop they went into Martin bought her a dozen pairs of silk stockings and put a little yellow hat on her head.

You make everything beautiful, he said. He turned and looked at the shop girl. I'd like a pound of coffee, he said.

I'm so sorry, you'll have to get it next door, said the shop girl.

In the shop next door, Martin put a gleaming brown bean of coffee in his mouth.

I'm going to write poetry all night, he said to Hannah. Give me a pound or a kilo, he said. Hannah, I'm in love with you. It's roasted exactly as it should be. You won't see anything of me until morning. I'll come back to you when I've written an entire book of poems.

Suddenly he put his handkerchief to his mouth. With his other hand he motioned to Hannah behind his cough. And then he went out into the car. When she had paid for the coffee and came out to him, he was sitting still behind the wheel.

It's all right, he said. I was scared for a minute. When I chewed that coffee bean it stuck in my throat and choked me like the real thing. For a second I thought I was going to. He started the car. Listen, he said. We'd better talk about it now if ever. If it happens, the first thing you must do is to get a swallow of this stuff down me.

Oh, Martin, cried Hannah, it's too beautiful! Turn and look at the lights of Cannes! They're hanging like earrings all the way to your shoulder!

Listen, said Martin.

You have nothing to say to me! cried Hannah. Look at Grasse ahead like a flight of geese with their tail-lights lit!

Listen, said Martin. We'd better settle this now. I can't speak when it gets me. If I can't get flat at once, it goes at a great rate and that gets me weak. So I just lie down with a spoonful of this in me, and that cuts it short.

Will you shut up, Martin? said Hannah. She put her hands up over her ears.

Listen to me, said Martin. That thickens the blood and gives you time to get the doctor to stick something into me. Once in Scotland Eve had to walk seven miles for a doctor. You see what I've let you in for, he said.

Will you keep quiet now? said Hannah. There's not a word of truth in what you're saying. Will you look at your château ahead which is your own home to you, and stop lying to me? she said with the little wax angel melting soft in her hand.

CHAPTER IV

The restaurant blazed as they walked into it, slightly drunk, looking about and looking at each other in admiration. Hannah saw that three women at least had glanced at the mirror and settled their hats on their heads because Martin had walked into the room.

At the other tables people were sitting as if sick of their own faces and of each other, and there was even illness in this mountain town. This was strange to Hannah and Martin and they turned their heads away from the few sick men eating lunch with little blankets laid over their knees and coughing behind their hands.

There's no way to keep them from making a show of it, said Martin. Public exhibitions of the agony which is death in all these towns. It would be nice to be away somewhere else, he said. As for me, I still have time.

They began their lunch with slices of sausage off a great twist of it, with the Italian proprietor slicing it off before them on a plank. The three dogs were of great interest to the Italian, and he put his hand with the close gold rings and gems on his fingers upon their brows and looked into their faces. He knew that to be here in a restaurant was not right for three such big shaggy animals who belonged to the hills.

Hannah was thinking it was a good thing the dogs were learning to be patient and not to yawn aloud in public places, but now the sympathy of the little Italian flattered them so that they were filled with their own importance and began wrangling amongst themselves under the table, with their voices yaw-yawing, and their teeth clicking aloud as they played. When the Italian had great crocks of soup brought out and put on the floor before them, Mirette became bold enough to lift her muzzle to the table and lay it on Hannah's hand. She stood this way, watching every mouthful they ate, and listening to them, with the cool blasts from her nose blowing the cigarette ashes across the cloth.

Here you are very far from the north, said Martin. Put suddenly in the sun with wine poured into you and everything insisting you must put on another skin.

Everything is very gaudy here, said Hannah. Do you know there is no need for a thing like Christmas even. In the north it must be because there is no other kind of wealth at all that there is Christmas, a sign for glass bells and elegance. Sometimes, do you know, Martin, the cold would refuse to be bought, refuse to be thwarted, and then we would put music on because the bed would be too cold to get into, and we would dance all night to the music. It was just a dance for warmth, there was no joy to it. Dilly would go dancing about on his feet with his face set, jogging steadily about the room all night, stopping to drink rum out of a cup every now and then, until he would slide under the stove where the fire had gone out.

Until they got after us with the *gardes champêtres* to fine us unless we kept the gramophone still. All down the road they were angry. They put an end to it, and they must have sat home in satisfaction, sitting behind their windows holding their cold hands in their laps, satisfied, and thinking: who shall we be after now? Turning their thoughts in their heads and their lean noses sniffing the scent: who shall we be after now?

The Italian proprietor was smiling at them, and when they smiled he said: You must come back when you are finished into what was his own place, and see his dogs as well. In the back of the restaurant, in a garden, was a runway with his dogs in it. They stood swinging their tails and pressing their moist noses through the little round holes of the wire. They were nice silky fellows, and when Mirette saw them she turned away in depression and sat down in a corner of the yard. There she averted her head from the sight of their beautiful bodies.

But Hannah's two other dogs walked straight up to the wire with their tails held high and their mouths snapped tight, but smiling. They were so happy to be making friends that their ribs swelled out as if their hearts were bursting. Their great heavy tails smashed back and forth in the sunlight, and one of the yellow Italian dogs began to whimper in fine whistling cries through his nose.

The sun was as warm as rain flowing over the backs of Hannah's hands and across her neck, out over the grass that here in January was bright green between the stretches of mud in the yard. The two dogs stood quiet before the sudden agitation of the Italian's dogs who were leaping back and forth on the other side of the wire. Suddenly, one of Hannah's dogs lifted his leg and quietly watered the yellow strangers—but absently, for he had lost interest, and it was of no real importance to him whether he insulted them or not. Then he crossed the yard and sat down near the bitch, Mirette, who had never turned her head. There he set to licking his own parts, quietly, tenderly, and with the greatest care.

The Italian and Martin had no French or no Italian to get on with, but still they stood talking together in the yard. Sometimes Martin would ask Hannah for the French words he wanted, looking directly at her with no recognition in his eyes, thinking only of the words he wanted to say. Then, said the Italian, you must come back and have something to drink with me. Back in the restaurant the two men began to smell at the corks of brandy and made signs at each other about the dates on the bottles.

When Martin had taken three little glasses of

brandy with the proprietor, he began to dance gently with his hands in the pockets of his grey trousers, began to dance gently through the restaurant, skipping before his own reflection that was skipping before him in the same way in the glass. The Italian sat smiling at the table, sipping at his brandy and beating his foot on the floor with satisfaction that there was someone at last who had time for all this. He himself liked to sit still, not taking commerce to heart, but there were not many people who came through the town who would linger a long while and drink.

Presently the proprietor's wife came in and watched Martin, who had begun to thumb his nose at himself as he danced. She spoke in Italian to her husband, saying that the place would have to be cleared up and out for any English people who might come in for their tea. So Martin and Hannah said good-bye and went off with the dogs in the car down the road to Cannes, over the white Italian road that was filled with deep gulfs of shade.

When they were still deep in the countryside, Martin stopped the car and they got out and sat down in the shade with the lace-handkerchief flowers opening out all around them in the grass. Below them in the valley they could see a red plaster house, and workmen busy on the roof of it, and in the garden a woman and a little boy, very small, walking out and working in the sun among the short roses that would later be going to the perfume factories in Grasse.

On this afternoon, Hannah could see Martin's eyes scorning to take any notice of the handwritings on the letters she had put in her bag and forgotten to open. She slit the envelopes with her finger, seeing Martin's eyes turned off, refusing to show any interest in who was writing to her.

When are you going to give up letters and realize? he said suddenly. He threw his cigarette away in irritation.

What part of your life or your vanity or what is it that you must be having letters every day from everywhere? he said. Can't you get over the past, or what is the matter with you that you can't leave your husband alone, for instance? Even if I have friends, there's nothing I can find to say every day in a letter to them.

As for Dilly, said Hannah, there are some things, there are a few things still to be settled.

Every time Hannah spoke Dilly's name, she saw the dogs lift the ends of their ears and listen for him.

He doesn't know how he is to write to his mother to tell her about me, she said. I had to send him a letter for his mother and one for Tante Dominique with his name to them for him to copy out. He is unhappy, too; he is unhappy because there is no one, for example, who knows how to starch his collars the way he likes them.

Don't tell me, cried Martin in derision, that Dilly wears starched——!

But all collars must be a little starched, said

Hannah, even soft collars, just dipped somewhat.

Even the kind you turned on the shirts for me, said Martin.

Yes, all collars somewhat.

Martin sat staring down into the valley, turning his face in anger against her to where the woman and the child were out working, very small, among the stiff rosettes of the trees. Mirette was idly chewing a grass blade and one of the other dogs pursued, in slow sudden leaps, a cricket that was escaping down the field.

I don't believe you, said Martin. He stopped in fury to light his cigarette. Now you are beginning to lie to me, he said. I have called you honest, the only honest woman I ever met, and you're far from that. You're far from the wife down there who goes simply out into the garden and works for someone she loves with no bit of the past hanging over her and no remorse in her making her heart a double thing.

At his words, the tears began to fall down Hannah's face and she put the letters into his lap.

Here they are, she said. They are yours to do as you wish with them.

Mine! cried Martin in anger. Mine, are they? Don't blame them on me. I've given up Eve, he said. I don't know where she is even. Don't blame your letters on me when I at least have had the courage to cut off with the past!

In his anger the light of his cigarette had expired, but he did not see.

CHAPTER V

But when there was peace in his heart, it was when the window at night stood open, filled with the black tails of trees and with starlight. The last of the fire dying in the room set a tide of warmth running out to meet the cool Mediterranean night, and the dogs lay as still as dead men before the hearth.

Hannah, he said, poetry is not a shirt you set aside at night. How can I explain to you. It is a white shadow running behind.

Martin, said Hannah softly in the glowing dark, you're a stranger to me. I've seen you five times in my life, no more.

A white shadow chained to the heels, said Martin. If a shadow had followed Oliver Cromwell, chilling his too arduous blood, the ankles of any girl running the roads of Drogheda might have persuaded his then purified spirit to spare Ireland and immortalize England.

Martin, said Hannah, what kind of a man are you?

I'm Alibi Ike, said Martin. I'm as slick as they make them.

Sometimes it comes into my head, said Martin in the dark, that when my jitney hit the ground, I never came out of it. The nose of it went a mile into the mud, and the motor went through me like an arrow and came out the other side. Could any man have? Did any man survive it? I have an idea, said Martin, that I didn't come out of it at all.

But then if there was someone, let us say, if there was someone like Eve, for instance, who cherished the thought of me, who ate me and drank me and had me for dessert every night, I simply couldn't be extinguished. She said my nephew this and my nephew that and my nephew's a poet and my nephew's an editor, until a couple of other people began to see me, a little bit, not very clearly. And one night when she was alone and extra fond of the dream or the vision she had of me, she stood up and shouted: you must come over and meet my nephew! Hey, hey, she said. And over you came to the table with Dilly. He wasn't the one to see me, he kept looking the other way. And Eve went on talking, making up a nice young man in her mind for you, Hannah, because you were lonely and cold in the heart and too young to keep still.

That isn't the way to speak of love, said Hannah.

How can I tell you, said Martin, that when you spoke to me. Or tell you. How can I explain to you that all the dead men in my veins woke up and surrendered?

I could tell you a lot of things about Eve's nephew, said Martin. He came to a good end at the close of the war. If he hadn't he might have lived to cause a lot of trouble. The truth was never in him. It was always somewhere else, nosing behind him, with its foul nostrils breathing in his ear. One day he got the idea of walking across America with a friend of his, from one water to another. Pacific to Hudson. They dressed themselves up smart in khaki, with leather motoring caps strapped under their chins. They slept six weeks in hayricks or places not so nice as. Working for food from farmers, drawing the fever out of his blood for somebody left behind him.

That isn't the way to speak of love, said Hannah in a cold, still voice.

She wasn't my love, said Martin. They got into Chicago at one in the night, and this nephew of Eve's, with his young man beside him, they walked into the Blackstone Hotel all covered with dust and glory and walked right up to the night clerk at the desk.

I beg your pardon, spoke his villainous tongue, but we want a room and a bath. Can you give us something particularly comfortable?

Indeed I can, said the clerk.

I took off my motoring cap, said Martin, and set it down, careless like, on the desk. We wrote our names in the elegant book, and I said:

Is the hotel garage open, or shall I try that one just down the street?

If your car's not too big, there's room enough in our garage, sir, said the night clerk.

It's a touring Pierce Arrow, said I with modesty.

In that case, said the clerk, you had better drive down to the other one. I'm sorry there's not a bellhop on duty, or I'd send him along to show you the way.

My young man was shy of the story. He stood before the desk and the night clerk, looking to me for aid. Go up to your bed, my dear, I said to him. I'll join you at once as soon as I've put the car away. Turn down the sheets for me. I'll bear in the luggage. But luggage there was none. I had to walk in to the lobby again and sing out good-night to the clerk at the desk and wave him my hand, and swing in my tracks to smile at him. I'll have to buy a new tyre to-morrow morning, I said. If you could send up the name of a reputable shop, with breakfast rather early.

The bed, said Martin, was as fresh as dawn. I'd seen too many. I was tired of being a cold man seeking warmth. My heart was quiet enough, and the trees, for once. Sharing the bed of horses and cows had suited me badly.

In the morning, said Martin, do you know what we did? We telephoned downstairs for breakfast, after our bath. I remember it very clearly. We began with grape-fruit. And then we had omelette, and fried potatoes, and bacon, and lamb chops, and hot biscuits, and coffee.

You were awfully greedy, said Hannah.

And we had two kinds of jam, Martin said. We had no money of any kind in our pockets, but we dressed up in our motoring khaki clothes and took the elevattor downstairs as easy as fine gentlemen.

What will you do? said my young friend in a whisper. His teeth, poor child, were shaking in his head. He would rather have stayed with the farmer's daughter who had fallen in love with him the night we spent in their garret in some state or other.

I'm going to buy a new rear tyre for the Pierce, I said. Will you send up a boy for the bags? said I to the day clerk who had never laid eyes on us. I threw down the key of the bedroom on the counter. I'm going to get our car out of the garage. Will you get our bill ready?

And then we walked out of the door together, arm in arm went down the street, my young friend and myself, and turned the corner. On Michigan Boulevard we ran pretty fast.

And another time, said Martin.

Hannah, he said suddenly, do you think I'm not an honest man?

In the dark even, she could see him, a strong gay man, with his eyes turned bold by the words in his mouth.

Ah, but did anything ever happen to you? she said in terror. Martin, did you ever get caught?

Nothing ever happens to me, said Martin.

When he drove the car like a man of ease over the

mountains, you could believe in it. He would swing the car around the high barren roads, with his hand on the wheel as white and wiry as flax. But if ever he stopped the car and started running up the land, the breath and strength were sucked from him.

Nothing ever happens to me, said Martin, beside her. His fingers moved over her face. We'll live high and arrogant as hawks, he said. We'll never stay more than a day and a night in any country. Has it ever come into your head? Would you like? he said, in the warm enveloping room. I've always wanted a child to myself. He added quickly, in shame: but that needs a special power. It needs a special worldly gift that I haven't in me at all. I have a thing that tastes like poetry, but it would furnish no bones for children. You must possess a worldly gift of belief in money or power before you can be a father to a child.

You could give it, said Hannah, the gift of the gab.

CHAPTER VI

They were so alone that a lady driving up to the château, one day, in a car from the station, sent them flying in four directions.

Maybe it's Dilly's mother, said Hannah, when they saw her hat dip under the arch of the stairs.

Maybe it's Eve come back for something or other, said Martin. His face was as white as paper. You can stand in the closet for a minute or two behind the coats until. . . .

Martin skipped down and opened the door, and when he and the lady came past the closet where Hannah stood, she could hear Martin saying:

If you will sit down in the . . . I will call my wife who is. . . . The servants for the moment are. . . .

He closed her away and he came back to Hannah in the closet behind the coats, and he said:

It's an authoress who has some stories to print.

She was sitting there in the room that had been theirs for a long time, smiling at them, with her white hand shaking as she reached the salted almonds out of the dish. A great gold-headed woman, a breasted apocalypse holding the thin cocktail Martin poured out for her up to the light.

I found the address, she said, on the back cover and took a sporting chance that you'd be good enough not to shut the door on me. I have a story or two, she said.

Her flesh was white and shaking from fright, from smoke or liquor. She had a face as round as a doll's, very clear and thick, with no rouge on it. Her hair was real, and smooth and bright, like the skin of an orange. There were a few yellow freckles across her nose and neck.

I took three drinks across from the station, she said, before I came to face you.

She laughed, with her pink, pale mouth tilted up sideways in her face. If she was forty, she looked very young for it.

I didn't know either of you would be such babes, she said, and solemn.

Her name was Lady Vanta. My Lady, Milady, Your Highness, Your Royal.

Everyone who likes me at all, she said, calls me Van. She drank down her cocktail and reached for the almonds. Are you Eve Raeburn? she said.

This is Hannah, my wife, said Martin.

He stood cold and stern by the table, separate and still, as was his way with strangers.

I'm such an old sinner compared to Hannah, said Lady Vanta. Is she as nice as she looks?

The third cocktail sent her sliding on the leather arm-chair under the table, and she too indolent to recover sat with only her white lashes remaining and her hand lifting now and then over the edge to fetch the almonds to her mouth.

I've not had a mouthful since last night. I'm on my way to friends, she said. I'll pick myself up and leave in a moment.

Have lunch with us here then, said Martin.

I'd like it, said Lady Vanta and her face shot up on the other side of the sweating cocktail glass.

Martin looked tenderly at Hannah, with the drink beginning to glow in his dark deep eyes.

We'd better eat here, he said, and not bother to go out.

Down in the garden, the mailbox stood empty at the gate. Another time, and the cheques had not come before their money was gone. Hannah thought of the kitchen, gaping in darkness across the hall.

We'll have one more cocktail all around, she said with her thoughts on the butter, the eggs, the bread that were not. Absent the steak, the side of lamb, the new potatoes. One more drink, she said, and then we'll make up our minds.

Our minds, she thought, our minds, our minds. It was an easier thing by far to listen to Martin's words, to hear his voice declaiming:

There should be written more odes and sonnets to food. Some free verse on the excellencies of the roast served in an entire joint with nobs of half-burnt crusty goodness forming a prow and stern to it. A few lyrics to crisp fried bacon and fresh iced celery and snappy green lettuce.

Stop, stop, cried Lady Vanta, I'm perishing for food!

I'm afraid there's nothing in the house, said Hannah.

I'm afraid we can't eat out, said Martin looking into her face.

We can go to an Italian place, said Hannah. She thought of the owner drinking and tapping his foot on the floor and watching Martin dance. Martin put down his cocktail glass and smiled at her. Two scarlet flowers were blooming in his cheeks.

I'll get my coat, he said, and he went out of the room, swaying a little at the doorway. Hannah could see the hair growing soft and black and tender in his neck.

My lovely poor one, said Lady Vanta's voice suddenly across the room. She had turned her hard yellow eyes to Hannah. Lady Vanta caught her underlip in her teeth and shook her head at Hannah, and for her impertinence Hannah could have slapped her face. But she stood facing the English lady with her glass held up in her hand and her eyes, because she was curious, saying:

Yes, yes, Lady Vanta. This is the way to win me. Yes, yes, go on.

My lovely child, said Lady Vanta, and then she heard Martin's feet returning down the hall and she turned her white face down to the almonds.

Shall we put our hats on? said Hannah. She was busy getting the olive with the end of her tongue out of the glass.

You ride in the back with Lady Vanta, said Martin, and a sorrow fell on her. We haven't far to go.

The coast had been such a deception that Hannah could not countenance it. It was there below them with its pretty, neat villas and its shops displayed by the sea. But once behind it you drove straight into the heart of desolation. Gleaming on the shore below was the cat-white face of Cannes, and behind them the great heedless mountains shouldering one upon the other, with no concern for the time of the year.

And Martin's back rode steadily before them, with his hair as tender as a child's and his grey hat on the side of his head. The sight of him turned the love in Hannah's heart to milk and kindness, and suddenly Lady Vanta leaned over and clutched her hands.

I've heard the whole story of it from someone I've forgotten who, said Lady Vanta. You too, you too, she said, you too. Your life like mine will now be an escape from the scurvy, the stale, the tongues that have gone between so many teeth that lies are as fresh as ice to them. My life is nothing else but getting away from them, and now you, my precious, with the pack at your heels.

Her broad white hands closed tighter and tighter on Hannah.

Talk to me, she said. Tell me everything. I know

you're eating your heart out. You're such a babe, she said. Suddenly she tilted her yellow eyes up in her face as if to keep the tears from falling from them. Take this me back into the unborn again, she said, and give me—give me some kind of prenatal strength. I'm afraid, she said, of the running. I have run so far. I'm afraid of everything the stale scurvy of talk can say about me, finishing me, tracking me down.

As if Martin might be giving ear to their talk, she shook off her anguish and talked clearly and quietly.

Once when I was a little girl, I was walking with my own brother in the public park, in Kensington, and we put our trekking feet square on the tip-end of a male peacock's tail, and every feather came out at once in a piece as if they had been stitched together. The dirty purposeful boots of us smearing and ripping out the what-is-it of peaboy and the feathers of his stricken glory. That's what they do to you, my heart, the best of them, with their dirty mouths that you've loved with your own life's blood, taking the beauty out of you in a piece.

I was at Malta, said Lady Vanta, gripping Hannah to her, and the fishermen there, God love them, had sweet kind children that soothed my heart. My part was to have a new smile for each of them and a sweet or two or what they liked on sticks or twisted in waxed paper. It was all the sport I had in Malta, and my own true love who shared the same bed with me, he wrote me a letter sent by a chasseur, mind you, saying that to be friends with the fishermen's fish was not to be seen with his good red herring. The scurvy of the mouths of my own kind, the filth and the venom. You must take either fishermen or gentlemen, for in the same lifetime the one swallows up the other.

Take this me, she said softly to Hannah. You're so young you can spare a little. My stories, she said, you must tell me what Martin thinks of them. Take this me back into the unborn.

CHAPTER VII

At the table next, there was a bunch of flowers in a vase, red flowers and crocuses like the sun, such as should never have been out at that time of the year.

How nice it would be to take that to someone, said Lady Vanta. To someone sick in bed somewhere, not too sick, of course, but to someone with a touch of colic or a cold in the head.

Martin dipped down the Chianti bottle in its basket. All about them on the cloth, the lunch lay finished in crumbs and empty grape-skins. Martin looked up when he had filled their glasses, and called the Italian proprietor over with his chin.

The lady, he said, would like that bunch of flowers.

He could or he would speak nothing but English in whatever country he was in.

The flowers, he said. He smiled at the Italian. I'll pay you anything you like for them.

Because the proprietor could not understand, Martin jumped up and reached them off the other table. The Italian stood smiling and smoothing his rich olive hands.

Lady Vanta pressed her white face into the bright stiff flowers.

How can I keep sober? she said. Me, out of England, with its fogs still like a noose around my neck. I'm not used to red so red, and yellow breaks my heart. You two, she said, you belong to the south. If I come very close to you, I can warm my hands at the flame.

The south of Ireland, said Martin. A lot of comfort that will give you.

He was such a young man that he had no need for aid or comfort, and a woman asking for it seemed a strange thing. But whenever he opened his lips to smile, a veil of understanding and beauty fell over his features; he lifted his proud face in pride and two black lanterns of wisdom sprang to light in his eyes.

You two, said Lady Vanta. I want you for ever. She looked into their faces with something turned suddenly sharp and canny in the ends of the eyes. Before I go, she said. Just let me say a word about my stories. They may not be your sort of thing, but such sweet things have been said about them. Mr. Eliot wanted one—the longest one—for his magazine, except for the moral side of it. He didn't know if you could, quite, have sailor-boys—I mean, considering the British navy, or the American for that matter—and I couldn't argue with him. I just kept my peace, knowing that somewhere, somehow, there'd be some kind of literary adventure on, and I know I've found it. There's nothing else like you in the world, Martin. Lady Vanta looked sideways at Hannah. *May* I say Martin? she asked. Will you allow me to say Martin and Hannah, too?

Oh, the English! said Martin with his mouth turned up with laughter.

Do you like us, Irishman? said Lady Vanta tossing her yellow head.

It's your reserve I like, said Martin.

It's part of our training, said Lady Vanta stubbornly. Blood and bone to us. We give nothing, nothing, really, to an outsider. Unless, of course, she said eyeing them deeply, unless something has happened to lay our hearts bare.

Martin called out for another bottle of wine.

A half bottle maybe, said Hannah. Martin stopped smiling and looked at her. Then he put his hand into his inside pocket, and brought it out again.

That's true, he said. He smiled at Hannah. I'd forgotten. Maybe a half bottle will do.

A half bottle, said Hannah. She got up and followed the Italian proprietor into the kitchen. In every mirror as she passed, she could see Martin and Lady Vanta sitting side by side on the plush bench, with a forest of smoke set thickly about them. Martin and Lady Vanta, with their hands on the table, fingering the remains and stems of the empty glasses, and talking about the places they had been. As she went through the kitchen door, she saw Martin, the side of his face turned proudly in the glass, turning to Lady Vanta to light her cigarette.

Could I see the dogs again, Signor? she said to the Italian man. He was wiping the soft mantle of dust away from the shoulders of the half bottle of wine. I left my own *cabots* at home to-day, she said.

The Italian walked out into the garden with her, running a little ahead on his small feet, and here and there with the toe of his boot, kicking an empty sardine tin smartly out of the way. At the wire, she took her cigarette-case out of her pocket and opened it before him.

A Milan case, said the Italian. His plump dark forefinger and thumb selected a cigarette from among the others. It's very pretty, he said.

It looks very pretty in France, said Hannah.

All the time in her head the words were turning and twisting of how she was going to ask him, tell him, explain to him without explanation: could you lend me a hundred francs until to-morrow, or could you? Would it put you out in the least if I paid for our lunch at the end of the week, or next year sometime? Or, I forgot my money to-day, I left it home, if I could run swiftly, swift as a hare, a doe, cry aloud as parrot or peacock, spring like an arrow from here to Washington, to Washington, D.C., and back, Signor.

Listen, Signor, said Hannah. She put her hand over the wiring and stroked the dog's blond brow. I wonder if you could or would or if it would put you out to. I wonder if you could cash a cheque?

It would be a pleasure, said the Italian. But I have no cheque, thought Hannah. That was not the right way to say it.

Or better still, she said, or even better, if you could let us pay for the lunch, and the flowers, some other time, to-morrow. I left my pocket-book, she said, where I put it I can't remember. But we'll be in for lunch to-morrow, or the next day, if that would do.

The Italian man was concerned with his dogs, and the spray of hair of one front paw that was twisted in the wire.

Now gently, gently, he said to his beast. Now, calm yourself, my little one. If you pull, it will hurt you. If you stand still, I'll have it free in a moment.

He stood soothing his dog and untwisting the soft fringe of yellow hair.

Now, gently, gently, my little one, he said. The light of the sun ran over his smooth dark foreign hands as they worked at setting the dog free, and his voice was as sweet as a father's speaking on the spring January air. He bent in solace and love over the dog's wild whimpering form, and his warm voice cajoled it. Now, gently, gently, he said, and no harm will come to you.

Even when the dog was free and had leapt away to shake his coat out, the Italian spoke soft words after him. All around the edge of the yard a shadow of afternoon had now begun to fall, and it edged towards them across the sunny soil, deeper and deeper, like a tide of winter night. Hannah felt a shiver through her blood.

If you would be kind enough, she said. She took another cigarette out of her case, and she saw her own hand was shaking.

The Italian wiped off the tips of his fingers in his handkerchief. At each knuckle, the rich oily flesh was bound delicately in as if by a silken band. When he had finished, he turned back to the dogs.

I once had a place as a chef in London, he said. But I'd never do anything like that again because you cannot have your dogs or your family as you like. I knew an Irishman there, an Irish *garçon* to wait on the table. He was as different from the English boys I had as the night from the day. He never went home to sleep when the restaurant closed up in the evening, for one thing. He'd drink down a bottle of whiskey and sleep in my kitchen all night, under the table, or else he'd go out across the court and sleep in the stable in the hay. He was up before anyone else in the morning, singing like a lark. He had the best heart of anyone I ever met out of Italy.

Hannah saw that the Italian's eyes had turned very bright with his tears.

When he was dying, said the Italian man, I took care of him.

The dogs were whining for more of his attention.

They put their paws on the summit of the wire and reached out for love. But the Italian's heart had gone far from them. He stood with the tears on his face, and his eyes looking blindly past to the blade of the winter afternoon travelling across the grass.

He caught the pneumonia, he said. And his lungs filled up on him.

Suddenly he looked at Hannah.

It's a sad thing, he said softly to her, when a young man has to die.

Yes, said Hannah with her eyes upon him, wondering, for such words were strangers to her. Yes, it must be a sad thing, she said.

I took care of him there in the stable, said the Italian. It took my taste for London away from me. It was the streets and the fogs of the city that finished him.

If he could have come down here to the sun, said Hannah. In her mind she was thinking, impatient to be off, of the ride they would take down the clear white road to Cannes.

He was a young man, said the Italian. Not thirty. Young men and death, he said, are not related. When you see them together, they stand out in a crowd.

Suddenly the Italian, seeing that her mind was elsewhere, or in apology, took out his leather purse.

Please, he said. It is a great pleasure. Will you have two hundred, three?

CHAPTER VIII

You were gone a hundred years, said Martin. He sat at the table, looking at her eyes and her earrings and the lipstick on her mouth.

Do you think she was gone such a long time? said Lady Vanta.

And suddenly Hannah's heart was laid waste at the thought that they had been sitting there, side by side in the empty restaurant, the time she had been away. She sat down on the bench beside them and examined Lady Vanta, as if the eyes in her head were Martin's eyes and the British voice were wooing a young man's love. Perhaps this was the type, the sort, the one that would shut like a vice upon Martin's life and not release it. She looked at the small pale ears, and the orange point of hair on the cheek above each ear.

My husband, God bless 'im, Lady Vanta was saying, is the biggest crook on the Continent.

Oh, the English! said Martin, laughing. The reserve that will not down.

Lady Vanta sat between them, a channel of separation, smoking her cigarette deep into her throat and crooning and rocking her laughter.

I read his translation of the *Fleurs du Mal,* said Hannah.

Whatever had happened between Martin and the English lady had closed her out of their interest in each other. Nobody heard her when she spoke or turned an eye upon her.

I read your husband's translation, she said again. She blew a cloud of smoke between their faces. Of Baudelaire.

A rotten one it was, said Lady Vanta. But things are all done by ways and means. And Duke, a friend of my husband's, was reader for a house in London. He put it over. He once sold a book of mine for me, too. Perhaps I put up with him a little for the sake of that. One has to be nice to people, you know. Duke and Phyllis, said Lady Vanta, musing. I wonder if you'd mind, she said in a minute, driving me as far as their door? You'd be such loves, she said, to help me on my way.

Like a sleep-walker Lady Vanta drew on her gloves, buttoned her green coat over, and stood up. Slowly, as if feeling her way through sleep, she walked out of the restaurant with them, with the bunch of flowers over her arm.

We should strew them before us as we go, she said, as though capturing the words slowly on her tongue as they went by. My loves, she said, my loves. She plucked off a scarlet flower-head and tossed the petals down before them. It's like stepping from winter and old age into the heart of spring, she said. My darlings, my lovely ones, when do you go to press, my loves?

You must take note of the fact, said Lady Vanta as she rocked behind them in the car, that Duke, who was my husband's friend, has a bit of tooth off in the front, just in the front, right where a lady would have hit him if she had, in fact right where a lady did.

Her laughter rocked slowly, slowly, as though in a cradle of anguish behind them.

Duke had been in our diggings, said Lady Vanta as they rode, up to the Temple to dine one evening a couple of centuries ago. And after my husband had taken a lady home, Duke hung on like the queer devil he is. The others had cleared off, mind you, everyone, which was all very well until he began knocking off what remained on the table, at the same time removing the rest of his clothing, and coming straight for me. Poor Duke, poor chappie; I'd done a bit of boxing that year and learned amongst other things to fling my weight. This I did neatly and ripped open the knuckle of this.

She swung her broad blanched hand between them.

D'ye know, it took the breath out of him quite as well as that bit of his tooth. The eyes he pulled were quite a show. The truth is, said Lady Vanta, that I've kicked him over most of the Continent until I kicked him into Phyllis's way, and she found him presentable for a couple of more years of it.

He may tell you he's been to the war, said Lady

Vanta with her voice turned sly behind them. But that hobble of Duke's was given him by a better lady than I. I was not in at the death but I saw the run, and the corpse too, poor Duke, after the dogs had been at it. He has to do his work out of England now because so many people have the laugh on him, though they do buy his books from him, blast him. The peeress who unseated him has gone unscathed for the rest of her career. But it's Phyllis who's got the corpse nice and stuffed as it is with high reasons for why it's a writer, and why it's a man, and why it's bloody dead.

The twilight had come down on the hills all about them and Hannah rode in silence beside Martin, with Lady Vanta travelling dreamily behind. Suddenly she cried out, as though something on the roadside had aroused her from sleep.

Ah, here we are, she cried. Here's the house!

Lady Vanta started up and climbed out, leaving the door swinging open behind her. They saw her feeling her way up the path towards the garden gate in the falling darkness. Her voice was crying out in the direction of the windows.

Phyllis! she cried, with a ripple of joy sounding out in her throat. Duke! Phyllis! Come, my darlings! I've some dear, dear friends in the car waiting! Bless you, bless you, she was calling out to them. Bless you, my own hearts.

Martin and Hannah sat still in the car, listening to her words cried out and the response of a man's voice in the early evening. Hannah felt Martin so close to her that his foot touching the brake was her own blood in motion, and yet there was a chasm of silence there between.

Martin, Hannah, they both whispered at the same moment to each other. They looked in terror into each other's faces. At the instant Martin said: You're in love with the Italian man; Hannah said: You have fallen in love with Lady Vanta.

Before them, the lights of the car were eating a soft dusty path through the accumulating dark. And here the claws of cactus and teeth of pine were at them, and the stones that lay about on the slopes were as white and lofty as the moon. Here the stones were so plentiful that they might have dammed all the waters of earth and heaven. There was no wind blowing, but this great wind of night seemed to blow past their faces. There were no longer any voices speaking, and before they could answer each other their hands fled together and their mouths fell upon each other in famine.

PART II

CHAPTER IX

There was only one room in the house that was safe and their own room, and that was the kitchen. At night they came back from wherever they had been and shut the kitchen door and made the fire. The other rooms in the house were filled with dust and darkness. In the kitchen were their books on the table, and the pigeons to pluck, and the new potatoes in their thin white skins.

Rain on Rahoon falls softly, softly falling, said Martin's voice. He held the book up in his hand before him and drank a glass of wine. When he spoke again his voice was quenched and fresh as though after rain. Hannah sat on the other side of the clean timber table, pulling the heads and the stringy tails off the beans, and watching the shape of Martin's mouth saying Love, hear thou how desolate the heart is. If he drank a glass or two of wine before dinner, then he read poetry aloud like a 'cello played sweetly and deeply in the room.

What was it you thought, said Martin suddenly, of the first copy of my magazine when I sent it to you?

It looked very expensive, said Hannah. It had paper as thick as a slice of bread.

It cost a lot of money, said Martin. Eve's money. Sometimes, he said, I think I care more for the magazine than for anything else in life.

With his hand he shielded his face from her for a moment. Then he said in another voice: I had a letter from Eve to-day. She's in Saint-Raphael.

She made you wonder a long time, said Hannah, and to herself her voice seemed bitter. Read me some more poetry, Martin, she said.

Love, hear thou how desolate the heart is, read Martin.

Hannah stood up from the table with the beans gathered in her apron.

What's Eve doing in Saint-Raphael? she said.

Playing in the casino, I suppose, said Martin. A strange sorrow had fallen on his face, and his voice was like another man's speaking.

And why must she come alive now? thought Hannah in impatience. She stood by the stove slicing fresh petals of butter into the smoking pan. Why must she come alive now? What does she want of him, for she was careful to take with her whatever she really wanted when she went away. She didn't forget her pretty printed dresses that look so well in the casino. For all her heartbreak, she didn't leave anything she really wanted behind.

She's had the flu for two weeks, said Martin. That's why she hasn't written.

She left you wondering a long time, said Hannah. Suddenly she felt the anger mounting in her and she slammed their dinner down on the stove.

Everything she had no more use for, thought Hannah in anger, she was careful to leave behind her. The tubes of used-up tooth paste and the slivers of soap, she left them in the bathroom when she went away.

One by one Hannah sliced the onions' crystal hearts into the frying pan.

Even Martin sitting up in bed coughing in the morning, she left behind her. What if I hadn't come on that train or on any other? She'd have left him sitting here with a month of anxiety and sorrow to chasten him for his flighty ways.

She says she thinks the magazine might as well come to an end, said Martin.

Hannah watched the crescents of onion charring.

The bisque dolls with their ruffled skirts and a raincoat in the corner of the closet, she thought. Anything she didn't want any more she was careful to leave behind. From the remnants left you could piece her together, put rouge on her mouth and a book in her hand and watch her skip from under.

Can she bring things to an end? said Hannah in anger. Is she strong enough to write death to this or that before your very eyes?

She paid for the magazine, said Martin.

There's other money in other places, said Hannah, flinging the potatoes into the pan.

Not shaking loose for me nor my obsessions, said Martin. Hannah saw the look of grieving in his face and her heart went soft within her.

If you went over and saw her, she said. If you went over to see her it might change things. If she's lonely it might make her glad.

A wave of pleasure ran up to Martin's eyes and he jumped to his feet and put his arms about her. He stood behind her, holding her back against him in his arms.

It occurred to me too, he said softly, that it might be the best thing to do. I could drive over to Saint-Raphael one day and have lunch with her.

In a moment he turned silent.

She doesn't say anything about you, he said.

Hannah lifted the potatoes out of the pan and let the butter run over them.

There's nothing for her to say about me, said Hannah. I'm the outsider. I'm the dark horse. She couldn't feel any other way.

You're the dark Irish filly, said Martin. He kissed her in the back of the neck. You're the most beautiful woman in the world.

Martin, were you ever in love? said Hannah sternly. He was standing close over the fire with her, watching her draw the pigeons out from the stove.

I was in love once, said Martin close to her. It's a very special feeling.

But I mean before, said Hannah.

Yes, said Martin, when I was seventeen. He danced off from her side and did a few steps with his hands in his grey flannel pockets. I worked in a big laundry, downstairs, underground all the time. I was in love then. And I was in love when I was twenty. I was selling real-estate in Florida then. And when I was twenty-five I was in love with Isadora Duncan because I saw her walk across the street.

And what did Eve do, said Hannah, when you were in love those times?

Eve wasn't there, said Martin. Eve was always in another country.

But didn't you fall in love in Scotland? said Hannah.

Yes, said Martin, I fell in love with my trained nurse when I was sick in the fogs there, and Eve packed up and went away.

The next time you fall in love, said Hannah, I'll go away too.

Eve cried like a Madeleine, said Martin dancing.

I'll cry like Saint Swithin, Hannah said.

Listen, said Martin, and suddenly he sat down at the table and opened his fingers out before him. I want to make you a picture of my life. If you see me as anything else or in any other way, then you must change your mind around, Hannah, and see me as I shape myself to be.

She sat down beside him. In the roasting pan on the timber the bones of the pigeons sizzled and snapped as she carved them in two.

A stream in its bed, said he, never flows direct or quiet from its beginning. It chatters and pauses, turns and twists, it is shallow, and deep, and devious, whatever its source may be. And I am these things, he said with his square white hands open and his face veiled with concern for the truth he was speaking. Although it may alter the respect you have, I am devious. To get where I want, I jump, sink, turn, coil, twist with intention. I do not meet obstacles. I go around.

You're a very young man, said Hannah, mocking his gravity, to know as much as you do.

Even poetry, said Martin as if she must know the bitterest part of him. It is a means to me like any other. If I want to get there, somewhere, anywhere, I do it by devious methods, by poetry or prose.

They sat close to each other at the table, eating bit by bit from the prongs of the same fork.

I want my magazine, said Martin suddenly. He sat close to her, like a child with his spirit sapped by the hours of the day. I want my magazine, Hannah, every month the way it used to be.

You'll have your magazine, said Hannah. It's such a simple matter. You'll see Eve for lunch to-morrow. If you love someone, she said, you can't just put them away.

She saw the open book of poetry lying before her on

the table with Eve's name written in in her slanting English hand. And she turned it quickly over, face down upon the boards.

You put Dilly away, said Martin softly.

Then it's because there was nothing but a couple of sticks and chairs between us, said Hannah. But you can't put it off forever. Some day I'll have to see Dilly too to dispose of the things we shared.

I'd take it hard if you did, said Martin, looking into her face. To-morrow what will you do?

I'll clean house all day like an honest woman, said Hannah. When you come back everything will be shining.

I want, said Martin, sitting close and weary beside her, to be a simple honest man, and I cannot. If I could give up one or the other. But that I cannot. Not you, nor Eve, nor the magazine and what it gives me. I love the best someone out there, beyond, whose name I do not know, wherever he is writing a poem, painting a picture. I love him more than I do you or as much as or else I could relinquish. But I shall, I must have you all. I shall jump, turn, sink, coil, twist with intention. Now you'll have me, now you won't.

He fed her gently, in little pieces, the soft breast of the bird, kissing her mouth as she ate, and saying:

If you will only remain with me, if you will stay by me, Hannah-cool, patient, quiet, possessed, I am yours forever, possessed, if you will have me devious. Only your tears and lamentations for my truth could ever frighten me. If you remain Hannah-beautiful, gambolling, caressing along the brink of what I am, I will always be there for you.

Love, hear thou how desolate the heart is, he said, is not for Dilly. You must never lay eyes on the man again. There are a few other descriptions of myself I might give you if you care to listen. Scamp or scoundrel. Have you any use for them? Bully or wretch. Will those do you? I might think of some others.

No, said Hannah. They won't do at all. Now eat your potatoes and the onions black as your hat.

CHAPTER X

The place was built so near the mountain that in the kitchen the windows shook from the strength of the falling water behind it. The air drove in through the open window solidly and slowly like a team of white horses and stopped against the stove. Martin was up early in the morning darkness, ready before the sun was high for the long drive over the hills. Because his heart was divided in two in his body he had no simple words to say to Hannah. There he sat by the table in his fine grey suit and drank the coffee down.

The flame in the stove was not strong, but it halted and staved off the cold's advance. And the three dogs, seated upright on the tiles, leaned close to it, harking, for some change was in the air. They never turned their eyes from Hannah, as though looking to her to make a sign, and she had no time for their curiosity. She made the toast in silence because of the displeasure in Martin's face.

What in the world will you do all the time I'm away? he said to her with his voice turned sharp in irritation. He had slept so little in the night that his face was as pale as wax. He had slept so little, with the thought of the magazine springing up again and again like a fountain of joy in his heart, and whenever he had closed his eyes to sleep, then the memory of a poem written by some other man came to stir him, or the remembrance of how some other man had laid paint on a canvas or made a shape from clay. All night he had started up from bed with these words on his tongue, his voice as strong as an eagle's arched open wing, and his weariness fallen from him. And the night could not silence him, for all her moaning and grieving with rain up and down the roadside, nor could the hours passing thicken his tongue with slumber. Every word he spoke in the darkness was sweet with wine, was good to taste; every thought that passed through his head opened out like a flower.

When a man was ready to bequeath something to his heirs, said Martin, he prepared an instrument to bind time, and thus printing came to life. And with it came!

And whatever he said or however he said it might die and perish, thought Hannah, for the thing that gave his flesh and his speech beauty was his belief in the things other people did and how they did it; and this faith survived long after the sound of his words in the room was dead.

Are you sleepy, Hannah? said Martin.

No, said Hannah. Feel my eyes, they are wide open.

With it came words, and words said one after

another are in themselves a reason for existence. Measure the gold, the axis where the rails run into the sun. Take it home, measure the miracle. Put your finger on it, that's what I mean by making a poem up and getting it down on paper. It remains to be proved that there is any dimension to grandeur, or that an open door leads anywhere except beyond the threshold of a man's heart. That's what I mean by a magazine, he said.

At three in the morning, Hannah made a little supper of yellow cheese and bottles of stout, and they ate it on a tray on their knees, sitting up among the pillows, side by side in bed. And Martin sang with his mouth full of crackers:

Tell me what thy lordly name is on the night's
Plutonian shore

and in the bedroom window a warm blush of dawn had begun to spread across the trees.

And now he sat, a stranger to her, drinking his coffee at the kitchen table, with his voice turned alien and harsh.

What in the world will you do? What can you possibly find to do to pass the time?

I'll have all the windows open and the rugs out for an airing, said Hannah. I'll give the dogs a walk in the afternoon.

And at night what will you do? said Martin. It's not at all certain that I can get back here to-day.

Suddenly he jumped up and buttoned his coat over. He put his hat on the side of his head and pulled his smart gloves on his fingers.

Well, good-bye, he said casually. They stood looking at each other.

Will you send me a wire, Martin? said Hannah softly.

My God! said Martin. You're as hard as flint! What kind of a woman are you that you can let me go this way?

But what can I do? cried Hannah, wringing her hands before him.

It might have come into your head, said Martin, to come along with me. That never occurred to you, did it? he said. I'll leave you to your solitude.

I thought of it all night, said Hannah. Do you think I thought of anything else? You don't need me there. It's between Eve and you.

Martin went out the door and Hannah stood there on the threshold, looking after him. He went down the garden path, a slender young man in a grey coat, with his hair growing long in his neck and his fingers twitching in his pockets. Out in the garden, the sun had begun to flow gently over and wipe out the wet blue shadows of the rock. The vines and leaves were upright: the cactus plants as thick and white as the bellies of serpents and the great horny tusks of grander species rearing out of the ferny bush.

Martin stopped still in the pathway and looked back at Hannah on the doorstep of the house.

Have your solitude, he said politely. I couldn't, wouldn't deprive you. I wouldn't think of. Have your solitude, my dear. Wash it and scrub it clean and hang it up to dry. But before I go may I speak my mind in passing, may I utter? You have no life, stamina, strength. You have nothing I can rely on. Shine the floors, do the silver, don't let me deter you. I have a rendezvous somewhere else. I have business to do with people whose emotions are tapped once, at the source, once and for all. You wouldn't know the meaning of it. I have important things to say in the desert. Take my old neckties, clean them, turn them inside out. I have something of less importance to you to say somewhere else.

Now you know what I think, he said, and he walked on again towards the gate. And besides, he said, and he turned his head back at her, it might put you out if you were with me and I happened to fall ill on the way, of course.

Martin, Hannah cried out suddenly, would you take me along?

It's rather late for that now, said Martin. There was no change of pleasure in his face, but he lingered where he was as if to wait, touching the ivy leaves at the gate with his lifted hand.

But if you did come, he said, I couldn't very well open the door of the car and say get out, move on, could I? I couldn't very well say: if you wait long enough here on the roadside somebody else will come along and cherish you. You are easy to cherish. Nobody could pass you by.

CHAPTER XI

Had it been the heat of summer on them, or a trip to be made through an evil city, the despair in their thoughts might have set their sorrow afire. But it was a long shadowy road they had to follow across a flight of mountains in the early day. They drove up from the palms and yucca of the coast, up through a mock-sunlight of mimosa, steadily soaring into the black firs, the pines, and the strong separate nameless trees growing up the mountain side. The rocks were dark and bare like savages; they were wigged with long green dripping mosses and had set their bony faces against the wastrel south.

In the north, thought Hannah as they rode, the streams must now be breaking clamorous and wide. The chattering roofs of ice must now be slipping and parting above the waters, and the earth gone soft and wooing under foot. She rode thinking of how long it had been now since she had walked out, for despite the falsity of the season about them, it must now be spring. And now there would be a change for love, she thought; it would take strength from the time of year and lift its head and flower. She put her hand through Martin's arm and drew it close to her.

Take my vanity, she said, and do what you want with it, Martin.

I'll wear it in my buttonhole, he said, and he kissed her. Vanity doesn't become you. I'll put it behind my ear.

His ear was near her mouth when she spoke to him, white, with the soft black hair growing down from the temple, and in the hollow temple, a wild tender pulse of life was beating there. His shirt was open at the neck, and when she looked at him her tongue became so heavy that she could not answer. She sat silent beside him with her breath taken in and out with care, as if something might alter. She sat quiet, in trust for whatever direction he might be taking her.

Layer by layer as they climbed the land changed for them and the clear air poured in upon their faces. Behind them hung the dogs' warm muzzles, their noses dewed and eager and quivering with spring. The trails of wild things escaping or scents they crossed, sent the dogs whistling with grief and impatience against the windows of the car. Far below on the sea level drifted a yellow haze of heat, but here the mountains reared on either side, high and mighty, out and away from the muck of sodden light.

However high they went, the blue craggy land ahead proceeded, range upon range. The alps, the lower alps, the seaward alps, and the foothills unworthy of a title lifting their antlered heads against the first retarded slopes, led on through hedgehog, brier, bramble, thistlecomb and melted upon the horizon in cones of sugar-loaf. Hannah was sitting close to Martin and looking ahead to the steeples of snow when she saw the priest standing in the road before them.

There he stood, dark and grim, a man of fifty maybe, with his slovenly frock hanging down in the wet clay. His queer little black bowler hat was smeared with mud and had slipped over on the side of his head. As the car advanced he held up his hand to them and looked them severely in the eye.

You'll have to do something for me, he said through the open window when they stopped beside him. You'll have to see that I'm properly taken care of. I've broken my arm.

What's he say? said Martin.

Hannah reached back to smooth the dogs' brows and still their mutterings.

He's hurt himself, Hannah said.

But for all the picture of the complaining priest before them, there were other thoughts in Hannah's head. She was watching the changes that came into Martin's face and his delicate hands on the wheel fallen helpless in pity at the sight of another man in pain. Someday I can look the other way, she thought, and know from the past what it is that sucks the colour from him or sets it to burning there. When I come to know him well, there'll be no need to spy on him. Poetry can open his eyes like fire, and the words of a stupid man turn him white as frost. And now he leaped from the car and put his arm about the ailing father.

I slipped on my bicycle in the mud, the priest was saying to them. You'll have to take me to wherever a good doctor may be.

There was no prithee please in his voice, nor his eyes asking, and suddenly, loud enough to startle them from their skins he broke into loud lamentation.

My God, My God! he cried.

In the back of the car, the dogs drew off among themselves, uneasy and suspicious of him, and Martin assisted the dark lamenting figure to the open door. But the eye of the priest had caught sight of his own bicycle left by the side of the road, and with one foot on the running-board he turned his head and measured shrewdly the length of it and the spaces of the car.

It would be easy to put my bicycle on the side of your car, he said to Martin. I'll stand right here and wait.

He had a lean venal face and his fleshless jaw was blue where the beard was piercing through it. His ailing arm lay clutched across his bosom like a puny infant swathed in deepest black.

No, not like that, he said sharply. The front wheel

up higher so it won't be injured. I find that details, he said in a moment, are gradually growing dim.

My God! he suddenly cried out as if his pain had stabbed him anew. Now if you can secure my bicycle with a bit of stout cord, he continued in a conversational tone. The tyres are new and I wouldn't want them fractured. No string? No cord? The priest looked from Martin to Hannah, and then his eye fell on the three dogs sitting erect with their brows furrowed with concern. You could take a strap off one of these great beasts, he said nodding his lean unshaven face in their direction. Oh, mother of Christ, he said in a bitter voice of complaint, and he nursed his arm close on his bosom, wherein have I sinned?

But Hannah's thoughts were sweeping in solicitude about Martin's head as he tied the bicycle in place and came forward to aid the priest into the car. Here with the hills behind him, and the thick stems of the mountain trees, he seemed a delicate man to her, with the weight of the black graceless priest leaning across his shoulders heavier than he could bear. He did not stagger, but she felt Martin's breath as if it were her own, escaping with difficulty, in and out, running a scale and hesitant, as though obstructed by his bursting heart. Whatever there was of strong life in him, a narrow torrent of twisted chains of strength, was suddenly knotted, halted like a cascade fresh at the brink, stopped for the moment and not allowed to fall.

She put out her hand as though in fear and said: Martin!

At this the priest took off his own weight to himself and looked up at her in suspicion.

Am I in danger from these big dogs? he said. You could very well take them in front with you, he said, if you are afraid they will attack me. You could take one on your knees and one on the seat beside you. The other might easily fit down under your feet.

Ah, they're harmless. You need not be afraid, said Hannah.

But nevertheless, she drew the two dogs in front with her, blindly, with weakness in her hands, squeezing them down in their great bulky coats beside her and between her knees. Behind, as if fearing the touch of the holy man's cloth, Mirette slunk off in the corner alone.

Why did you call me? said Martin softly as he took his place at the wheel. What made you afraid?

I don't know, said Hannah with shame. She looked into his face and saw it strong and fair, and she did not know.

Behind them the priest too had settled down in his skirts, thrust out his soiled masculine boots from under his draggled hem, and begun rocking his wounded arm to sleep with prayers. He had entered into conversation with the holy family, speaking naturally and intimately with them, telling them in detail of all that had befallen him and where the pain was sharpest. Now and again he cried aloud as though stabbed with agony.

Can I give you some cognac? said Hannah turning her head to him.

Ah, no, said the priest. I'll be patient until we get to Frejus.

He sat huddled in one corner, murmuring his lament, and Mirette sulked off from him in the other. Each was a scourge to the other one, and the black eyes of the bitch and those of the priest spied on and reviled each other and moved away. However firm were his belief and virtues, the priest was now a skeleton shaken with misgiving.

The young gentleman, said the priest in a moment, could easily move over a few centimetres and take this other dog beside him. As long as his feet are free for the manipulation of the car, I see no reason.

And then he cried out again in pain, and Mirette rattled her anger in her throat. The two other dogs sat close to Hannah and turned up their eyes in supplication to her. When the priest shouted out in anguish, one lifted his wide paw and laid it in entreaty upon her shoulder.

I'm afraid there's no more room, said Hannah.

Of course, said the priest, you might put them out and let them run behind.

But Martin was driving carelessly at the wheel. The road was narrow and from its outer edge fell a great wide valley of desolation. It was still as a desert here, with no sign of human life or beast, or any traces, except for the ruined walls of abandoned houses gaping in the sun. There was no shelter to turn to, no direction to take as choice. Far ahead and below them was the uncertain vision of Saint-Raphael melting in vapours and tides along the edge of the sea.

The descent was as swift as flight, and on the plain the soil beneath them turned gradually to sand. The fir trees grew lavishly from pure white beds, their boughs luxuriant and black with needles and their roots firmly set in sparkling white. Down through the sandy outskirts of Frejus they drove, past a few colonial soldiers scattered here and there on the roadside, with their wide yellow faces turned idly to eye the passing car. The priest laid bare his tortured face at the window and the Mongolian eyes looked blandly at him, as cows turn their heads, roll their cud over, pause, and again return to their purpose. The soldiers, indolently set upon their own direction, were making their way under the remains of the Roman aqueduct out into the sun. Beyond in the fir forests where the barracks stood, they had built themselves a place of worship in the shape of a pagoda. The turret of it, painted like a top, could be seen through the spangled branches of the trees.

At the crossways in the town, the priest leaned forward and said: Stop here a moment. I want to ask this gentleman for the closest doctor.

He beckoned with his sound arm through the window to a tidy *agent* in blue. The *agent* lifted his hand in salute and came over to the car with his short little cape swinging over his shoulders.

I've met with an accident, said the priest hugging his arm across his bosom. Where will I find the nearest doctor?

Did these people run you down, my father? said the *agent*.

The priest hesitated for a moment, puzzled, for the idea had not occurred to him. Then he said, in haste:

No, no, oh no!

The *agent* looked closely at him, and at the faces of Hannah and Martin. Surely he suspected that the holy man, in his generous forbearance, was shielding the two strangers from trouble.

There's a doctor in the next street, my father, he said. I'll go with you while they drive you there. He stepped briskly up on the running board and held to the frame of the open window. I'll have a look at your papers after that, he said to Martin.

CHAPTER XII

Martin sat still in the police station at Frejus, waiting, with the telephone receiver held to his ear. Everything in him was upright and attentive, peeled for the voice that would sound at the other end. Whenever he looked back across the little dark room at Hannah sitting quiet with the dogs about her, he made sweet mouths at her. In a moment his head swung up and he cried out: Hallo!

The dogs lifted up their ears and watched him. An *agent* in khaki was writing in a long ledger on the table by the door.

Eve? said Martin. Eve! This is Martin. His voice was shouting as if she were a hundred miles away. Yes, I'm in Frejus, he said. He looked around at Hannah and nodded and smiled. Yes, in Frejus. I've had some difficulty.

He stood silent a long time, moving from one foot to the other and listening. Then he said:

There's nothing to be angry about. It's simply that they stopped me here the way they do sometimes and asked to see my papers. And of course you carried the driving papers of the car away in your bag, you know.

I haven't a thing, he said. Not the driving permit or the grey card thing.

You're an angel, Eve, he said in a moment. What?

Hannah saw the colour run into his face, and he pushed his soft grey hat on to the back of his head.

Of course, he said. Of course I'm alone. I say OF COURSE. Can you hear me now? Of course. Don't be silly. Why in the world would I come to see you otherwise. . . .

He looked over and smiled at Hannah in reassurance.

Yes, he said. It won't take you fifteen minutes. I can't move a step from here until you come. Hurry, he said. Come as you are. I can't wait. Yes, of course I'll wait. OF COURSE. Good-bye. Yes, good-bye, he said. I said GOOD-BYE.

He came gaily across the room to Hannah, his hat on the back of his head and his black hair damp on his seamless brow.

Tell them tell these bastards, he said. He lifted his hand as if to thumb his nose at them, but thought better of it. Tell them the papers are on the way. My God, Eve's deaf this morning! *Toot sweet*, he smiled at the *agents*. *Toot sweet*, he said. Just bide your time.

Hannah, he said and he sat down beside her. I had to explain myself as best I could to her. You saw that. I couldn't have said you were here with me. I'd never have seen hide nor hair of her again if she knew that I'd brought you along what? Had I a drink, said

Martin, I could give this situation the attention it merits.

Can you never say the truth to her? said Hannah, for now they both seemed strangers to her.

At the moment alack and alas come first to my lips, said Martin. I'm afraid to risk speaking the truth to her at present.

Maybe she'd use it different than you think, said Hannah.

I've known her a long time, said Martin. The side you knew was another.

It will make things simpler then, said Hannah, if I go right away.

She stood up and wound the dogs' straps tighter through her fingers.

I can't spare you now, said Martin. The place is too dark without you, my throat too dry. A spot of drink would give me courage, but instead of it if you could give me a small sentence spoken out clearly, a word or two or three words even to bind on my forehead like a miner's lantern. Without you, he said softly. He sat looking down into his open hands and she could do nothing in her love but sit down again beside him. Without you for half a day even, he said, I might go astray.

She saw his face beside her, and she thought that she who was in confusion about all things except her love for him, could never be any aid to him. He had lived through thirty years of life and this seemed like an age of reason to her and she could find no words adequate to say. On one side of her heart he stood with his gravity or merriment, and his wild wondrous talk that led her into endless places, and about him the flare of his spirit such as she had never known before nor thought could be. And on the other side was her misgiving that her own spirit and strength could match him. She was humble before him, and speechless, because of the belief and purpose in him that was never turned away.

Say me a word that will remain, urged Martin. Do not speak to me, or preach to me of honour. I have my own and am content with it. If you begin with the words of someone else on your tongue, there is no issue for us. It is time to believe in discovery, he said, and to me discovery means that your own life can rot in filth and perish as long as your senses are identified with what is being wrenched out in pure and lasting form from the lives of other people. For the poet in Italy, he said, is more my own existence than mine. And I'd sell my last shirt to read two lines of Mr. Alaric's prose. Now it is time, Hannah, he said softly, to believe in me.

The minutes had passed away under the big hand of the clock in the police station, and when Hannah saw this, she stood up with the dogs' leads in her hands and said:

Now I must go, Martin. Why should I complicate things for you? There's a café across the street and in the afternoon you will find me there.

Unless you speak the words to me, said Martin, you cannot leave me.

He stood up before her with his hat off his head and his hair back smooth and bright from his brow. The love in his eyes and the curve of his mouth were wooing her heart. But now I must go, she repeated blindly.

But he held her still with his eyes and she could not go.

Fifteen minutes! she said to him. Eve will be walking in on you.

I don't care how many Eves walk in, he said softly and bitterly to her. You must give me what I ask before you go.

Hannah looked into his eyes, awed by the strength that grew and flourished in him at times when it seemed that it must falter. He stood before her quiet and patient, waiting almost nonchalantly before her, with his clothes worn carelessly at ease and his grave eyes warm with light. Such a sweetness and love now shone in his gaze that when he moved his tongue and spoke, his words came forth like a miracle to Hannah.

Everything is setting out for us, he said. We are on the edge. Everything is beginning.

When she herself began to speak, it seemed to her out of the slumber of long deep draughts of wine.

Yes, she said. Things come to life because of you. I shall never feel any different.

She felt her senses swimming in her head, and she stumbled down the stairs in darkness, drunk with his strong hands and his beauty. The pressure of his mouth was still on hers, and she knew that the dogs on their straps were dragging her cruelly out into the relentless light. When it struck her face in the street she lifted her hand as though to ward off the blow, but the three dogs had already torn her out of the dark hallway, across the road, and on to the dusty square. There she stopped still for a moment, looking about in bewilderment, with the dogs on the ends of their leads swinging their tails in the sunlight and yawning in content.

She stood there in the little square wondering at the warmth, for now it was noonday and the sky was a strong dark blue. Plane trees were planted along the walk and handfuls of little green leaves shook on high in the branches. The spring had no more than begun in the sap and the earth here, for the mistral often blew up the plain and laid it bare for sharper weather. But now the air was as mild as though the sky were sponging a warm healing liquid far and wide.

Hannah spoke to the dogs and turned towards the open café. The tables were empty and sitting out bare and lean in the sun. She slipped off her coat as she walked and carried it across her arm, and behind her the dogs paused to smell at a tree, to turn back and forth and lift their legs and water the dark bark as they passed it. When she sat down at a table, the dogs turned once or twice and then settled down outside her shadow. They laid down their bright noses, like jewels alight between their forepaws, and waited with their eyes alert for whatever she would do.

Hannah looked up in surprise at the waiter when he came, for even the sound of Martin's words still remained to her. She looked up startled into the waiter's face and ordered a small red drink; warm and burning as a coal it lay in the round belly of the little glass. She had lifted it to her mouth to drink when she saw a taxi drive up in front of the police station across the square. She set down her glass suddenly and watched the woman it bore step out: a tallish woman dressed in white with a white hat set on her curly locks and a white woollen coat hanging open over a frock that scarcely covered her knees.

There's Eve, she thought. She looked wilder, shyer. Even her slippers were white, with the feet in them bony and narrow like an Englishwoman's foot was often, and the toes that hastened to the driver's seat curled up like the toe of a sultan's shoe. She was not a young woman, but under her white hat her face was shining and eager, and the hair was curled permanently up from the neck and the glasses she usually wore laid off her nose. Hannah could see her well as she turned to the chauffeur of the taxi: Eve in a flurry of love for Martin, impatiently pressing her thwarted gaze and her suspicion close on the taxi's lying meter and the chauffeur's face.

She stood there peering at the taxi man and at his meter with her great white pocket-book held open. Her sight was short and she trusted no one; she could never be sure and she looked close at the figures so there would be no mistake. Hannah could hear Eve's voice distinctly as she spoke to him. It came ringing across the quiet square, the broad English accent in the French tongue, with an echo of deafness and suspicion in it.

If that's your price, said Eve, then I won't give you a penny's *pour boire*. You said it would be fifteen francs from Saint-Raphael, and now it's eighteen!

Eighteen! she snorted, and she paid out the bills of money to him. At the sound of her voice berating, the window in the police station opened over her head. Hannah saw Martin there, leaning out and calling Eve's name to her, but Eve was deaf with her fury and she did not hear.

What's that you say? she was shouting to the chauffeur. You want a *pour boire* on eighteen francs of robbery? You're a scamp! she cried. You take advantage of people when they're in a hurry! My nephew is here in the police station, held by your wretched police who can't tell an honest man from a criminal. If they're really looking for business, I'll hand you over to them and let them deal with you, if they have the wits to!

My God, shut up! cried Martin out of the window. Surely he understood little that she said, but this uproar and scene before the police had bleached his face with fearfulness. He waved his two arms at her. You're mad, woman, he cried, you're mad!

Then Eve lifted her head and saw him. He was leaning out from the window with his hat off his head, and now the police had gathered behind and were looking down on the angry woman storming below. Hannah saw the colour clotted in Eve's face, dark and menacing over her elegant white clothes.

If you keep on like this, shouted Martin, you'll finish by having me in jail!

In jail! cried Eve in derision with her sore face lifted to him. I've come to get you out of jail! You're lucky to always have me to fall back on, young man. You're always in trouble, like a heedless child! Why couldn't you stay home where you belonged for once instead of traipsing out over the country after people who don't want to see you?

No matter why I came! cried Martin. Come up the stairs and bring me the papers. All you need do is show them to the police here and keep your mouth shut and they'll let me go.

So it's the papers you came after, is it? said Eve with triumphant suspicion. That's what put it into your head to come driving over to Saint-Raphael! You thought you might need your old papers so you routed me out with your usual thoughtfulness for others!

She stood on the walk before the police station with the sunlight shining on her head. Her queer shy smile was on her mouth, but for a moment Hannah thought she was going to cry. Then she turned her face down to the contents of her open bag.

Ah, your old papers! she said to Martin. She was searching for them with her close gaze pressed down and her fingers scrambling. It's your own fault, she said, making me come off in such a rush with your telephoning and your shouting at me as though I was deaf or daft or whatnot! I left your papers at the hotel, she said.

My God, cried Martin out the window. You had time enough to doll yourself up like Queen Victoria!

He held his tongue for a moment while she sought wildly through her bag.

You look like a trained nurse in that outfit! he shouted at last, as if he had found the jibe that would cut her deepest.

What's that to you? cried Eve in fury. Trained nurse or not, you'll have to sit where you are until I find a taxi to drive me back to Saint-Raphael to fetch the old papers for your car.

CHAPTER XIII

Whenever you walk into a restaurant, said Martin, look up and down to be sure, for Eve has no suspicion.

On the third day it happened that when Hannah walked into a restaurant, a simple one so it seemed to her, on the port, she saw Martin and Eve in the window's bay, sitting there. The side of Martin's face was turned to her and he did not see, and as Hannah stood for a moment at the door, she saw that he was talking and that a full warm smile was blooming on Eve's mouth. There was even rouge on her lips for the occasion, and her head was cocked and her eyes smiling to the things that Martin said. Hannah saw then how greatly she had altered, and how different a woman Eve was now that Martin was a holiday and no longer a natural matter in her life. She had spent out her money for elegance: for the shape of a hat, and the shade of her finger nails. She had set aside the English taste for fancy trim and buttons, left off her ropes of amber and put a wave in her hair. And she was harking to Martin as though to a lover speaking, and he, with his tongue wagging in his head, was letting his untouched food go cold.

Before Hannah went out alone into the street she saw this: the Scotch aunt cocking her good ear to Martin's voice and toying with the silver. There was even a flush on Eve's face as if she were playing a gentle duel of love with someone new and captivating and an entire stranger to her. For the first time Hannah saw that at moments in Eve's youth she must have possessed a sort of beauty; for now the suspicion had gone from her face and she was quick with delight. At times when men said warm things to her in her youth, thought Hannah, she must have been a fair young girl.

Hannah walked out into the street and up under the palm trees, remembering Martin's talk of Eve. His father had wanted her settled and safe, but there had never been any man that seemed good enough to her; and maybe the truth was that she had never known any man whose words could keep this beauty on her face. After her parents' death, she had run out of the room from a bald Scotch barrister in fear, for however he put the matter, she knew he was after what her parents had left behind. Whatever any man said, she had no faith in it, and on her physiognomy lingered suspicion of this one, contempt for that. Only the Irish nephew, come from the States with honey on his tongue, only this one could wipe the dovetails of rancour from her face.

Now if I were a brave and a simple woman, thought

Hannah as she walked away under the trees with her cap in her hand and her hair out in the sun, I would see sin and virtue and be able to distinguish between them. I only believe in sin when I see the fury on Eve's face, and I must be the sinner. When I see the look she has now with him I know there can be no virtue in having come between these two.

Only the matter of love could not be explained. Hannah walked a long way under the palms, with the sea as blue as heaven murmuring on her right hand. It was not rightful, nor was it wrong, she had no name to give it. What can you do with love? she said. On which side does it lie? If love is an element, like weather or wind, then it must go unchallenged. The virtuous can go to shelter, for their strength is in themselves. It's only the frail and the weak who need it; the strong have something else to do.

This sort of strength was Eve's, she thought; for all of Eve's unbearable delight in love she had taken it as foul weather always, and gone in the other direction. Only in the lingo and shape of Martin was it safe to her, like a shower falling in her own garden on her own soil: he was young, nephew, ill, and he could not come beyond. In her own heart Hannah grieved for this weakness in her own blood and Martin's, that they must reach out in frenzy for every vestige of love that might go.

The thought of the three dogs waiting and biding their time in peace made her turn back to the hotel.

It was the finest on the seaside walk, for Martin would have no other, and was built up in a garden of idle trees and tended beds. Whenever she walked up the driveway, she felt her clothes shabby and graceless on her, her shoes worn down at the heels, and her cap so inadequate that she swung it still in her hand. She ran up the stairs alone, with no wish to see her own face reflected whichever way she turned in the mirrors of the lift, and when she stepped into the great front room, the dogs jumped up from the soft carpet and flung themselves upon her, trying with their mouths to say her name.

She sat down on the bed with their paws upon her, and her thoughts went back to Martin. Her hands moved over the dogs' dark shining brows. If he were a child and spoiled like a child, then she must have wisdom for him. But where does one find wisdom? She thought this suddenly in fright. How does wisdom come?

She looked in anger about the handsome room with its wide white bath, and its ante-room, impatient that she and the three stricken dogs should be sitting shabbily there. What was this hotel but another drop of honey from Martin's tongue, a word of blarney because he in his life had seen too many smaller, simpler places? What were the servants in fancy dress but an affront to them, for they had never seen the dew hanging on the dogs' coats in the morning in the north when they came home through the fields with their moustaches dripping. She looked down at her own feet on the carpet and wondered if these were the same bone and flesh that had gone through the grass and sunk into the deep pliant earth of spring, had traversed water, and had paused while the dogs stopped to flash their tongues through the icy stream. The bottom of its bed would now be laid with heavy short green mosses, and long early grasses would be bellied with jewels and swimming in the current. Even with the thick hirsute armour of the palm trunks showing in the window, Hannah felt nearer the far soaking earth in February and the swampy ground that sucked achingly at the feet in colder places.

She was sitting still, stroking back the dogs' long hair when Martin came back in the late afternoon. He switched on the light quickly and said: What are you doing there in the dark? He had talked so long with Eve that his voice was dry in his throat and his eyes were hollow. What were you doing? Were you asleep? he said.

She went across the room to him and he kissed her.

You must pack the bags quickly, he said. We are going away.

Where are we going? said Hannah. She kept her hands close together, and something inside her seemed shaking with the cold.

Back to Vence, said Martin. Back to Vence together, you and me.

Hannah hastened here and there in the room, picking up this and that, smoothing his bathrobe over, laying things one on the other into the open cases.

Everything's fixed up, said Martin. He was changing his shirt and whistling softly to himself. Everything's just as it should be. We've talked out the entire next number. We've only a few contributions to decide on now. Eve's strong for Lady Vanta's work.

Everything's fixed up, he said. He skipped across the room and pushed the bell button. She's as keen about doing it as ever. Everything's turned out as it should.

And if there be sin and virtue, thought Hannah as she laid his handsome neckties in, then it is sinful to greet him now with a sour grieving face when things have gone well for him.

Martin, I'm glad, she said, and he crossed the room to her and pressed his head close on her shoulder. His empty white cheeks betrayed him, but when she had him in her arms she closed her heart to the thought of the defence, denials and mitigation his mouth must have shaped for Eve.

Darling, we'll be simple again, he whispered. In our house again, eating our meals together. We'll be simple.

She put her arms about him, about his broad slim shoulders and his delicate hips. She held him close to her, pressing him gently to her, bearing him against her as if to give him strength.

You will make me strong, he said softly to Hannah. His breath sighed wearily from his open mouth. And yes, said Hannah, yes, yes, I will cherish you forever. She set to packing the bags again with one arm about his waist, hastening from one case to the next so that they might speedily leave the place.

When the porter came to the door she dropped her arm from Martin and ran for the last things in the bathroom: the toothbrushes and Martin's yellow slippers by the tub. Martin himself sat down on the side of the bed and looked the bill over. In a moment he opened his pocket book and said:

It's funny, I haven't enough money to pay the bill here.

Hannah came out of the bathroom with the things in her hands and looked at him.

It's a very expensive hotel, Martin said. You can't imagine how much they ask for this silly room, for instance.

Martin stood up and handed the bill back to the porter. Then he waved his hand at him: Go away, he said. I have to go out and get some money from the bank or the American Express or elsewhere.

The man took the bill and closed the door, and Martin put on his hat. He smoothed the side of his black hair back and looked at himself severely in the mirror.

It's a great nuisance. It's just what I didn't want to do. I have to go borrow some money from Eve, he said.

CHAPTER XIV

She sat for a time idle in the room watching the palm blades sparring without the window, and then as the day went darker and darker and she could no longer make out the water of the sea moving through the branches, she picked up some work and began weaving her needle and wool through a tear in Martin's sock. To remain idle waiting for events to shape themselves was the bitterest thing that could come to her; she sat working with the dogs at her feet seeking not to think of her own impatience. For all of Martin's love, he, like a man, had the better part of his concern on other matters. She might listen, and sew, and cook his food for him, but he, as befitted a man, had his mind elsewhere judging, manipulating, and making things serve his ends.

But Dilly's mind had resided in her, and the thought of how he had tended her in illness, had come home from work like no human man and set aside his weariness to bathe her face and feed her, even this now seemed no more than a soft flurry of purity that had scarcely survived but melted off like shallow snow when the warmth of Martin's love or ire came. Even the remembrance of Dilly's letters saying: I might as well be dead, there is nothing left to me. *Je n'ai plus rien*, like a weak man, or a woman; she had no time for it. You're through with me now, she thought, so rejoice for it and let me be. Or he wrote to her: If you are not happy, you must tell it to me, for I could not bear you to suffer, and this went in one ear and out the other at the sound of Martin, if it would be Martin, coming back to her from Eve down the hotel hall.

She thought of Dilly going to Paris and facing strange men in business and asking work from them, and every day he woke up his face would have differed some, and his figure changed, and the lines of his mouth gone sterner. Dilly would alter as every year of their life together had changed the look in his eyes and his jaw's edge and the smile on his face. He had no wild need for the sound of other men's might, or fame, or wonder. He thought he knew very well what he wanted for success, for it would be something that he could touch with his hands.

She saw him with sorrow, a dark sallow man in his corduroy riding breeches, throwing one thigh over the saddle of his wheel. She could see him, as she had seen him every morning, pedalling down the road from her, smaller and smaller, with his shoulders humped in discontent and the small of his back drawn in with irritation. He hated the rain on his face and the mud on his heels four times a day; his family had brought him up to expect something better. He wanted to own things: perfume, and silk, and elegant cars, and the countryside that he could not possess had made him bitter. Ocean liners and clubs he had a taste for, and his venom came out at the dogs at times as if they stood in his way.

She thought of Dilly now as she listened for Martin's footsteps down the hallway. Dilly in Paris, in a city as he had always wanted: she could picture the gleam of ambition for things that other men possessed that must now be burning brighter and brighter in his narrow eye. Whenever she had wept with him, he had taken her tears as his own, but all he could see ahead was wealth of his own and to what uses he would put it. She could speak to him of other things, but the words might as well never have been said.

He had hated the beets growing there in the ground and had wrenched them out by their tails in anger, but he had cherished her close whenever she was in torment. I am a hard woman, she thought, remembering how when she had turned to him for comfort he had succoured her as gentle as falling dew. I am a hard woman, and she thought how she had flung away from him with impatience because of his face gone black as night if a spark of dirt clung to the radishes and cracked under his teeth when he bit them. I am a hard woman, she thought. I can say these things of myself because I know what I've done to him. But Eve outside, with Martin, saying them, she could not bear.

When she thought she heard Martin's feet sounding

out down the hallway, she jumped up and ran to the mirror as if to wipe any sign of grief from her face. He had never seen a tear fall from her eyes, and pity she would not have from him, for his way of speaking in itself, in mentioning the weather or the commonest things, was such that stirred her courage. She wanted to be steadfast and calm for him, with patience for whatever he bade her do.

And what are these, said Martin's voice in her ear, but tears upon the pillow? Are there not enough soft-hearted women in the world that you must turn to complaining?

Hannah opened her eyes and saw him with the light of dawn coming through the window behind him, his mouth turned up and smiling and a yellow and red paper hat on his head. He was tickling her neck with a torch of crimped paper that shook in his hand, and his clothes were spattered over with confetti.

I've been to a gala dinner and dance. A cancan, a hornpipe, a minuet, a waltz. And you Niobe, white flower at the pale throat of night. Darling, he said, sitting down on the side of the bed, with his breath shaped with the designs of his absence, I've been to a jamboree all night with Eve.

He shook the torch of paper in her face and smiled.

In a minute, he said, the sun will be stepping into the room, warm and cheerful, like a fat bishop making his call on the parish. See me, said he with the paper cap slipped sideways on his dark heavy locks, see me as I was then in the early evening when I walked spruce as a lark but sprucer into Eve's hotel. I made no bones about it. I had none. I said without shame: Eve, I have no money again and yet again. I don't know how it is.

And fie upon you, said Eve the hearty. I couldn't count the laughter, so fast it ran out of her mouth. The truth was that it gave her a turn of joy to see me returning after my solemn farewells to her. There's a gallop, a strathspey, a junket, a wake to-night, she said. You're a young man and you should take advantage of it. As long as ye've stayed this late in town, then stay a little later. I'll dress ye up in my Boxer Rebellion gown and you can go as a gentleman for once, and won't that be a change for you?

Do you mind the time, said Eve as she dressed me up like all get-out, and the poor creature so full of rejoicing that she was fit to strangle her logic in tears, do ye mind, said she, when you fell ill in Paris, nor would you let me into the room because I had told the doctors you were a poor man with no money and it would do them no good to listen to you. And for your obstinacy and your temper they took you off to the hospital and there would have let you lie and die if you hadn't called for me two days without stopping. Poor you were, but you'd rather have eaten black bread than admit it. My nephew, said I to the medical man, is a pauper. He lives on what his government gives him. You can do what you want about that. And the bottle you threw at me was ergotine, black as your hat, that broke on the wall and left a scene there that my pennies paid for as usual, not yours my lad.

I remember it well, said I to her, nor will I forget that you came to the hospital at a time of night when visitors were put out at the gate, and shouted your own way in until even the dead men in other rooms sat up in their shrouds and took notice.

I hit the pompous one with the end of my brelly, said Eve, wiping the laughter into her handkerchief. It was the second quart of champagne that made things seem grievous to her.

All her life, said Martin suddenly tender and close to Hannah on the pillow. All her life wherever she was or however, she had the side of their boot to deal with or the wrong end of the stick. Whatever friends she had, if ever they saw her coming first they ran in the other direction. She was always too much for everyone and no one had time to stop. Her walk in itself would put you off, and her temper that rises whichever way the wind is blowing. You knew her before in a casual way, with her manners on and her shy mouth smiling. No one has ever had time for her, said Martin softly, unless it was me for a little while.

If you close your eyes, said Martin, can you see her stepping down out of a train and leaving her baggage behind her the way she does when she travels anywhere? Or see her eating her meals alone at table, and if anyone looks in her direction, her eyes crossing over in her head because she thinks they're laughing and mocking at her.

Martin lay still in Hannah's arms, with his weary face and the snow of confetti in his locks beside her.

If you close your eyes, he said softly, it might break your heart, the solitary kind of life she leads.

CHAPTER XV

But now they were restored to each other. He would wake up late in the day, wake up refreshed by sleep and they would start out over the mountains together. He now lay asleep in peace beside her, and when the first strong rays of the day came in through the windows, she slipped out of his arms and hastened across the room to close the vast curtains before the light should strike his face. When she moved, the dogs lifted their heads and looked warily at her, waiting for a sign from her that they might rise and yawn.

And now, thought Hannah, combing her hair out before the mirror, life must be led in a simpler way. In her hands she felt some great pure power, and her soul lay quiet. She could feel it, strong and motionless within her, like a presence, speechless, but filled with comfort as if a warm dinner eaten and good wine taken. Enough words, she thought, have been spoken. She thought of the château, and that it would be a cold place when they returned to it, shut off four days in the dark and chill. Once the fire was going in the cooking stove in the kitchen, she would take down the copper pan from the wall in the hallway and fill it with coals and lay it in the bed. Combing her hair out she thought of Martin seated in the chair by the stove, tipped back on the heels of it, and his voice reading: To-morrow will be beautiful, for to-morrow comes out of the lake.

She remembered very well one evening when Martin sat in the kitchen saying: What of æsthetics? Let us have them once and for all out here, between the thumb and forefinger, one at a time, like a flea escaping. And at that he had tipped his chair back too far and gone completely over.

Now why do you laugh? he had said, sitting upright on the tiles. Is it so funny to see a man sit down?

Martin had smoothed his beautiful black ruffled feathers into place and risen to his feet with dignity.

I must have looked a fool, he said, straightening his tie.

No, no, Hannah had cried, but even now as she combed her hair she started laughing into the mirror. We are going back, back. She had to bite her laughter into place. We are going back. I'll cook him pigeon for dinner. I'll put his money away in a box so it will be safe.

She bathed and dressed and made the bags afresh. There was a grinding void in her belly because she had not eaten lunch or dinner the day before. She thought of rare roasted dishes with their odour curled in steam around them, and when she saw Martin stirring as if he might wake, she rang the bell for coffee and bread. The dogs could bear their hunger no longer and came and dropped their jaws upon her knee and looked into her face. She fed bread and butter to the dogs and rang for more of it. The tray was waiting by Martin's side when suddenly he opened his eyes and sat up and began to eat.

He sat up, awake, but he had few things to say to her. Slowly she began to see that there was something strange between them. The soft torrent of words that he had poured out upon her heart in the early morning had been released by the wine he had taken, and now he had nothing more to say.

He asked her if the weather were fine, and for answer she threw open the windows and let the sun fall in upon the bed. But still his face was remote, and his eyes veiled, as if a weight of displeasure had fallen on him. He had no sight for the strength of the sun, and when she questioned him he gave her a long cold look that turned her words away. He did not seem like a man who was ailing as he ate his bread in great mouthfuls and drank down his coffee, nor was his face weary. He did not seem to be sorrowing, but the wild reckless tipsiness that he awoke to on other days was gone from him. He was brooding on something that had come and in which she had no part.

He dressed himself like a strong indifferent man

who had no time for her; led her out to the car and tossed the bags in. The dogs climbed after her while he settled the hotel bill with Eve's money: leaf after leaf of it lay fine as silk in his purse. Then he stepped into the car and drove them down the promenade. Between the bearded trunks of the palm trees, the sea shone smooth and colourless in the glaring sun.

Hannah put her hand under his arm as he drove, and moved with his motion as he guided the car from town and out into the country. Now they were restored to each other, and she would have patience; he would speak to her of the things that were on his mind when the time came. She had exhausted none of her patience. In a little while, when I am twenty-four or five maybe I'll find a tongue for my pride.

Now they were restored to each other, but she would have asked anything rather than this stubborn set of his face against her. They were alone now, the world having receded and left them to each other; for all of the past and the magazine linking them to other people, they belonged to each other and they were quite alone. When she thought of this, her heavy patient calm forsook her, but she could not speak out her joy for fear of saying a thing that might not seem to him simple and clear from her heart.

But she could sing, could shout her pride, could wreathe the pleasure in his ears. Whenever she sang the long dimples in his cheeks came out, winked, and went away again.

Hum-ho, fee-fi-fo, and a rum-tum-tiddle-dee-oo,
Twist your apron, cheery.
Wash the dishes, so pick up the rooms, put a thorn-apple branch in a pitcher of water, listen twice to the bob-white call.
Hum-ho, tiddle-dee-oo——

I'm going to miss that, said Martin driving. There was no smile on the side of his face.

Going to miss it, going to miss it, said Hannah laughing high. Hum-ho, tiddle-dee-oo, going to miss it when?

Then the words sat still on her mind, set down their heels and ceased to dance.

What do you mean, Martin?

Going to miss it when I'm dead.

But that was not what he had it in his mouth to say. She saw the lie descend his cheek, sour his lip, and slide away.

Hum-ho, tiddle-dee-oo, he hummed, don't mind me, I'm talking through my hat. He swung the conversation up and over: Eve's strong for Lady Vanta. She's written to her in England, taking her stories for the magazine.

But Hannah sat quiet with a chill nameless knowledge in her.

She liked the one best, he said, about the English lady, single, who lived on the Continent and never took a lover. The high, the mighty, the proud, who might have made her choice from amongst a number but never stooped.

But the thought lay cold and terrible in Hannah's heart: where are you going, Martin, that I can't go along?

Out from the houses they drove and straight into the sweeps of desolation. The stony slopes of the hills led them deeper and deeper into their own silence in the abandoned land. There was only one way through, one road to follow, winding and gripping up through the hacked and scattered boulders. The higher they climbed the redder blushed the blasted rock, and the soil turning red stained the harsh steep country.

Martin did not speak again until they were almost at the top of the pass, and then he stopped the car for a moment, and they stepped out on the earth.

Eve's intuitions are straight, he said as if in defence of her.

Maybe she sees herself like that, Hannah said. Like the lady in Lady Vanta's story.

Maybe she *is* like that, he said.

It was a long time since they had set their feet on soil, and Hannah felt its life springing up through her body. The sun was shining, but as if from no central source, but cast down in pure hot slabs of light upon their heads. A fire of spring was burning over the wastelands, and the dogs stretched out their bodies and went leaping through it. Hannah could feel the heat under her feet as she walked: the vegetation dry as kindling; tough stalks and close rosettes of thistle. And the scorching wind at mid-day over them like a sheet of flame.

The wind gave them no peace but stretched their locks out before them and slapped their coats out behind. Hannah turned her face from the false bright coast below, from the islands basking near the mainland, and followed the wind across the barren country. To leap, to glide upon it, from stepping-off place to dip over the forests thick as midnight in the valley; to descend the wind, or swoop or rise without roar of artifice. Within hand's reach were the shaley ridges, upright against the sky, and under her feet the volcanic land cracking wide.

She began to run, jumping the rocks and the seams in the dry soil, turning her head as if in escape from the sight of the fawning sea coquetting with the shoreline far below. She went exultant over the land, shouting in the hot wind for all the men who had passed that way before and left no name or sign behind them; she saw with joy the fir trees stealthy advance up the slope through the boulders, seeing them as the Skrellings in another country and knowing that if she cried out and slapped her breast with her bare sword that they would take to their boats as they had before Eric's daughter. Her heart was leaping for the battles that had been fought there in the open, in the wilderness: I could have crossed swords with you as fierce as any warrior! At the edge of the unfolding valley and plain she could see the sea water cringing and lipping in. To balance like an albatross I would give my eyes away!

Suddenly she wheeled about and cried out Martin's name in the deserted place. Her breath was still coming deep, but even, and she could have walked another hour and climbed higher for a wider sight of the sea. But in her frenzy she had forgotten him, and when she turned around she saw him sitting far down near the roadside. He was so far and small that she could not make out his features, but her heart smote her that he seemed to be waiting as though in weariness for her to return to him. The crown of her own head was hot as flame when she put her hand to it, and she called to the dogs to follow and hastened down the land.

CHAPTER XVI

The last days of February were part of the fairest season here, and when they returned in the late afternoon the town seemed welcome to them. They could see their own place, still with the sun on it, high on the hillside, with a few little evening clouds beginning to gather about its head. It stood so far and clear from the other houses on the hill that when the weather was low flocks of clouds passed continuously by its windows, and in stormy times long wisps and shreds of cloud gathered, as if seeking shelter, under the tall white pillars at the front.

It may be that I will want to be out of the house as soon as I am in it, said Martin, and across his face even there had gone a gentle tide of peace, but now it looks full of cheer, with the light shining on the panes.

There'll be a hundred letters for you, said Hannah. When it's warm you can sit down and read them by the fire. And to-morrow we'll be up early, or you stay in bed, as you like, and do your writing there.

But when she spoke to him in this way, his face darkened again as if in anger. He drove the car up to the flight of steps that led through the château's wall. How he could keep his tongue from speaking out his mind seemed strange to Hannah. Now say it, she urged him in her heart. Now speak it out so I may know. Now tell me, and he brought the car to a halt, what change has taken place and how I can touch you in your isolation. But Martin got down from the car in silence and walked up the steps.

Hannah went out, and the three dogs leapt after her. A faint but odorous chill of evening resided in the stone and in the shade of the garden, but Hannah was rejoiced to see again the same tough subtle plants flourishing near the walls. Back on the hills in the open country the wind had blown, but here there was no trace of it. The cactus and yucca stood thick and motionless as if beneath a weight of glass.

Martin had gone up to the door, and now he called out her name to her.

For God's sake, come down to earth and tell me what this blue paper is? he said.

When he put it into her hand, she read it out to him. It was a notice pinned on the door from a man who signed himself a *huissier*, and it advised them that bills which had been given him for collection would and must be paid within twenty-four hours or all the property of Mr. Sheehan would be seized and confiscated. It was dated the day before.

Bills? said Hannah. What kind of bills, Martin?

Bills, said Martin in irritation. Lots of bills. The

wine bill, the milk bill, the garage bill, the cleaners' bill. And then, if they're really going to be difficult there's the rent.

The rent? said Hannah. Her mind was working slowly and laboriously. Haven't we paid the rent? she said.

Eve took the house in December, said Martin, and paid a month in advance. We've been almost two months here and haven't paid a cent.

But we don't need a château, said Hannah. We can just pay what we owe and go away.

How can we pay what we owe? I haven't so much as a thousand francs on me. And we have to eat, he said.

He put the key in the lock of the door, pushed it open and stooped to gather up the pile of letters that lay there.

What we can do is, he said, we can pay not a goddamned cent and still go away.

Then I'll pack, said Hannah.

And while you're packing, said Martin, the *huissier* and his bag of tricks will come up and seize the car.

Then I won't pack, said Hannah. The dogs had come up beside her, and suddenly her hands fell on their necks. Martin, what if they took my dogs? she said.

Martin looked at her bitterly.

What about all the back numbers of my magazine

in there? he said. What about all the manuscripts submitted, and the letter files, and my books? What about Eve's pictures, and my clothes?

Then we'll come back and pack, said Hannah. We'll come back in the middle of the night, shall we, and park the car out of sight, and carry the things out one by one.

We'd better clear out now, then, said Martin. In the stress of the moment he forgot himself and took her by the arm. They may be up here after us any minute. We'll drive down the back way to Cannes and settle things in a café there.

They ran down the steps to the car together, hand in hand like children, with the dogs shouldering behind. Once driving down the long white road in the dim light, Martin pulled out the letters from his pocket and laid them in her lap.

Open them up, he said, and read me the nice things people say to me.

The first was from Italy, in the square blue-green envelope of the poet who lived there. Within it were five or six sheets of his story, typed out on pages as thin as onion skin. And it began: I know that what little truth my closed fist of sick man may let escape is in this writing. . . . And upon my love I shall put a seal and throw the packet in a hidden corner of my heart. There to grow or die, to blossom or shrivel, to increase or to dwindle away, to remain or to go. If they are roses they will bloom.

A strange awe and wonder now came into Martin's face as he listened, and he said:

Go on, go on. Don't stop there.

With his head inclined towards her he listened to all the words of the Italian poet's story, and at the last of them they were already entering the outskirts of the city.

How am I to go on now with the miracle of putting other people's things into print and down on paper so that, began Martin wildly. Where can I beg, borrow or steal the sustenance to impart. Put your hand on my breast here, under my coat, Hannah, and feel my heart beating. When you read me his words it opened out so wide that it could not strike against my ribs any more.

He drove blindly through the lighted streets and the bright windows of the shop displays to the post office. There he stopped the car and turned to Hannah and she had never before seen such wild grief in his face.

Come into the post office with me, he said, and she stood beside him at the desk as he wrote down the name of the Italian poet and the address where he lived in poverty alone. Every word that Martin set down on the coarse telegraph paper seemed to spring up fresh and untouched from his reverence, and now would the poet be a rich man when these things reached him for they bore such praise and courage as almost took her breath away. It stood as a document and seal for the allegiance, the glory and pomp, and the sun rising according to the prophets and the sacred inscriptions. Every word of it was so simple and clear that it could have no other meaning: You will be remembered.

When he was finished he handed it to Hannah to read, and his dark stricken eyes were pressed on her as though in speech.

You will be remembered; and Hannah thought of the young poet in Italy lying ill and reading these words to himself: You will be remembered for your beauty and wisdom. You are new and fresh like a child. Your anger is a benediction. Your gusto blows through the wasteland and other minor poems and sows them with rich crops. The wrath of the lion is the wisdom of God. You will be remembered for the deity within you. You tell me you are not a fairy but this you have just written would be denial of any such weakness. The frail men will tremble forever when they see the passion in your prose.

Then he carried it over to the telegraph window, paid out a hundred francs for it and sent it away. Even when he walked out of the building with Hannah and led her down the avenue along the sea front, his belief in the miracle of things spoken out or written lingered with him. They sat down side by side in a café, and the glass of pernod he drank only released the more the glibness of his tongue.

Can anything be acquired or gained in life without

paying dear for it? he said. Can poetry or love even? The poet in Italy, he pays for it with his health broken in two and his fine locks falling. As for me, I've never been asked to pay any price at all.

He asked for another glass of pernod, and with the end of his finger he ripped open the other letters that had come. In the first was a poem with a man's name and address typed to it.

If ever you write a line of truth out of the sorrow of your own experience, said Martin, then it's one more deviation on the Via Salaria that runs white and strong from the mouth of one poet to the ear of the other. It is a sharp taste, coming from the sea and briny from the rock, and among poets it exists, the covenant of salt made over sacrificial meals and bloodshed. You never find it in fruit, for fruit rots and falls, but it's there in the root solid, and in the flesh of fish. As for me, said Martin, for all my love of other men's poetry I've never made any sacrifices at all.

And would you have me sit still, he cried out, and hear the words of the poet in Italy, or of any other with that taste tickling his pallet, and turn a deaf ear to him? The music of certain men, he said, will rouse me when I'm dead.

His eyes were so black and deep that there seemed no end to their descent, and such grief was in his face that Hannah put out her hand and touched him gently, fearing the covenant of salt would break and fall from his eyes.

How can you ask more than being a new season to other people? she said to him. The season when skies change their stars and the inwards of things alter.

But Martin put his hand up over his face and said: I am none of these things.

He shook his bowed head slowly from side to side and she put her arm about him.

How can you be sad she said, when everything is now turning out as you would have it? There's the work on the magazine to be done, and it will keep you going like mad. I can type very well, she said, if you'll let me. And I can stick stamps and things on the wrappers.

If I have courage for others, said Martin with his face concealed, still I have none for myself. I have none left to me. I can only have the magazine, he said, when everything is finished between you and me.

Hannah sat quiet beside him, listening to the meaning of his words. Whatever she had thought would come, she had never foreseen it would be this.

Is that what Eve said to you? she asked him after a moment.

When I would give you up she'd have me with her again, said Martin. She said that we could go on together as soon as everything would be over between you and me.

CHAPTER XVII

They each drank down another pernod and then they began to laugh together. They sat close, side by side on the bench, and began to laugh aloud with their grins drawn up sharp in their faces, like people gone suddenly out of their heads. The rain was falling without, and a gust of it struck sparkling against the glass roof of the café. The wind swung strongly in and out about the terrace, and in the street beyond the lights were drenched and all but extinguished by the sudden burst of rain.

Hannah sat close to Martin with her laughter shaking inside her. If she could quiet the thoughts that reeled in her head, she would know what it was they had to do next. Hum-ho, tiddle-dee-oo. Twist your apron, cheery. The door's wide open, Miss Hannah. It's time for you to go. Oh, what an elegant fool I've been for asking! *Where is it you're going, Martin, that I can't go?* It's you that's to go, Miss Hannah, it's time you was on yo' way.

Then what'll you do? she said aloud to Martin. She sat shaking her teeth like dice before him and her whisper was wild and shrill. Hoops, my dear, Miss

Hannah! She knew very well what he would say. He would look up into her smiling face and answer: I want my magazine the way it used to be.

But Martin suddenly put down his head on the table in the face of all the people in the café. She saw that he was crying and for a moment some kind of hope leapt up in her, and then she knew at once that this answer was as final as any other.

Surely you don't want me dying here of shame for you, she said. Now lift up your head, Martin, for we must go out and eat. You were up the entire night and you've driven all day and are ready to fall to pieces. Put your hand in mine. You've been brave through so much in life, do you think it's a little separation from me that will rob you of your strength?

And even now that she said the word separation, he had no will to deny it. She could hear her own voice chiding and urging him.

Come now, we must eat well, and then we'll drive back to the château and get our things away. Whatever comes after that, we'll take care of it after.

Now she would think of the details, she would fill her mind with the objects, the large and the small, the books and the pictures, and the unwieldly bags and cases to be borne out from the château under the sheets of rain. She would think fiercely of the hot-water bottle in its crocheted shirt, and of the dish-cloths, and of the dogs' red wire brush to keep their back bushes in order. But in spite of it all a tide of bitterness and fury was welling up in her. She went out of the café with him, holding him still when his head spun at the door, talking to him, but of the thing that was now black between them she would not speak. Only when the gall of despair turned sour as poison on her tongue did her speech falter.

They drove to a tavern opposite the station and sat down for dinner. Martin ordered lobster and Pouilly, blindly, without thought, as if repeating words he had once heard somewhere. He sat beside her, frail as glass, and listened to her talking.

This is where we had our first drink together when you came, he said bitterly, in a moment. But she made as if she had not heard him speak, and she called out to the waiter. When he had brought them a map of the region she spread it out before them on the table. Martin's eyes never wandered from her face, taking her features softly apart and putting them together again in his sight. And one by one came back to her the things he had written out to the Italian poet, one by one returned to her mind as though it had been a message from his heart written out for her as well.

You will be remembered, he had written down. You will be remembered for this and that and the other thing.

And can people, she asked herself in terror, become strong again after having been as weak as water? Can their pride return to them like a staff they have set aside?

There was the map before them, and La Moure seemed a far enough place to escape to, lying as it did concealed in the hills between Vence and Nice. They could get to it by country lanes that night, with their car packed up with all their belongings, and hire a room in the hotel there.

The hotel will do you for a while, said Hannah. Simple and therefore cheap, of course. And Lady Vanta's friends live just outside the town, and they will be near by you, and perhaps Lady Vanta visiting them now and then, and anyway. Now *you* talk to me, she cried out suddenly, for she felt her own sorrow wringing her voice of its last drops of love.

But when she looked at him, she saw he was frail and worn, he was weary and bowed with the conflict in him. His shoulders were failing and his hands were clenched, and what are we but two leeches at him, she thought? What are we but two empty women turning to him and sucking him dry for a taste of life? The tears came into her eyes and she said to him gently: Now speak to me, and tell me of the loves you've had, Martin, for it gives things a proportion.

His face flushed dark with blood when she spoke, and he took down another glass of wine.

Something becomes of a man's fidelity, he said, when he gives it to a number of women or tries it in a number of places. Had I kept mine more to myself, there might be more of it left to speak of now. When I gave it at first I gave it so entirely that the whole supply of it suffered and wilted and the seeds of it were carried away. Now where they went, I have no idea any longer. There was some of it given to an American poetess who had no use for it. And some more of it was given to a Russian girl who played the violin.

I was living with her, said Martin, when Eve first came to Paris. We couldn't so much as leave the violin on the piano but Eve would cut the strings of it. It was the cat who did it, or the cold that snapped them, or one thing or another, but however it was I found Eve with her nail scissors cutting the throat of the E string one day. Whenever they came to words, said Martin, you could hear them all over Paris. If I wrote down the wind, the wind, I'd have their brawling on the side of my face with a vengeance. How could I sit pretty writing down poetry with the two of them calling each other forty names at the same time?

Suddenly Martin opened his fair white hands out on the table.

But the truth of everything is, he said, that I've come so close to death so many times that I've gone as far as one can get from women. Close to it, Hannah, on the very threshold, there is no one else, you are quite alone. And if to be near death is like death itself, then I am not afraid to be alone.

I am not afraid of how people will speak of me, for of them all there will not be one who will be there. It comes down like a glacier, without motion, antlered like a glacier, steep and castellated. I have stroked its horns. It has beautiful clear seracs that horn the heavens. And growing along the side of it in certain months, there are arnica and gentian flowers, made sharper and brighter than any others because of the deep draughts of ice and death that lie in their stems. Can you imagine, he said, how words of praise or condemnation would shrivel in that air?

Hannah, said Martin, but he did not turn his eyes to her, I wanted to see a glacier again with you near to me. And Venice with all her floods can go down to the bottom, can be forgotten forever as long as I can't show it to you.

The weather outside the tavern was softly shaking the breath in his throat. They sat still beside each other, looking down at the strong simple lines in Martin's open hands, at the untouched lifeline that carried on deep as a gorge of life to the very end.

You can't go away from me this week, Hannah, he said. You can't leave me right away.

As he spoke the door of the tavern came open, and in from the rain came Lady Vanta's friends, came Duke and Phyllis. It was Duke who saw them first and walked over the hall to them. He was a rough, tough, thickset man of forty-five with a mane of curly chestnut hair. His colour was high, his paunch was swelling, and his hobble gave him a lurch like a seaman walking on land. And Phyllis followed, short and broad, with her wide bosom thrust out before her and her eyes aster-blue. When she shook off the hood of her cloak her hair looked a richer yellow than on the night that she had welcomed them with Lady Vanta into her home by the roadside. Her curls were short and bright and bound with the silver meshes of middle-age.

Have you heard anything from Van? Duke and Phyllis asked in one breath, and then laughed aloud that they had spoken the same words together.

But Martin's cold remote mask with strangers had fallen on his face, and he could scarcely bring himself to speak civilly to them as they sat down at table. Bit by bit was he drawn into their talk, slowly, as though he were waking up from sleep and must come slowly to see the objects in the room. They ordered more wine and talking amongst each other they drank it down while the wind blew wilder and wilder outside the door.

Now Van, was Duke saying, is never a writer, for my own definition of that is a story-teller who puts down his pen on the paper and lets it run off with him. The tale takes him in hand and he's written a story before he knows where he's at.

Is it a writer who worries and fumes, takes this word, discards that, with his head so empty of anything that he had no tale to tell in the end? It reminds me, said Duke, of the story they tell of the priest who——

As the time went by, Hannah could hear Martin joining into Duke's laughter, and even exchanging stories with him. The Englishman seemed a man with a wealth of talk, for he had been a naval man, and half the time both he and Martin were speaking at once, and neither was listening to the other. But Martin's cheeks were dark with pleasure and his voice rang out loud while he talked.

When he said: My wife and I have been thinking of running over to La Moure to stop for a while at the hotel there, the faces of Duke and Phyllis filled with light. Oh, and Ah, they cried out, as if this were a promise of nourishment made to hungry people. It was a terrible thing, thought Hannah, the sun that drew people from their own lands and set them off in isolation. In this part of the country every foreign ear was cocked for the sound of English, and when strangers found others who spoke their tongue they did what they could to move closer together.

Oh, you must surely come! cried Phyllis. The hotel is no more than a *bistrot* there, but it's full of sunlight. Duke will stop in and say a word to the landlord that friends of ours are coming. And we're so *near*, she said. Hannah and I can talk *chiffons*, can't we? As for a bath, there's none at the hotel, of course, but you can come every day and use ours if you like.

In a moment they all stepped out into the wet windy street.

Heave ho! Avast! Duke's hearty voice sang out through the storm, and Martin and Hannah ran off under the blowing rain to the car.

CHAPTER XVIII

When they awoke in the morning, the sun was in through the strange small window after the night of rain. The room was dwarfed and distasteful, with the ceiling lowered almost upon them, and the foul smell of the dogs' wet coats hanging on the air. Their own familiar things that belonged elsewhere, their coats, shoes, paintings, were cast about as though a flood had swept them on; and the books, piled one upon another, were drying out before the dead ashes in the grate.

Hannah could still feel the rain in her hair, and Martin's locks were back, dark and wet, from his pure brow. The dogs would never be done licking their tails and their paws into shape after the wild wet night in and out of the château. Hannah's shoes were scarred and running with the three hours of it, and Martin's handsome brown shoes from London were black with rain. She would make a great fire on the hearth to dry them all, and she stepped out of bed and ran across the floor. The timber had been so fair when they entered the room, but now it was defiled by the rain and mire they had brought in with them, and down the heart of the room was strewn a highway of needles where the landlord had got up from sleep to draw in the pine-boughs for the fire the night before.

There was no servant in the place, but the man himself and his wife to cook and tend, and Hannah crossed the hall to the garret where he had shown her the pile of pine-boughs that would serve to warm them. When she stooped in her nightgown to take them in her hands, she could feel the quick rivers of strength stream down her arms and her lungs grow stout with the smell of the wood. They were so fragrant that it seemed the sap must still be living in them, and when she bore the great boughs out, they caught on the jamb of the doors, and on the chairs in the bedroom, as if they were human men seeking to cling to life. She flung their heavy shoulders down in the chimney that was in itself as big as another room, and when she set a match to them they went up like rockets. She stood watching the roaring flame that filled that side of the wall, dusting her hands off and thinking that they must have lain a long time in the loft drying under the sun.

Martin lay silent on the pillow, with his eyes turning to see the furious fire. It cast an angry glow upon the walls and ceiling, and lit the mirror like the setting sun. This is our room for a little while, thought Hannah, and she went about putting their things in place. The dogs came to life and crept close to the blaze and there crouched down, but warily, ready to leap away if a bough snapped in two. In a miraculous torrent of flame, the fire poured up the chimney, and Martin stretched out his hand to it as if it would thaw his silence and warm the speech upon his tongue.

She saw him easy again, smiling at her as she moved about the room in the sun and the firelight, and it was like the first days they had come together.

I am glad we are out of the château, he said. It was black as a tomb.

His eyes were guileless and without treason, and when she thought of Eve her heart went sore in her bosom. Between the two of us we'd make a coward of him. But when I go off by myself, she thought, I'll have no will you come back to mes or will you nots. I'll have my own way, or I'll have none at all. I'll arm myself to the teeth with pride and work until I fall stiff and worn into bed at night. I'll remember him the way he was, and not torn with indecision.

You'll get out of his life as quick as you can for him she thought, but Eve will never put up with this place, let me tell you, for the cabinay's no more than a hole in the floor. Nor would Eve climb the flights, or partake of the meals in the *bistrot* maybe. But I'll not have anything Eve made of you, she thought. I'll get out in a minute or two, but I'll have you as you were.

Hannah looked up from the books and the letters she was sorting out of the wet, and she saw Martin's head as beautiful as a flower on the pillow.

Wait a shake and I'll go down and get your coffee for you, darling, she said, and she buttoned her bathrobe over and ran down the stairs.

The red wine in this place was so new that it turned them sick the first day, and Hannah came down to dinner tired and sick, leaving off her earrings in the bedroom and thinking that the lobes of her ears must be hanging out long and naked. She sat down looking at Martin, and reproaching herself that all day she had been too sick and tired to think of Martin and his legs touching her under the table. All about in the café were the men playing the Italian game with their hands, throwing their fingers out from their palms, and shouting aloud the numbers. In the evening they came in out of the fields and from the work they did and sat drinking at their glasses and reading their newspapers out over the table. Martin and Hannah sat and talked with them, Martin moving his cigarette and nodding when he understood them, or leaning his ear to Hannah so that she could tell him their words.

Martin was lost in their eager faces and talk, but Hannah turned away from their voices. For she had had enough of speech, and now when she said a thing it was to be done. She went out through the café and into the kitchen where the landlord was scalping the trout and drawing the guts out of them, and she told him that she would cook the trout herself for dinner. He was happy to show her how much butter went into the pan, and how neatly the lemons peeled off his knife and fell like crescent moons among the stiff fish corpses. He said it was the lemon frying with the trout that gave them their blush. Hannah tried to curl them up on toothpicks and make them *truites en colère*, but the landlord said it was never done that way.

He said she was not to touch the onions because of the smell and the stain they left behind, but it was a thing she liked to do: to cut them up in patches and wipe the tears off her face that the onions stung from her eyes. He rubbed the fine skin off the potatoes with a heavy cloth and then he dropped them over the fire, and the sparks from the boiling oil set the two of them jumping back from the stove.

Then the landlord began talking to Hannah about an illness which gets you in the lungs. He drew a picture for her on the top of the kitchen table, showing her what was a lung and how the disease would be like a rank marsh spreading through it. His idea of a lung was the shape of a ham and he thought of it being solid with meat and the disease devouring the meat away from the bone. The place where the good part of the lung was he filled in with flour, and the brown papery onion skins was the disease attacking the flesh.

He made the picture very pretty on the table top, and then he said: Your husband is very ill, as though it was that that he had been saying all along.

Oh, no, said Hannah, and she smiled at him because

she could explain to him now how it was. Yes, ten years ago maybe, when he first fell, he was very ill. He ruptured blood vessels all the time, but now he's all healed over and that part is past.

The landlord shook his head at her.

Oh, yes, said Hannah wisely, you see there's a time when it gets you, and if it doesn't get you then, then you never die from that at all. He might die from almost anything else now. There might be an accident in an automobile, or anything.

She went over to the table and began to show him how after a certain time the lung closes up of itself. She pushed the flour across with a spoon and said:

You see, the disease is closed away in here now, and it can't get out.

It gets out, he said. I know. I've seen people with it.

Hannah was sitting on the table's edge, and she picked up another onion and cut it through the heart.

Oh, no, she said, there's a difference.

The landlord looked at her and shook his head.

A little bit later when the season comes, he said, there won't be a free room in the hotel. Maybe you and your husband had better start looking now for another place.

Hannah threw down the knife and went back into the *bistrot*. Now what was Martin's look, she thought in anger, that another man could read that in him? She went in the door and he was still sitting there among the other men, and when he heard her coming he glanced up quickly and watched her walking across the room. She looked sternly, like a stranger, at his face, and it was white and delicate, but she knew it was a tough flower and not a fading blossom. The landlord had filled her with distrust, and she came looking at Martin with a cold and arrogant eye.

Beside him was a working man in a broad black hat who was drinking red wine out of a bottle and singing to himself, and when Hannah came up to Martin she heard the working man say to Martin that he had a fine wife.

You have a fine wife, he said, and he made signs at his own bottle of wine as if Martin was to drink with him. Martin was happy for this sign, and he picked up his own empty glass and held it out to the peasant. He looked up in pleasure at Hannah, and she saw his face transfigured, and he said:

Look, this is the first time a Frenchman has ever offered me anything. And he has been admiring you, do you see?

Hannah looked bitterly at Martin, wondering how they could see any illness in him. Not in his eyes was there any illness, nor in the way his mouth moved around his words. He sat there holding out his empty glass to the workman, but it was not this at all that the Frenchman had wanted. His own bottle was empty and he had wanted to flatter Martin into buying him more. But Martin was so good that he could not believe this for a long time, and it was only when the workman at last moved his own bottle angrily away across the table that he saw that it was so.

When Hannah sat down, Martin ordered the peasant another bottle of wine, and he said: Now just leave us alone.

He looked at the workman and spoke in English to him, holding his nose tight between his two fingers as if he didn't like the peasant's smell.

Drink it and leave us alone, you bastard, said Martin.

But Hannah saw that he was silent, and that it was difficult for him to eat the food before him because he was thinking that he had been deceived, that he had believed in the peasant offering him a drink and that it had not been so.

Listen, Martin, said Hannah, you must eat.

Yes, he said, I must eat.

But he had no heart for it, and in a moment he got up and went out of the place. He went out and stood in the early evening in the square, and when Hannah followed after him he was standing watching the mountain goats coming down in haste from the hills to drink at the fountain. Down they came running on their tough little hoofs, and Martin took sugar from his pocket and fed it to them in his hand and pulled their beards and questioned them.

Do you believe in it, in Love, he said, and they tittered together like old men and slid their yellow eyes in their faces.

CHAPTER XIX

Each time I strike a key of my typewriter, said Duke with his whiskey blooming in his face, it means a cocktail at the Majestic.

He stood on the floor of his own house, the beams of his dining-room laid dark and heavy over their heads, and his own glassware shining in the candle-light on the table. There was the bit of his tooth knocked out in front when he smiled, just as Lady Vanta said it would be.

Just one more drink of this, he said, before we sit down to supper. One line on my typewriter, and he filled their tumblers again with ice, means another bottle paid for. He lurched with his seaman's hobble back to his own chair and sat down. I know how it feels, said he, and he crossed his legs, the shorter one over the other, to be a young writer trying to make his mark. I used to write on duty, on deck, or home on blighty. My advice to every poor begger who's got the itch, is to *write*, and the devil take theories about writing. If anyone can prove to me that a theory alone ever wrote a novel, then I'll pay up my money like a man.

Martin sat sipping his whiskey on the other side of

the table, less blood and bone than a shadow when faced with this fleshly ruddy man.

Now why should there be any pretence about it? said Duke with his strong English voice ringing out in the rafters. Every man's after the selfsame thing, whether it's John Doe, or the chappie next door, or merely you and me. Every bloody one of us wants a house built to his liking, a car that eats up the road, and money enough to eat and drink as we please. He leaned forward genially with his glass in his hand and tapped Martin on the knee. I always looked forward to being a man of means and fame, he said, and you're looking ahead to something as like it as a pea. But how are you going about getting it! said Duke, and his mouth filled up with laughter. By writing poetry! By writing *poetry* of all things, he said.

His breath and his strength had blown all the colour from Martin's face, and now Martin set down his glass on the polished table and cleared his throat as if he were about to speak.

Ten years ago I had ideas myself, said Duke instead. I don't deny it. But there's not an idea going that will put four walls around you and keep a roof over your head. If you looked at this house, he said, and he threw back his heavy head on his neck to eye the rafters, would you think it was built entirely out of words, out of one sentence coming after another, would you think every stick and stone of it was an empty poetic idea put to a better use?

Martin's dark glowing eyes moved over the furniture, over the provençal tables and chests and chairs in the low-beamed room. When his gaze returned to Duke's face he cleared his throat again as though he were about to answer, but Duke's voice rang out before him.

I've seen your magazine, he said kindly, but look here, it won't do if you bring a mission to writing. My God! Where does it get you? It's like going around in a loin cloth and sandals! Writing's not the place for fanatics. We haven't room. Now take Van, for instance. Take Lady Vanta. She wrote a fairly good book, for that sort of thing, but the principal scene was staged around incest. Incest! he repeated. He pointed his finger at Martin. Take it out, I told her, just like that. Take it out and I'll sell your book for you. She put up a little fight, art for posterity's sake, and one thing and another. But now look here, Van, I said to her. Who in the name of bloody decency reads the by-ways of past writings to-day? You keep right out on the big open highway of writing and you can't go wrong. Study the people around you, look what's going on inside of *them*. Don't get carried away by some little quirk in your own way of thinking. A thing like incest, he said with contempt. Who's going to give a rap for incest, except a few perverts, either now or a hundred years from now?

No, said I, take it out. After a bit she came to see things my way. And I sold the book for her. I swear I don't know what you fellows are after, he said, and he swung the dregs of his whiskey in the bottom of his glass. I swear it. What I mean by writing is something entirely different, which doesn't mean that I didn't take time off to read radicals like Wells and Shaw when I was your age too.

Hannah sat quiet, listening to him, and the dogs lay at her feet. Their black brows were lifted and winking in interest at the wooden cage on a side table which held captive two small thin marmosets. The two little beasts were crouched in a corner seeking warmth from each other, rubbing their skinny blue hands over and over, and peeping out like evil men.

But poetry! was Duke shouting out in contempt. My dear man, poetry!

But poetry, said Martin, speaking simply as though the words he was about to say would at last make everything clear to Duke. Poetry is where the search for literature begins.

Eh? Eh? cried out Duke, for Martin's voice was so soft and strange that Duke could not bring himself to hear it. What? he shouted, and then he tossed out his arm to the shelf of books behind his chair.

There are *some* of my own short stories and novels, he said. I've written more. I don't know what you're talking about when you say you're searching for literature. But what I say is that if a man has nothing to write about, then let him turn to something else. For I've noticed one thing in life. And here Duke leaned confidentially forward and narrowed his sky-blue gaze. If a man's a good writer, then he's a good soldier, he's a good swimmer, a good dancer. Do you think because of this hobble I got in the war, said Duke smiling, that I let it hinder my activities or cripple my outlook on life? Why, I walk more in one day than a sound man in ten, and I write my books besides!

Now take Dickens, he said, and he leaned back and clasped his shorter leg with his open palm. There's a case in point. He was a writer, we'll all agree on that I presume, and he was an editor. And he could play the mouth-organ, push a market-wagon, speak on a platform. He had something to *say*.

He had something to say once about Edgar Allan Poe, said Martin. He spoke of him as a miserable creature, a disappointed man in great poverty, to whom I have ever been most kind and considerate. . . . And suddenly Martin's warm laughter ran out. The chill of that kindness and consideration! said Martin, buttoning his coat over. Don't you feel the shiver of it on your spine? There, he said, you have them, right in that wooden cage behind you, Poe and Virginia, holding hands and trying to keep warm!

The sight of the two little marmosets sitting there in misery took all the patience from Hannah, and she jumped up and went across the room.

As for literature, said Martin's voice at the table, it is not a vocabulary. Literature is a taste, and if you can give someone else a taste for it, then you are a writer.

Phyllis followed Hannah to the monkeys' cage and there she put her arm around her.

It's so seldom, she said in a low voice to Hannah, that Duke gets a chance to talk shop. And he revels in it! Just look at the happy faces of our two boys!

Take Walpole! was Duke shouting out, but Hannah could only look into the frail physiognomies of the two little marmosets who watched bitterly through the bars.

They can't get used to the climate, said Phyllis to Hannah. She had made a bed for them of a roll of cotton, and had laid little coverlets of wool over their couch so that they might warm their quaking bones. She put her broad freckled hand into the cage and picked them up, first one and then the other, and laid their brittle bodies down upon the bed of cotton. When they whistled with fury and tried to rise, she held them down by their skinny shanks.

Now do relax, do sleep a little, she said to them. Now cover yourselves over and be sensible, do.

But however she pressed them down, they sat upright again; they sat up in their little bed eyeing the two women and clutching their woollen blankets up under their quivering dark chins. There they sat rigid, with their thin lips twitching, and their eyes shining out in their blue-kid faces.

What do you feed them? said Hannah, and behind her she could hear Duke's voice speaking.

Oh, I've got a use for magic, he was saying. I bring in magic when I need it, here and there. And I've got a taste for language, if that's what you fellows want. I wrote a little story the other day and I brought three different dialects in.

Bananas, said Phyllis in a low voice, answering Hannah, but because Duke's voice came to a halt at that moment, the word rang out clearly across the room. Duke and Phyllis looked quickly at each other and laughed as though some subtle vein of humour bound them.

Martin opened his mouth to speak, but a clock in some other part of the house began to strike and Phyllis lifted her head and listened. That's Chuzzlewit, she said fondly. In a minute you'll hear Barnaby Rudge.

Just a moment before you begin talking, said Duke to Martin eagerly. He fixed Martin's unsmiling face in his blue eye. You see we have eight clocks in the house, he said. It's rather an amusing idea. They all keep just a slightly different time, a matter of a minute each. Four of them are characters out of Dickens, and the fifth is Ellen Terry. You hear that silvery ripple? he said, and now the chimes of the different clocks were following upon one another from every room in the house. That's Ellen getting ready to strike, he said.

He sat with his ear cocked while the painted clock in the corner of the dining-room struck out eight times, and then he tilted his head towards the stairway before she was fairly done, in expectation of the next chime that would issue from above.

There's Benvenuto, he said with hushed delight as he harkened. You know—Cellini.

And then Phyllis cried softly out:

And now our hero, Garibaldi!

They all sat about the table in silence while the deep dooming strokes fell.

And the last one—William Tell! said Duke, chuckling at the humour of it. He *tells* the time, you see, once and for all in no uncertain terms. Each stroke is like the famous arrow shooting home.

Phyllis nodded wisely at him across the room and the candle light as the eight full notes rang out, and when it was done, Duke leaped up and drew his chair close to the dinner table.

Now you sit here, Martin, he said robustly. Martin? That makes things easier, doesn't it? And my name's Duke, you know. You can take the handle right off and throw it away. And Hannah here, right on the other side of me, he said. He took his seat and he said: By God, when I was your age, Martin, I had a wife, my first wife, and three growing offspring. That's enough to keep a man down to fundamentals, I tell you. I had no end of ideas myself how things should be written, but I never had the time to set them down —I was too busy *writing*. And now when a story of mine appears in America, then I change the scenic effects and the names of the characters, and that self-same story makes a hit in a London monthly.

Martin looked up from the grapefruit he was eating with the lace napkin laid over his knee, and his eyes were drunk with whiskey. He set down his spoon and smiled richly at the Englishman.

I then asked Ezekiel why he ate dung, and why he laid so long on his right and left side, said Martin softly across the table, and the soft sound of his voice was so irritating to Duke that he cupped his ear in his hand and seemed unable to hear.

Eh? said Duke. Eh?

And Martin went on: And what did he answer me but the desire of raising other men into a perception of the infinite! This the North American tribes practise, and is he honest who resists his genius or conscience only for the sake of present ease or gratification?

That's a modern way of putting it, said Duke grinning at Martin.

Then your William Blake had a modern turn of mind, said Martin, turning back to his food.

Highbrow or not I used to think the way you do, said Duke hastily and with impatience. You'll see, young man. You'll change your tune when you're forty-odd!

Martin took a swallow of the clear wine and looked at them all around the table.

Then you know, I think I'd rather die young, said Martin.

But the mention of death made Phyllis shake her

yellow curls at them. Even in this imperfect light could be seen the silky strands of grey in their meshes.

Let's talk of something else, she cried out, now that you men have had your say! There's always the subject of clothes or love, for women at least, she said laughing. And taking advantage of Hannah's and Martin's guileless faces she said: Now, tell us, Martin, did you fall in love with Hannah at first sight?

Hannah saw Martin's face go cold with fury that this woman should step so boldly into their life. He set down his fork in silence and turned to Duke on his right hand.

If this is a subject that interests women, he said, for myself I think it a dull one for men.

Duke gave a hearty laugh and slapped his thigh as he swung around to Hannah.

Well, Hannah, you tell us, then, said he, what it's like to be married to a poet who refuses to talk about love!

The colour ran up in Hannah's cheeks, and she could not answer for shyness. All about her she saw their faces, the three of them, like enemies watching: Martin's dark glowing eyes in the candles' halo, and Duke's tongue, like a bloodhound's, showing between his jaws. And Phyllis on the other side, impatient for her to speak and be done so that her own dripping story might be told.

Hannah sat speechless, looking into Duke's bright saucy eyes. And she was thinking: do you know what

Martin can do for you? Do you know he can give you a taste for living that is sharper than all the beauties in the world, and whoever can give you this is the strong light of the day coming to shine on your youth. If you sit with this man thinking that his clothes are different and his words different in a queer way, then maybe you want nothing else of living except the seeking and the finding of your own kind so that you need never know that your humour is a sick thing and your art a hollow thing and all your words fall as heavy as stone into the heart of the man who listens to you.

And Duke's shining eyes were on her in contempt: Ah, yes, were his eyes saying to her. Ah, yes, but you're in love!

CHAPTER XX

The truth is, said Phyllis at last grasping a moment of silence to drive in her wedge, that Duke and I fell in love at first sight at my husband's dinner table!

She looked all about the table, a broad middle-aged woman with her curls going grey and her bosom pouting before her.

We're all pretty much in the same boat, my dears, she said with a laugh. You know Duke and I are not married yet either.

Either! said Martin, aroused by her inclusion.

Oh, come, said Duke, smiling. Van told us the whole story.

What sort of a story did Lady Vanta tell you? said Martin.

The story of you and Hannah, said Phyllis. Van had heard it from somebody else.

But the English! said Martin, setting down his knife in amazement. Their aloofness. Their reserve. Now what happens to it, may I ask, when you bring it to another climate? It seems to expand and blossom, like a tropical flower. A man-eating orchid that lives on juicy bits. It's only when the English have secrets of their own to keep, said Martin with venom, that they settle down in this part of the world.

But the healthy, hearty laughter of Duke, refusing to take offence or to allow it to matter, stretched open his mouth and brought his hale hand down on his knee.

And feed it bananas! he shouted uproariously at Martin. But Martin sat grave and white, looking into his face. A frown had come between Phyllis's brows, for the story of her own romance was on her mind and she wanted it told. She looked swiftly from Martin to Hannah and then she opened her mouth.

International marriages are no go, are they, Hannah? said Phyllis. You tried it out yourself and found that out, didn't you?

But she had no time to wait for Hannah's reply. Instead she went on explaining that she had been so sunburned that her face and neck were red as fire, but Duke had fallen in love with her—perhaps the white dress in contrast to what the weather had done to her complexion—and from the first instant they knew how it was going to be.

I didn't waste a moment, said Duke openly. The next morning I went out and bought a gun, a pistol that slipped easily down in my pocket, and I went right to Phyllis's house. She was married to a Russian chappie, still sentimental as hell about her. But her life had been a raw deal from every point of view for the past fifteen years.

My husband was an archæologist, said Phyllis. You can imagine.

When he'd come home at night, said Duke, he'd leave Phyllis sitting there for hours in absolute silence, his eye glued to a microscope. It was no fun for a lively woman, I tell you.

If a clock so much as struck in the house, said Phyllis, it gave him the jibbers.

You can picture the life she led, said Duke. A woman still young, with the best part of her life before her. I tell you it made my blood boil! After dinner, back he'd go to his study and leave her to entertain the guests as best she could.

It was sometimes difficult for me, said Phyllis modestly.

My God, exploded Duke. Old fogeys with beards down to their middles!

Duke tossed on his chair with indignation, and Phyllis spoke patiently over her folded hands.

I must say he was awfully big about it when the time for the break finally came, she said.

The whole thing reads like a story, said Duke. There was I with all her wrongs on my mind, standing in her parlour that morning, me with my pistol in my hand and she just out of bed, surprised by my early morning call. If you don't come away with me to-night, I said to her, I'm not responsible for what I do. I'd rather you were dead, and myself too, than to know you were sleeping another night under the roof of that boor. But the children, she said. Her first thought was always for them. One thing at a time, said I, and hand in hand we went in to face her husband.

Were you still holding the pistol? asked Hannah.

Duke turned to Phyllis.

Did I have the pistol in my hand then? he asked.

No, I don't think you did, dear, said Phyllis.

No, said Duke, we just walked in simply and naturally, like two children, and went right up to him, hand in hand. He was sitting there in his study looking over some old relics or what-not, and although he had seen me at dinner the night before, he was so absent-minded that he didn't know me from Adam.

But that was just for the first moment, said Phyllis. Afterwards he behaved really nobly.

The thought of her husband's nobility made her flushed blue eyes swim warmly in her head.

I put it to him bluntly, said Duke. I said, Sir, your wife loves me. Well, the old duffer looked up through his spectacles, said Duke, and there was a hint of some affection in his voice. Are you absolutely certain, said the old boy, that you love my wife? If so, I have nothing more to say.

He even gave us a dowry! cried Phyllis. Of course I had money in my own right, but he gave us a lump sum down to make things easier for us. And he agreed that I could see the children whenever I wanted. It wasn't as if they were small enough to really need the constant care of a mother. Fourteen and twelve they were at the time and off to boarding school, what I call the height of independence. Oh, he was really superhuman, the way he made everything easy for us! It's always the women who act badly, said Phyllis with a little grimace. Duke can't get his wife to divorce him.

Suddenly she turned her full warm gaze on Hannah.

Did your husband act in a big way too? she said.

I—don't know, said Hannah in confusion. I've never seen him since.

Oh, when the real thing comes along there's no two ways about it! cried Phyllis. It's got to be faced. There's no quibbling with conscience. You can't turn a cold shoulder to the real thing.

It's all like a dream to me, said Duke in a soft brooding voice. How we went off together, my resignation from the navy which followed soon after. I had a stormy life behind me, I can tell you, and now I could devote all my time to writing, follow up one book with another, something I never thought would come to me while I was still young enough to enjoy it. That was five years ago, he said with emotion, and he turned to look at Phyllis. And this little girl's stood by me through everything. Twelve novels and God knows how many articles on foreign travel. Phyllis has the best sea-legs of any woman I ever met. My God, she's gone through author's squalls and temperamental hurricanes by the score with me and never turned an eyelash. She's done everything but *write* the blamed books for me. She's read up on Garibaldi till she knows the subject backwards—she knows the fighting position of every one of his subordinates. There's a man for you—Garibaldi! said Duke, and he smote the table lightly with his clenched fist. If you don't know the ins and the outs of that little skirmish, I might say you're missing one of the best stories that was ever lived.

They saw themselves so clearly, these two people. So clearly in their own minds they saw the shape of themselves and their actions silhouetted against the ethereal quality of life and event that whether they saw themselves with justice or not was of no real matter. They thought of themselves as two proud possessed people living unconfused and creative, and this endowed them with a blind thick power and conceit.

Now tell me, Hannah, said Martin, when they had bid them good-night and were outside the door in the darkness, now tell me: if Duke is a writer, then what am I? And if I am a poet, then what is Duke? And if Duke is real, then what am I after all?

He flashed on the headlights of the car, and she saw him standing outlined against the clear stream of light. She waited there silent while he stooped to peer into the glaring glass, his slender sloping body flung back against the golden flood. But for all she saw him so clearly, what he was or what she was in herself was obscure to her, hidden, like a veil cast down. Her own self she could not see, but when she thought of being far from him, in another city, then she could see herself, clear and bold, as if living the life of another woman: tall and thin, with her hair cut short and rouge on her mouth, living alone and working, with a secret pride in her own might.

She stood hugging her arms over her bosom in secret satisfaction, waiting for Martin to start the car and drive them back to La Moure. In the end I will be all the things I have never been. I'll have a sharp hard edge, she thought, and she could taste her pride like a good flavour on her tongue.

In a moment Martin had the lights fixed to his liking, and he came back to her and said:

What were you thinking about all this time, Hannah?

He was troubled because she had not answered his voice out of the dark.

I was thinking how I shall live like a woman of rock forever, she said.

She stood hugging her own self to her, secure and apart, and Martin turned his head down towards the invisible road.

I've never been a strong woman because I've never remained to myself, she said. Now I'll be solitary. I know very well there's nothing that can ever again splinter me in a hundred ways.

You can't make yourself over, said Martin bitterly.

He stood there drawing on his gloves and he could not bear her to be so.

You're soft and gentle, he said, and your heart will always be melting like butter for somebody or other. What do you intend to do with yourself? You'd do better not to try to find work. You'd do better to go back to Dilly, poor man, and make him happy.

Before she knew that her hand was lifted, she had struck Martin hard under the mouth. And he raised his own hand in amazement and stepped back against the car, nursing his jaw.

Whatever it is you've left me, she cried out, I'll keep for myself, if I have to fight you for it! It isn't love, it's something the Dukes and the Phyllises haven't had their hands on! It's something better than that! And when I go I'll take every bit of it with me. It's something of you that you can't destroy, and Eve can't snap it in two!

She heard her own voice crying out, strange and menacing, and to escape it she turned and fled down the road. The hand that had struck Martin was ringing with shame by her side, and the words she had spoken now lingered without meaning in her head. Even before the lights of Martin's car had turned to follow her, she felt her knees failing and the tears falling weakly down her face.

CHAPTER XXI

In the morning, when the sun was scarcely in the room, Martin sat upright in bed and reached out for the vessel that came under his hand on the table beside him.

Get up, he said through his teeth. I'm going to bleed.

His voice betrayed no fear and he sat quiet, waiting, while Hannah slipped out of bed and stepped on the timber of the floor. Then the thing within him leapt at his throat and seized him there, clutched fast to his wind and shook him like a rag. His own voice was throttled, and in its place rang out the frenzied barking of a wild fox pursued and almost at the death. Hannah stood wringing her hands before him, seeing the fox fly yapping in agony and terror down through the thundering woods and out again in anguish over the white hot plain. She could see the beast's small frantic eyes and its gasping tongue curled up in its jaws and charred by fire. But Martin she could not see for the sound and the frenzy of the thing that hacked him dry.

Then in deliverance, the fox escaped and fled from

Martin's mouth in a pure exquisite flow. Over his lips in brimming mouthfuls the torrent of blood fell, quenching his thirst with full deep draughts of red. Now, enough, enough, she thought as she stood shaking before him. The vessel was full and she thought she must seize it from his hands and bear it away. He has drunk his full, he has had enough, now he is through, she thought in madness. If I take it from his hands he will fall back and go to sleep on the pillows. Now let him be through, she said to her heart. Now let it be finished. But still the flow came coughing from his mouth, came bubbling and soft as if from a throat of laughter. And suddenly Martin's lips turned up like a tautened bow and he smiled.

Get me the brown bottle, quick, he said in his soft unshaken voice. And his words seemed to Hannah to stem the running tide.

She ran to the cupboard and brought the bottle down from the shelf, and she stood with it in her hand while he wiped off his mouth.

Pour some out in a glass, he whispered to her, and take this thing away.

Slowly and warily he lowered himself upon his pillow and sipped the brown stuff through his scarlet mouth. A strange white beauty had bloomed on his face, and his eyes were bold and fearless. He lay there, peaceful and gentle, with his smile of love arching in his eyes.

You know where the needles are? he said. I mustn't

speak much now. Get out the needles and boil them on the lamp.

Now that it had come, a miracle of relief had fallen upon his features and he lay quiet. The curse was off his head now, the threat had spent itself and no longer breathed in menace in his ear. He lay still, waiting in peace and watching the sunlight come slowly over the room and fill the mirror.

Bring it to me, he whispered, but he did not turn his head to her. Put them here beside me and I'll show you how they fill.

He raised his hand, almost without motion, and grasped the glass tube firmly between his finger and thumb. With a slow deep lingering pressure, he drew the white liquid from the capsule's broken mouth into the heart of the needle. Then he handed it to Hannah.

Clean my arm with ether here, he said.

Ether, thought Hannah, and she ran across the room in the sunshine. Ether, ether, the fierce odour of rotting flowers corked down in violent spices. When she opened the bottle she could see the trail of stench it left behind on the air. She washed his arm clean above the elbow, and whenever her sense reeled and failed she looked into Martin's quiet eyes.

Now stick it in, he whispered.

Hannah held the needle over his flesh.

Pinch up a bit of the arm in your other hand, he said.

I can't, said Hannah. But there were his soft wooing

eyes upon her. He lifted his own hand carefully and between his fingers held the flesh in place.

Now run it in sideways, he said. And while his voice hung calm and quiet between them, she thrust the needle into his steady arm.

Press the end slowly down, said Martin. Let the liquid go in gently as it will. You do it very well, he whispered and he smiled into her face above him. My Hannah, he said.

Hush, said Hannah, don't speak. Save your breath to tell me now what I must do.

Ice, said Martin softly. And close the sun away.

Hannah put on her clothes, picking them up from the floor in her haste and her confusion: a stocking of one colour and one of another, blindly putting her sweater on inside out, and hastening down the stairs. She walked into the *bistrot* where the landlord was sitting at the bar reading the paper.

It's a beautiful day, she said, and her teeth were shaking. I'd like a piece of ice to take upstairs.

Ice? said the landlord. He set down his paper and looked at her. Ice? said the fellow, and then a wary look came into his eye. You want ice? he said. You and your husband weren't down for breakfast this morning. Is he feeling ill? he said.

He's tired this morning, said Hannah. He's staying in bed for an hour. We were out late last night. Can you give me some ice to take upstairs?

I have no ice here, said the landlord. It costs money

to get it from Cannes, but I can order it for you. Here's the bill for the week you've been here, so you can pay for the ice and the week at the same time now.

Hannah put the bill in her pocket and went upstairs to Martin. And where's your money, darling, she said. Just point, don't talk.

Martin shook his head on the pillow.

Expecting it to-day or to-morrow. Poste Restante at Cannes. How will we get it? he whispered. You can't get it. I have to be there with my passport.

Hannah was standing by the window in the little room, and through the half-drawn blinds she could see the far hill against the skyline, fashioned and broad like the hill that reared up under the château beyond Vence. She saw the black edge of the trees across its mild bluish brow, and then just below the melting curve of shadow they cast she perceived the tall pale pillars of a big house that stood there, far and high. She stood reflecting on what next she should do, seeing the hill and the house built on it almost without sight, and then it struck through her like a blow that the pillars she saw standing forth in the sun were truly the portico of the château they had fled from, outlined on a clear day against the dark trees for her, scarcely a dozen miles away. And the anger of the shop people and the houseowner's just fury must still be storming against those walls, she thought. The sight of the château shining out white and flawless in the sun stirred her, and she cried out to herself: I must send money to those people! This is not a way to be!

She turned back to Martin in haste and softly laid her hand on him.

Now do not think of it, she said. Put the money out of your mind for the moment. It can be settled in a hundred ways.

Now put it from your thoughts, she said. You are a poet and a man of wisdom and have better things to think of. If I had poems of my own to write, I'd be singing another tune. Now leave me the womanly cares and I will deal with them. I'll have ice in a jiffy for you, and your cheques from the government too.

But don't leave me for long, whispered Martin. At times it begins again, a little while after.

I'll have ice in a jiffy, she said, and she ran the comb through her hair at the mirror. She put rouge on her mouth and smiled in the glass at him. Ice in a jiffy she said. And because of her words Martin's face went soft and gentle again in peace. I'll get your ice, she said. Just hold your horses. Don't you worry, Mr. Sheehan. She put on her jacket and took it off again. She whistled to the dogs, and then she sat down in a chair.

Martin's face lay soft and trusting on the pillow. His eyes were closed and he seemed to be drifting into sleep.

Now where can I get ice from? she thought to herself and then a scream rose up in her throat. If anything happens to Martin, she thought in fury, I'll kill the whole God-damned countryside. But she knew that he would not die, because now it was over. The lung was healing now with every breath he drew, and he was falling into sleep.

In a moment she reached out her hand for paper, and she began writing a letter to the Poste Restante at Cannes. Whatever mail there was must be sent to them here. Martin's passport was lying among the books, and she opened it and copied his signature from it, each letter formed miraculously like the other: Martin Sheehan, as well as he might have written it himself, for her mind had gone from her and, whether the need was there or not, her senses were sharpened to craft.

Softly, so as not to awake him, she called to the dogs and moved over the floor. But Martin's eyes had flashed open and were on her.

Who did you write to? he said in a whisper. She showed him the address on the letter. She stood at his side, and he said: You must promise not to borrow money from Duke and Phyllis. Promise me. They've too much conceit as it is, he said in a bold whisper. They've got health and a house of their own, and I won't have them holding their money over me too.

CHAPTER XXII

Now that it was March a sultry spring, like the breath of the sirocco stirring, blew hot over the hills. Every house that faced on the square had drawn its blinds, hoarding the clear darkness within, and old women sat in the doorways knitting and watching the water in the fountain fall. Hannah came out the door of the *bistrot* and in the deep dust the lizards slid off for shelter, slipping hither and yon like quicksilver running in the dust. The old women's heads went up in their bonnets and they watched Hannah cross the square in the sun and go into the village Poste.

There were no flowers abloom in the town, and no colour in the garments of the people. For all that they spoke a *patois* soft with Italian here, they had no indolence or grace. Hannah bought a stamp for the letter and put it in the box, and turned to see the children gathered close in the doorway. In their puniness and dirt they might have come in off a city's rancid street; they might have been bleached white in the face for the lack of sun in tenements. They had soiled faded eyes and sores about their mouths.

Wherever she went the dogs came after her, carrying their tails high and waving them like kingly wands whenever she spoke their names. They were out at the elbows and shabby now because of the time they had lain in wait for action on the tiles of southern floorways. It was like an afflicted town she led them through, with the clothes of the people and their country faces mourning for nourishment and air. Yet all about below there thrived the fields, and in the valley the rose plantations flourished. It was so early in the season of heat that the stream at the hill's base had not yet parched and perished in the sun. Hannah could tell the way it took below by the thick tall stems of emerald grass growing up through the faded grasses.

Hannah went running down the road, hastening through the countryside to Duke and Phyllis with the craft of getting money from them sharpening in her head. To borrow from them, without giving it that name, so that Martin might bide his time until the place healed over. To go back to him with ice and money in her hand, and a lie of how she had come by it. Every thought that passed was choked and stained by the chattering fear that even now the blood might be spilling from Martin's mouth.

On her left hand as she fled, she saw the cemetery. It was hung with great bouquets of wax and silver blossoms. The steel wreathes on the tombstones shone out like diamond rings. The whole field of dead men was alive with painted likenesses and vases of red and blue and white refulgent flowers, with a treasure of golden bars and glittering anklets, and long deep corridors of dark where the shade of the tombstones fell. For their dead the country people had turned their pockets out, and Hannah fled past the spectacle of their extravagance.

She went through the gate to Duke and Phyllis's house and she saw the elms and the ivy stirring. The china cats and the porcelain doves sat quiet and plump under the eaves in the sun. When she pulled the cord at the doorway, a cascade of bells sounded out through the halls.

Martin is ill, she said. She had said it again and again to her own ears, but now Duke's beery face was there before her. Martin is a little bit ill, she said smiling, and I would like to have some ice.

She felt that she must say no more, but as if Martin had bid her, must keep some shame from strangers. The courage of meeting the eyes of other people wide with fear had failed her, and in cowardice she smiled a soft fearless smile into Duke's uncertain glance.

Come in, Hannah, and have a cocktail, he said. All the ice you want, Hannah. What's the matter with Martin? The dinner party last night too much for him? I'm sorry he's not up to scratch.

Give me the ice, please, now, said Hannah. I'll take it in a bowl or a bucket. He's tired. I can't let him stay alone.

Ice, said Duke, and he took her arm and drew her

into the house with him. Phyllis has driven the car down to Cannes for the market. Now let me see.

Ice, he said, and he turned around in the gleaming dining-hall. Poor old Martin, he said. That's hard luck.

He rang the bell for the serving-man.

Now let me shake you up a cocktail, he said to Hannah. I suppose you want to give Martin an ice-pack on his head? That's a sound idea. Takes the fever off in a jiffy. I used to know a chap who had tropical fevers—wrote about him in one of my books, by the way—and he used to keep an ice-pack on his head when the fever came back on him.

Ice, said Duke. Of course, we make it ourselves in our refrigerator here. But it's one of the most compliant things in the world.

The serving-man came in with the cocktail shaker white with ice, and Hannah said: Duke, please, I'll have to go.

But just a minute, said Duke. The fellow will tie you up a bucketful. He shook the liquid hard and swift in his hands. A swallow of this will set you up for the climb up the hill.

Ice, said Duke as he poured the amber juice forth from the shaker's silver snout. I like every manifestation of it. We take it for granted in Great Britain, of course, but take India, for instance. Do you know, Hannah, that in a climate such as India's, ice can be made on clear cold nights by leaving water, you see, in a porous vessel. The evaporation through the pores does the trick.

Duke handed her the little frosted glass, but Hannah paid no heed to it.

Duke, I've done the maddest thing, she said. I don't know how to tell you.

Oh, come, Hannah, said Duke, as though he were grieved to the core.

I was rather upset, she said, and she saw her hands were shaking. And I went in to send a letter to the Poste Restante at Cannes about our mail. I had five hundred francs in my hand, a bill of five hundred, you know, along with the letter, and when I came out and started down the road to ask you for ice, that five hundred franc bill was gone.

I feel such a fool, she said, and her voice was shaking with nervous laughter. There was a crowd of children around the door, and I suppose one of them picked it up. I went back and looked at once and asked the woman at the desk, but no one had seen a thing, or at least pretended they hadn't. Of course Martin's money will come from Cannes in a day or two, but in the meantime it makes things pretty tight.

I say, you *are* running in bad luck! said Duke. He brought out his purse with the seaman's crest on it and opened it before her. All the bills that were in it he put into her hand. She counted it out on the table before him, and her shame was burning hot in her face.

That makes eight hundred, she said.

Don't think of it, said Duke, filling up his glass. It makes me think of the time Lady Van——

But the servant stepped in through the doorway with a pail of ice tied fast in a dishcloth, and Hannah leapt to her feet.

The ice, she said, and she was about to seize it from his hand, but Duke bade him carry it up the hill beside her. She ran out of the house in haste, calling good-bye to Duke, leaving him standing there with his cocktail still in his fingers.

The presence now of ruddy upright people had become like an affront to Hannah. In the *bistrot* she paid out the money owed the landlord, and his thick neck and his wrists in his shirt seemed foul to her with health. His nails were black with soil or some other element of well-being.

There's fifty francs extra, he said with a smile, for the pine boughs and the view you have from your window. If you'd taken a room on the other side I could have made it a cheaper price for you.

He looked at her warily as he took the money in, and then he said:

I don't think the climate is suited to what your husband has. If you called the doctor in he might say it was better that you moved him away.

He's got a cold on the chest, said Hannah. He has a touch of the grippe.

The landlord shook his head from behind the bar

and smiled at her. His eyes were small and dark in the fat of his face, and his pores were glistening with grease from his lavish health or the kind of cooking he did for his customers. And his eyes, for all their scantness, did not spare her. I saw the thing you tried to get clean of blood, they said to her. I saw the pyjama shirt like a murdered man's stuck away in the corner of the loft where you thought no one would see.

CHAPTER XXIII

Phyllis and Duke came in the afternoon. They brought grapefruit and Perrier water, and when they came in the room and saw him lying there, they did not speak. They stood in the centre and the sun was closed out and fell through the shutters in angry welts by the wall. Like strong sturdy cattle they came lowering and shouldering into the cramped place, with light on their yellow hides and their eyes shining, and then they stopped short at the brink of the pool where the water lay in darkness, and they tossed up their short stubborn muzzles and would not drink.

The covers were folded neatly down over Martin's heart and his hands lay out upon them.

Oh, said Phyllis in a whisper. Can't he sit up?

In them there was a terrible fear and hate as if they were in the presence of death itself. Hannah stood between them and the bed on which he lay, remembering how they took the air into their own lungs with a deep special pride, and how when the wind came down around their house in the evening they turned their heads and spoke of it as if it were their own. They were older people, but they had in their minds set Hannah and Martin apart from all the rich possessions of life as though these were theirs and the young people were promised in each other to death. She remembered that they never took a cigarette out of Martin's case when he opened it before them, and that the woman would not lick the stamp that Martin had given her when she had a letter to mail.

But then as they stood there, Duke returned to his pomp, threw out his chest where the chestnut hairs leapt through his shirt and removed his canvas helmet from his head.

Well, they've laid you out in fine shape! he roared at Martin.

Laid him out! breathed Phyllis. Duke, what a thing to say!

But Martin had no words and no breath to waste on them. His courage was elsewhere, healing with respiration the hole that gaped within. His eyes were gay and eloquent and there in his face conversed with his guests and wooed aside their candour. He looked at the grapefruit swollen in their hands and smiled, praising the size and colour with such blandishment as the words spoken out of his mouth might have done.

Martin looked them strongly over and thanked them with his eyes. When he closed his lids they knew they could go away.

Oh, can't he speak? whispered Phyllis to Hannah outside the door. Her blue eyes were starting out of her head.

To-morrow, said Hannah with the latch held tight in her hand. He's saving his breath because he's tired to-day.

Which doctor have you called? asked Duke, and Hannah answered: Martin's been ill like this before. He can do for himself anything the doctor might do. He'll lie still to-day and be better to-morrow.

But Duke was shaken. He put his hand under her arm and wiped his brow with his handkerchief. He had turned yellow and rank as butter under the eyes.

Come down and have a drink in the *bistrot* a minute, he said.

Hannah went in the door and touched Martin's hand.

I'll go as far as the café with them, she said. I'll be up right away.

Martin smiled at her under his closed lids and nodded his head gently, as if a breeze had passed his face. When Hannah went down she found Duke and Phyllis waiting on the square.

They sat under the umbrella in the sun, for the landlord had fancy ideas enough and had set little tables around the door outside with parasols striped yellow and white to shield the alcohol and the delicate crowns of his guests from the vengeance of the sun. Each swallow that Duke drank down from the glass of green smoked white emerged again from his lips in portent. The wit and the courage of other men lies in these glasses, Hannah thought. She took down her drink, in haste to return to Martin's side.

You're a young woman, said the false courage deep

in Duke's green glass, you're a young woman, Hannah. Why don't you go back, Hannah, he said, why don't you go back, go back from where you came?

Why don't you go back? said the womanly echo lying in Phyllis's drink. One man is very like another. Why don't you pack up, Hannah, and go back. We can telegraph Eve Raeburn and get her here in half a day.

Why don't you go back? said the green drink in Duke's voice. Why don't you go back to the man you left behind? I'm old enough to be your pa. I'm talking like a Dutch uncle to you, darling. Why don't you go back before you've caught it too?

Why don't you go back? said Phyllis with her eyes as small as needles. Why don't you go back to your husband and make it up again? We heard all about it from Van. Lady Vanta told us how the old wretch went off and left you with Martin sick on your hands. And what could you do, with the nature you have, but shoulder the burden? But we'll get her back, Hannah dear, said Phyllis. We'll make it hot for her. I'd like to see her before me now and I'd tell her what I think.

It wasn't that way at all, said Hannah. That isn't how it happened. You don't know anything about it or why she went away.

Then tell us then, said Phyllis. Her long white teeth smote against each other in eagerness and she reached out and covered Hannah's hand.

But Hannah jumped suddenly up from the table.

I'm going up to Martin, she said, and she smiled quickly at them. Duke had brought his mandolin with him, perhaps thinking to play and sing for Martin to help pass the hours away. But now it lay forgotten by his chair, and the humorous songs he might have sung were humming in his throat, muted in disappointment because the invalid had no ear to hear.

Dear, you must count on us, said Phyllis. They both looked fully at her with the drink swimming in their faces. If you need—anything. Why don't you go *back*? said Phyllis desperately to her, and she put out her hand with the rings on it and clutched Hannah's skirt. I can't bear to have you—trapped, she said.

Hannah released Phyllis's fingers from her dress and leaned over them smiling.

Have another drink on me, she said. I'm going up to Martin.

She went through the *bistrot*, still smiling, seeing herself in her blue dress with her hair combed back, reflected through the painted trees on the glass. She ran up the first flight of stairs, and then she heard her own voice in her mouth groaning aloud with anguish. The dark snoring cries of someone in pain were coming from her mouth. She pressed her thin back to the wall and held her hands off from her in terror.

Martin, Martin, Martin, my love, she whispered fiercely, and she fled up the stairs.

He was lying quiet but fiery-eyed on the bed, and when she went to his side he turned in fury upon her.

You were gone hours, he said. How can you leave me alone?

Hush, don't speak! said Hannah. You must lie still, Martin.

You borrowed money from those people! cried Martin.

Not really, said Hannah. I told them a lie and they gave me the money. They really believed that I had lost ours. I'll pay it back when the cheques come.

You did what I told you not to do, said Martin. Why do you stay with me? Now that I'm ill you might as well go back to Dilly.

Ah, don't speak, don't speak, said Hannah, kneeling and pleading by his side. You will do yourself harm.

Why don't you go back to Dilly? said Martin, whispering sharply at her. I permit you to. In fact, I advise it. Save yourself while you can. It won't be the first time I've relied on my own black magic!

She had no words to say before his unquenchable passion, but she drew near to him and put her hand on his hair.

You've been down there talking of me and disease to those people! he said fiercely. Did they speak of contagion to you? Did they tell you how to fumigate your mouth and disinfect your lungs? Why don't you go back to Dilly? he said, and suddenly the tears came up in his eyes.

My love, my love, said Hannah, and they held each other close like children. They whispered words into each other's mouths, and when Hannah felt his tough white bones under her fingers she knew he would not die.

CHAPTER XXIV

For two days they sat in the room with the door closed, waiting. The sun came through, and gusts of summer wind, but the landlord sat downstairs, and the sound of his wife's voice shrewing the barmaid and the dogs of the village was all they had of them. When the letters from Cannes came he put them on the first step of the stairway and skipped down again with his plump glossy hand running lightly along the bannister of the stairs. Hannah above saw his toes winking in and out of the railing, down to the second, the first, and out through the café door. She stooped for the letters and carried them back to the room.

Wherever Eve was, she was no longer ominous in Martin's face, and now when he laughed he laughed silently with joy in his flat belly. He was ill and he could give his first thoughts to himself now; he need no longer brood on the single, solitary woman who waited his coming in another city. The books were there, like a crowd of hushed people in the room, and when Hannah opened them and read aloud he turned up his mouth and lay shaking with laughter in bed.

But, boy, you did your strong nine furlong mile in slick and slapstick record time and a far-fetched deed it was in troth, out of the page of Joyce to fill his belly and eyes with laughter.

Not on the bed was there room for her, for the books were all about, and the words read out into Martin's hunger lay softly here and there in the corners. Wherever she was, with her fine contempt and her pride, Eve was cocking her ear elsewhere, smiling at other faces over the sour pit of furious love in her body. She was not between the lines they read nor enmeshed in their speech like a thing struggling to escape upon their tongues. She now belonged to legs that strode and voices that spoke out above a whisper. If her hard voice had shouted once in the room, everything there would have crawled under its own shadow or that of the next, and spat. Whatever Eve would have said would have been strange words out of her situation with life, for conflict and love had gone by in her brothers' part in the Boxer Rebellion, and had left her a trunkful of Chinese coats and her unbroken will.

When Hannah came in the door, there Martin's hunger gaped on the pillow in his deep motionless gaze, there Martin's silent love waited. His hands fell on the open books and the words written on them as if they were beautiful stuffs, texture to feel between thumb and finger, the silk and satin of other men's mouths to fumble and touch.

Read me some more, said Martin's voice. Have them he would from the page on which they were written.

Read me some more, said Martin in his strong gay whisper. Read me some more, like a man starving that must know that elsewheres were men eating well and carrying their wine like gentlemen. Read me some more, he whispered, with his fingers twitching over the pages, another man's banquet served to his liking. Read me out of this book, read me some more.

All day they read, and half the night: *The Discovery of Kentucky*, William's *Discovery* which said: As an Indian to the wild, without stint or tremor, Boone offered himself to his world, hunting, killing with a great appetite, taking the lives of the beasts into his quiet, murderous hands as they or their masters, the savages, might take his own, if they were able, without kindling his resentment. . . . It was against his own kind that Boone's lasting resentment was fixed, *those damned Yankees*, who took from him . . . in his old age every last acre of the then prosperous homestead he had at last won for himself after years of battle in the new country.

This was the America with which Martin felt bondage, and the skyscrapers might never have been reared aloft. The country of Pocahuntas: a well-featured, but wanton yong girle, Powhatan's daughter, sometymes resorting to our fort, of the age of eleven or twelve years, get the boyes forth with her into the market place, and make them wheele, falling on their hands, turning their heels upwards, whome she would followe, and wheele so her self, naked as she was, all the fort over.

Dostoevski's Russia, or Joyce's Ireland, the Italian poet's Italy to which he had returned ailing when America had broken him in two.

But on the second night when Hannah had sat down beside Martin and opened her mouth to read, the lights had gone out in the room. She could turn the wings of the switch back and forth as she liked, but still no miracle of light came into the glass bulb over them. Perhaps the fuse is blown out, Hannah said across the dark room to Martin.

No, Martin's bitter voice had answered. No, I know very well. The landlord has closed the meter because we read too late. It's happened to me before.

She felt her way back over the room to him, past the elbows of the table and the black shins of the chairs. She sat down close to the bed, not daring to stir the springs by lying upon them. Tell me a story now, said Martin out of his wild clamorous hunger for words to be spoken. Hold my hand and speak. Defeat the dark.

But before she could begin he spoke again out of the obscurity that concealed his face from her. What do you think of Eve? he said.

Hannah sat a long time quiet in the silence that prevailed, pressing her hands together on her knees. After a little she said: You are the one thing left to her.

Hannah, said Martin, and his voice was strong and sweet. Do you think Eve could want you too?

No, said Hannah.

Ah, don't say that! cried out Martin in the darkness. It's the one thing I have set my heart on! I can't give you up, he said. I cannot do it. And I know that I could bring her to love you too.

There are a few things I do not believe any more in the world, said Hannah in a strange tight voice to him. She could not see his face, but she knew he was waiting with his eyes turned to her for the words she had to say. She held her own hands tight in her lap and she said: Ever since you told me the other night that you had to make a choice between us, and that you had made it, I knew that love is narrow as a coffin. It is not wide and warm, she said, like—like Whitman's love. It casts everyone else out. It is sharp and pointed, like a thorn.

But I believe in my own miracles, said Martin. And I believe that Eve can want us both.

What do you, yourself, think of Eve? he said again in a moment.

Hannah thought slowly and carefully of Eve in her mind.

I think she is brave and full of indignation, said Hannah. She is ferocious and unjust, and these things I like. It is only her cruelty that I do not envy. And the worship and contempt she has for man. She could never like a woman as well, for she thinks there is not so much prestige in winning another woman's love.

How would you like to live with Eve? asked Martin.

In the same house? said Hannah.

Yes, under the same roof, said Martin. Eat with her, share a place with her.

Is that what you want to do? said Hannah.

Martin stirred in the dark.

I'm putting a question to you, he said.

Hannah sat close and still beside him, and in the black churning emptiness before her, the things that she believed grew strong and clear.

If the room were not dark, she said softly, I don't think I could speak out this way to you. If that is what you wish, she said, that is what I will try to do. If this seems like weakness to you, then I am not afraid of weakness. However things were, she said, I would want to be with you. The other night you said to me in anger that when I left you I should return to Dilly, but that is as impossible as if I should say to you, now you must get up and walk ten miles to-night.

Then you must believe in me, said Martin in comfort. A great peace seemed to have fallen on him, and he seemed to Hannah so strong and far as to have no need of her. In his love for them both he was playing them one against the other, and when he is well, thought Hannah, surely my own pride must take me away.

CHAPTER XXV

But when the morning came these words might never have been spoken, for there was no sign of them in either of their faces. Their life lay still and composed over the pages of the open books.

Now read me this and read me that, until up came the landlord hippety-hop, with his mouth full of eye-wash, and left the letters from Cannes at the top of the stairs. And even when Hannah came through the door Martin had no idea of what she was bringing.

Are the cheques there? he said eagerly, as though nothing else stood between them and ease. There lay the long envelope, and Hannah said: Yes, Martin, the money's here.

God bless you, said Martin. We'll pay back Duke and Phyllis. His smile spread out and he opened his arms to her. It is time for spring now, he said. Now it is time for spring. Every thought that comes will be new sweet soft fresh out of the sod. Open the windows wide, said Martin, and he sat up in bed. Open the windows and let in the season.

There's a post card from Eve, too, Hannah said.

She put the card in his hand, the picture of the

casino at Monte Carlo, with all the geraniums painted in, bedded in the fair green lawns. Martin picked it up and he said:

Eve's in Monte Carlo.

He turned the card over, and then turned it sideways for the rest of the message, and then he held it out to Hannah.

You might as well read what she says, God damn her, he said bitterly.

It was written out clear and straight across the blank side of the card so there would be no mistake about it. Anyone who picked up the card could see it at a glance. Expecting you here at Palace Hotel, Friday. Engaged room. Magazine will go to press at the end of the month.

And up across the corner in a smaller hand of Eve's was written: Don't forget to bring the original Derains with you and the *two* Boxer coats. I wouldn't lose them for the world.

Hannah read the card with a feeling of shame rising in her. When she handed it back to Martin she saw the anger that had flared into his face.

She just mentioned the Derains and the coats because of you, he said, because she knew you liked them. She thought I might give you one or the other.

It doesn't matter, said Hannah.

I'll give her a piece of my mind, said Martin. His fingers were pecking wildly at the bedclothes. She thinks she can say anything and have nothing thrown back at her. She wrote it on a card, he said in fury, so that you'd surely see.

Hannah saw him sitting there in anger, plucking at the sheets and cursing Eve's temper, cursing her pride that blew her full of venom.

I'm going to ram you down her throat, he said. I'm going to dangle your picture before her. I'm going to talk about you until she knows what you are. I'm going to have your photograph all over my room and write poetry to you all my waking hours. If she won't have you, then she can't have me in her life.

Be still, Martin, she said. You'll go when you're well and spend a little time with her and see how it goes.

From every word he spoke she knew he would go to Monte Carlo. He was pulling wild at the bit to be gone and speaking his fury out to a fury that would match his own.

Ah, yes, I'll go, he said. I'll go.

Are you well enough this week? Hannah said.

Oh, yes, said Martin, yes, by Friday. I'll throw her Derains in her face and choke her in her Boxer jackets.

He sat erect in the bed with his shadow mimicking and writhing on the wall behind him. His black locks tossed wildly on his brow and his hands opened out and clenched in anger.

By God, he said. By God.

The fever came into his face and glowed there and he looked with his wild impatient eyes at Hannah.

I'll be a new man by Friday, he said. I'll be another man.

The knock on the door was short and sudden, and Hannah jumped up and crossed the room. When she opened it she saw Phyllis and Duke standing close together in the evil hall, hushed and imminent with fear in their eyes.

Hannah, dear, how is he? said Phyllis. The landlord told us he was worse.

Hannah stepped through the door and closed it behind her.

He's much better, she said. He's sitting up to-day, but he's been talking so much I'm afraid he's tired.

There was a thing so hesitant and placatory in their manner that she could not fathom it.

Hannah, said Phyllis, and then she halted. Duke cleared his throat and looked steadily into Hannah's eyes.

Now, Hannah, he said, you mustn't think we're unreasonable. But we know you're a sensible girl and that you'll agree with us about the proper thing to do. Now, Hannah, my good friend the landlord is very much disturbed by this illness of Martin's, and so is the rest of the village. Moreover, it's very uncomfortable quarters for the two of you here.

Duke put his hand on her shoulder and spoke directly to her.

We've done the only possible thing that friends could do under the circumstances. We've brought a good English doctor here to examine Martin—and, by way of precaution, he's brought an ambulance along.

An ambulance? said Hannah in bewilderment.

Yes, an ambulance, said Phyllis, and she laid her full bare arm about Hannah's shoulders. It's the only thing to do, dear, surely you see that? Martin will be so comfortable, and so well taken care of.

Hannah stepped back in silence and put her hand on the door-latch.

Please go away, she said. I don't know what you're talking about. Wait, let me give you the cheque to cover the money you gave me. Martin's endorsed it to you. He's almost well again.

But Hannah, said Phyllis softly and patiently, but Hannah, you must see things as they are. Martin, she faltered and she looked to Duke for courage. Martin is —dying. There's no use picking and choosing words, Hannah dear.

She had said it once and now she could say it again with relish.

Martin is dying, Hannah, she said, and you must give him a chance to fight for life.

What do *you* know about it? said Hannah in a hushed dry voice. She stood with her back against the door, facing the two stout sturdy people. If I could get my hands in *you*, she thought, I'd wrench the health out of you and make it serve a better purpose. She felt the life sapping out of her bones, but she turned swiftly and fled into the room.

There sat Martin, sitting up against his pillows looking to her for explanation. She turned the key in the lock behind her and stood with her back against the door, gasping for life.

What is it? cried Martin. What are you keeping from me?

Duke and Phyllis have brought a doctor. An English doctor. Do you want to see him? she said through her shaking teeth.

What good can a doctor do me? said Martin in irritation. I've seen two thousand doctors. There's very little left of me, except the part doctors don't know anything about. So what can they do about it? Prescribe bread and milk and chastity. You can't write poetry on bread and milk, and you can't grow strong on chastity. Well, bring him in, he said in a moment. Give me a cigarette, he said. I can sharpen my wits on him, anyway.

CHAPTER XXVI

The three strong people who entered the room where the man lay ill on the bed, now seemed terrible in their health to Hannah. Every breath they took seemed a wilful theft from the man lying ill. She stood with her eyes cast down, but she was spying upon them, as if to filch from them slyly the healing sap of a few warm drops of blood. Her glance moved stealthily across the doctor's broad stout back in his spotless tweeds, detected the healthy meat on his neck and the pink scalp carefully done beneath his thin white hair. All through his body ran sound fresh blood, and his chest was deep as a barrel. Even the golden fleece on the rims of his ears and in his nostrils she hated for the strength and purity from which it sprang.

Good day, sir, said Martin as though they were both strong men standing up as equals and wringing each other's hands. Make yourself at ease, if there's any to be found here. The one chair we have is as hard as charity, and you look as if you came from a cleaner country than any this hotel has been used to.

I come from England, said the middle-aged doctor mildly as he sat down.

My disease is not for the English, said Martin. He picked up the package of cigarettes from the table and passed them about. The doctor himself leaned forward and took one between his fingers, but Duke and Phyllis smiled wanly at Martin and shook their heads.

What I have, said Martin, pulling the smoke into his mouth, is for the outcasts. It should go off alone with a bell around its neck and cross the desert, or it should go to high places and end there.

I was going to speak to you about a mountain place I have in mind, said the doctor genially.

I've known so many, said Martin leaning forward. I'd rather you talked to me about England, for being Irish, he said with his eyes dark with delight, or at least as much as Poe was Virginian—being Irish, I have a curiosity for England that will never let me rest. When I see an Englishman coming along the street in a foreign city, I cross over to be on the same side of the street with him. I like the way his clothes hang on him, or do not, and the width of his shoes, and the way his neck goes straight into his shoulders. Englishmen walk very well, you know, said Martin, for all their feint of slouch and their careless easy ways.

I had a special place in mind, said the doctor quietly. I've recommended it to several patients and they found it remarkably beneficial.

Not Chamonix? said Martin smoking. Not Hauteville? Not the Swiss Alps, or the French, or the Italian? I've tried them all and they can't have me yet awhile. Not while I still have legs to carry me. They got me to Hauteville once, on a stretcher, and two nights later I made my getaway through a back window and walked six miles to the station. Everyone who knew me said I was a better man for the cure in Hauteville, and I tell you I was a better man for that walk under the moon.

Can you or any other man of wisdom, said Martin to the doctor, can you tell me anything of myself that I do not know already? If you could be anything else but the man outside looking in, then I might hold my tongue and listen. But I know very well that I have the advantage, for I am the man inside looking out. That is the fallacy of medicine: you cannot alter general knowledge to fit a special case. It's badly cut for any man's shape or figure. If you want to cure me, said Martin, then you have to begin fifteen years back when I started hopping freight trains. It's no mountain vista or eggs or milk that can work the miracle now. Something else might heal me, but if you'll pardon me, sir, it's nothing a doctor could do. It might be done by America restored to the Indians, or an entirely new race of proud men sprung up, or enough good books written out of the austere spirit of people who do not falter or conform.

Martin passed another cigarette to the doctor, who shook his head.

I suppose you've been told, said the medical man quietly, that smoking——

Yes, said Martin, lighting another. Yes, I know. Or drink. Or talk. But still being alive I find it hard to dispense with the gestures. There's time enough ahead to lie quiet. Once I made up my mind to take myself to heart like an ill man and I went up to a place called Beuil. Good and clear, and the air there turned my lungs to silver. I could taste them every time I took a breath. In a day or two I went out for a walk, and I had the premonition that something would occur. I couldn't walk fast enough to get me back before night. The mountains about were blue with snow, and the sun gone suddenly down before I could stop it, leaving a light like dawn all over the edge. In a minute the snow began falling, and then I felt this thing inside me, this wonderful spring of blood that starts up suddenly from the rock within and comes up deeper and warmer. I could see the snow falling, the air melting that way at sundown and dropping all over the sleeves of my coat. And then this thing inside beginning to bubble: melody, melowidy, meloody, melood.

The place was too high for what I had, said the doctor to me, and in a week he took me down to a place full of other doughboys coughing their way out of the picture, with gramophones and everything else about to make it pretty. I listened a while to the radio and read the things that were provided: Hoover addressing the eighteenth annual dinner of stick-in-the-muds.

And then I skipped, skedaddled, decamped; they never saw hide nor hair of me again. I've had almost all the advantages that my condition can offer me, said Martin, and I've used them meanly. I've got something else on my mind. I'm a poet, said Martin, and I still have voice enough to shout about other people's poetry. You can't expect me to be a reasonable man as well.

Now tell me, he said, setting light to a new cigarette from the stump of the old one. Tell me a word or two about England to cheer me, doctor. For whenever I'm led to believe that I'm in a bad way I remember the faces of men who have lived an entire life in the Five Towns, and God, how the fog must lie around their throats at night and throttle them, and how they must wake up in the early morning with the taste of smoke foul on their tongues.

Ah, the Five Towns, said the doctor. You're American, aren't you?

Yes, said Martin, sucking the white smoke deep within him and flinging the ashes aside on the floor. Yes, he said, and he looked about suddenly at the faces of Duke and Phyllis and the British doctor as though they were enemies closing in upon him. Yes, I am an American, he said.

This moment wherein he faltered and looked into their faces gave the doctor the space unguarded for which he had bided his time. He moved forward on his chair and spoke quickly to Martin:

Now tell me, how many days ago did you have this recent hæmorrhage?

Two days ago, said Martin. His eyes were fearful now and he opened his mouth to proceed to other matters, but the doctor raised his voice and lifted his hand.

Now here is my plan for you, he said. I know a delightful place, a really charming place, full of gay young people all aware of what they're up against and helping each other *morally* to fight it.

I know, said Martin. Comparing temperatures three times a day and discussing spitum.

No, said the doctor. Hear me out. They have dances, parties, charades. You can play cards, chequers, with young men your own age, and your wife here could be in a neighbouring hotel and spend agreeable afternoons in the sun on the wide terraces with you. And the whole thing reasonably priced.

By the way, said Martin to Duke, I owe you some money. Here's the cheque to make matters straight.

Duke stepped forward, hesitant, and took it in the end of his fingers.

Now let me try and persuade you, said the doctor in his quiet urgent voice. Martin turned and looked him full in the face.

What would you do, doctor? he said. What would you do if you were twenty-nine and me?

I'd try to show a bit of wisdom, said the doctor promptly.

Wisdom, said Martin slowly, and he opened wide his hand. Who is to judge, said he, what wisdom is? Wisdom may be the way a bird takes the wind, or how the side of a boat turns to decline the water. It's surely not wearing your shroud before the time has come for it. Wisdom, he said in a loud voice, and he tossed his cigarette from him, is to eat well and drink and be dressed for the banquet!

He sat fiercely back among his pillows, sat pressed back and looked at the strangers about him.

You and you and you, said his eyes to them, go! I have had enough.

They saw him sitting there silent and white before them, and a terrible vengeance and anger sprang up in their faces. His impatience and beauty seemed insolent to them, and they tossed back and forth in their well-cut clothes. For an ill man to fling his ailment in their faces, to flaunt it and boast of it as though it were a virtue, was an affront to them. He had no shame, and shame he must have for the evil thing that set him, like a leper, apart.

It seems to me, to us even, said Phyllis clearly, that you have no choice, Martin. You can't inflict, you can't expect.

I expect everything, said Martin sternly. His brow shone out serene.

Look here, old chap, said Duke, and he took a step forward with the cheque still hanging in his fingers. It's only a matter of the time being.

The time being is all I have, said Martin, and he smiled.

Oh, we've had so much talk about it already! said Phyllis shrugging her shoulders. Come along, Martin, you've got to take your medicine like a man. The doctor's brought the car with him. The ambulance is waiting outside.

When Hannah saw what now became of Martin's face, she caught up his hand and held it. And this, she thought in anguish, this I might have spared him! His cheeks had fallen away, had withered back from the two black lamps of terror lighted in his skull. His palm in her fingers gushed forth with sweat and he cleared his throat, ahem, ahem. Ahem, he said, and his teeth were knocking.

Please go now, said Hannah fiercely to them all.

Hannah, Hannah, cried Phyllis. Hannah, my poor child, don't you see what you're doing?

Get out! shouted Hannah, and she saw, like a madness, that her clenched hand was beating her own breast. The doctor got to his feet and inclined his head, and Duke took a step towards her.

Hannah, dear, said Duke. Leave it to people who know.

I know enough, shouted Hannah at them.

Well, the landlord won't keep you, said Phyllis in triumph, but her voice was shaking. The whole village is up in arms. They'll put you out by force, and I tell you it won't be pleasant.

Get out, said Hannah. I'll take care of it.

Hannah! cried Duke at last from the door. I didn't think you were such a bloody fool!

Suddenly Martin shot up on his pillows.

You shut the door or I'll knock your damned block off! he said.

CHAPTER XXVII

Now pack the things, said Martin, for we're out of here with a vengeance. He tossed the covers off him and a strong bright gleam of gaiety leapt into his eye. He stepped out of bed and his legs seemed strong under him although he had not eaten. Out we go, he said, and out rang his loud and youthful laughter. If they're gathered outside to see me borne forth on a stretcher they'll have to reconstruct their fancy.

And there through the window they saw the little group of country people around the ambulance, and Duke and Phyllis and the English doctor talking with the landlord at the door of their own elegant car.

To-morrow will be beautiful, said Martin, and he thumbed his nose at them out the window. To-morrow will be beautiful for to-morrow comes out of the lake. Lago di Garda. Chicago di Stockyarda. Can you picture the Italian poet sitting small and beautiful before the vile sight of Chicago and writing it. To-morrow will be beautiful, and what did to-morrow ever give him but a swift kick in the backside? And what did to-morrow ever do for him but make him a creed and a music for other people? Whenever I think of him, he said, my heart tunes up for better weather.

He talked boldly to her and dressed, watching her pack their belongings. He put his arm about her and leaned over the bag with her as she laid the pyjamas, the scarves and the socks into its depths. You're out of my own marrow, he said in her ear.

He shaved his face and cleaned his nails, sitting still in a chair and gathering strength by the window. He made himself ready with care while Hannah packed in his books and his pipes in their little casket.

We'll drive as far as we can get and eat like gentlemen, said Martin. The bastards, he said of the voices speaking in the square. I'll give them the scare of their years when they cast eye on me. They'll think me risen up from the dead.

You bastard, he said to the landlord as he paid out the last of Duke's money to him. When they stepped out on the hot white square, there was no one about. The place was still as the plague, but there was a whisper and rush of life behind every window, as though the people of the village were gathered and watching there.

Martin and Hannah crossed through the dust to their old faded car, and the dogs came obediently behind them. When they passed near the fountain Martin paused a moment and watched the frogs crouched in the slime at the edge with their creamy throats beating on the dark ruffled water. And now the whispers of the country women pierced through the drawn shutters and cried out as if his presence would pollute the fountain. What if I should spit in the water? said Martin idly, and then he walked on.

The dogs leapt into the car in gratitude and leaned upright in the corners. They had had enough and to spare of the blistering place. And even now the flies pursued them and swung in menace around their shaggy faces. Their jaws yawned and snapped at the insects and their tongues lolled out on the heat. Martin touched their brows as he climbed in at the wheel and set the motor going. The boy who had carried out their bags would not take the money from his hand. Martin tossed it out in the dust beyond and turned to thumb his nose at the deserted village.

Amen, La Moure, he said.

They had escaped from the one thing, but they had not escaped from the other. They sat down in a restaurant at the end of Nice, near the sea, and ordered their meal from the broad white *cartes* in their hands. And don't forget the coats, thought Hannah with the oysters. Your room is ready Friday with carpet on the floor. Don't forget the Boxer coats and all the pretty pictures. A lady with an income is better than a whore.

Hannah lifted her napkin suddenly and wiped the rouge off her mouth. Across the room she could see in the mirror a thin young woman in a little black jacket with her hair combed back from her ears.

You might as well take off that face and wear another, she thought. Let your locks go grey and your mouth down at the corners. I've put all your things, young woman, into your own bag, and all his in the others. Twist your fingers, cheery. The day after tomorrow won't be so pretty as all that, for you'll be on your way.

Between them there had been no mention, but Martin bent his head above his oysters in their shells and did not face her. What was to be said she must say.

Well, then, tell me something about the next number, she said. She squeezed out the half lemon and watched the delicate edges of the oyster shrink away. I'll give you a poem for it, she said. Don't forget the Boxer coats and *don't* forget the Derains. A lady with a background could never be a whore.

How can you speak of it so lightly? said Martin, looking up in irritation.

You mean speak of the magazine? said Hannah.

Hannah, said Martin suddenly, you know it's only for a little while and then we'll be together again.

Yes, I know, said Hannah, and she smiled at him, but terror then closed so tightly on her heart that she thought she could not draw another breath. She knew that Eve was somewhere in a fine room in a confusion of manuscripts, reading, and forgetting, and making notes to remember on bits of paper that fell to the floor and were swept up or dropped and perished in the fire as soon as they had slipped from her mind. And the work of Lady Vanta would seem good and brilliant to her, the work of another Englishwoman who had come to the continent as well and who could write with a hard British sentimentality of the persons of young men. Lady Vanta's longest tale would start off the magazine had Martin said, for in her Eve recognized some portion of herself. Whatever it was that snarled and skulked in Eve was written out golden and caressive in Lady Vanta's style.

Hannah could see in her mind how Eve would sit in the sun with her faint queer smile on her face and the loose pages of the manuscript of another woman slipping down off her knees and some of them lost or swept aside and what did it matter, for her thoughts would be off brooding on what Lady Vanta must seem to a man's eyes, and how Lady Vanta wore her clothes, and if Lady Vanta were really forty and still had the young men she wanted to walk on the streets with her and be seen carrying her books and her parasol. Eve would read a page maybe and then she would thrust the bulk of it off the table, or over the bed, thinking so much of the square little white face that Lady Vanta talked of having and of the little red flag of her hair that fell like a curtain down the back of her head, that out would Eve go with her toes turning up in her English boots and buy herself a sunshade with lace hanging off the edges, and all the way back to the hotel imagine herself the picture of Lady Vanta going out to meet another admirer waiting for her coming in a bright café.

Martin put out his hand and touched Hannah's.

There's no need for you to go as far as Paris, he said.

Oh, yes, said Hannah. I'll go to Paris.

Will you see Dilly? he said, and he seemed to be harking in impatience for her answer.

No, said Hannah, I don't think I'll see Dilly.

They drank down great white brimming tumblerfuls of wine.

You must believe in me, said Martin. I know what I can do with my own tongue in the way of persuasion. When Eve understands once and for all how it is with us, the three of us will come together. But now, for the moment, there's nothing else to do.

Yes, said Hannah.

You do believe me, don't you? he said. He pressed his voice urgently on her, as though in need of reassurance.

Yes, she said, but she knew that the three of them could never share a life among them. Yes, she said, but she knew it could never be that way.

In the warmth and motion of her sight Martin now looked more beautiful than he had ever before to her: his cheekbones were stained with wine and his thick black locks were brushed back smooth under the light. His eyes were as clear as bells, and deep and merry, as though he possessed some secret certainty of how their love would be. But above all it was his mouth curved up so rich and young that turned her blood to water.

Hannah, I have seen you angry, he was saying, and because it is such a rare thing it makes it even prouder. I want to finish my days with you. I want to grow old and white looking at your face. I have been a bad son, and a bad nephew, and a bad lover, but I might be a good father, he said.

I want to end my days with you, said Martin, and in the melting warmth of her submission Hannah did not know if he were speaking now or if these were words he had said to her before.

CHAPTER XXVIII

It was early in the day and the warmth on the southern water touched and destroyed the crest of rime that rode it. They were far from the frost here, but frost it seemed, and the great white icy shoulders of snow could be seen rearing up far behind the city. In spite of the tide of sun that took its ease upon the Promenade des Anglais, the place seemed chill and blighted to Hannah, and yonder the waves ran in without arch and almost without sound.

The avenue followed the sea's curve, but stiffly, with an alien face and no flavour in its air. Little could be said for the sea itself, for it was cramped and wary. Not one wave amongst them all had the courage to rise and sweep back clear to the foothills. If one wave had risen, then the others like hastening sheep might have followed after, might have drawn back a muscular current of sea to lap against the swelling ground and the fancy trunks of the olive trees sticking out of the sod. The roofs would capsize and the windows and streets flow over, and the city's shape would narrow into the sucking funnel of water travelling fast. The fish alone would pause, after the first mouthful had poured them out, hesitant in a gulf of sea packed thick with writhing life. Under their fins would the houses crumble and fall, fall slowly, brick by brick, like ruddy petals forced down through tons of mighty sea.

What are you thinking about? said Martin, setting his grey hat on his head.

Tidal wave, said Hannah.

She stepped into the car, and this would be the last time, she thought, but she did not let her mind dwell there. The dogs at her heels climbed in after and sat down with the luggage behind.

I'd like to see a tidal wave go to beat the band, said Hannah.

Yes, said Martin. He was waiting, uncertain, on the other side.

Come on, Martin, said Hannah. There's only twenty minutes left.

Martin stepped in but sat motionless at the wheel. The hotel porter closed the door behind him.

What in the devil are you in such a hurry about? Martin said, turning to look into her face.

The train, said Hannah. But Martin sat still with his hat on his head looking straight ahead through the windshield glass.

I have an idea, he said. Come as far as Monaco with me. Eve's not expecting me at any special hour. We could have lunch in that place near the station, and you could take the train after. There's another that leaves at two or quarter past.

But it will be just the same thing then, said Hannah. Martin, we'd better go to the station now.

The hell we will! said Martin and he set the car viciously into motion. You wouldn't put yourself out for anyone, would you? he said. I suppose it's too much to ask of you? said Martin. It's too much of a bother for you to buy a supplement ticket at the station at Monaco? Probably because you let Dilly know at what time to meet you in Paris! My God, when you've had enough of a person you make no bones about it! You're so anxious to get rid of the sight of me that I sometimes ask myself if you have any intention of coming back. I see your point of view, he said. It's not difficult to see it. I'm nothing so much as young men go, I can see that easily enough. You never really believed that I was still a sick man, did you? he said as he drove. Oh, yes, you knew I had hæmorrhages once upon a time, long before you knew me, some other time when they weren't your affair! But to see the thing before you, I suppose it's that that has set you against me? My God, what's your heart made of that you can hurry the matter of leaving me?

He swung through the streets and up the Moyenne Corniche. Down the slopes of the olive orchards, the houses dropped behind, retreated and disappeared. When they turned the curve at the summit, the city of Nice snapped out of sight and the rocky cliffs strode up on every side.

What if I were to fall ill again? he said. The hills

are practically deserted between here and Monaco. You'd have me sick on the roadside, I suppose, and you riding off safe and sound in your little train to Paris?

He saw nothing that was there about them save his own anger that must keep her with him. For a long way they rode in silence, and then as the houses of La Turbie showed out against the sky above them, he said: Listen to me. His voice was quiet now and he let the car glide into a slow rolling pace around the hills.

I have a cork leg and a wooden one, he said, and a curly wig for special purposes. I have a couple of glass eyes for pity and sometimes I roll them in agony in my head. I am afraid of the English and for them I reserve a boisterous ignorance. I give them a conversation carefully weeded of any names or standards upon which they might seize as a handle to me. And for you I have a host of angry men who will never cede you an ounce of right. When one lies down in me, another comes awake and shakes his fist in your face.

I've grown accustomed now to the entire family, said Hannah.

Martin laughed out and put his arm around her.

Will you mind very much, he said, when the lot of them are under the sod?

It won't be for a long time yet, said Hannah. I'll be sitting home knitting the socks with my hair getting greyer every minute, waiting for you in person to be coming home from the pub.

The pub, said Martin. God bless England. Where shall we live together, Hannah, when we're old?

I'd like to go to Ireland and get a brogue of my own, said Hannah.

And a child of our own, said Martin. To turn Eve's heart to butter.

Her name was back in their mouths again. They could not keep it away.

Now everything should be straight and understood between us, said Martin, before we go off from each other. The picture you have of Eve should be very sharp and clear. If you see her as a sour woman waiting to bitter and gall me, then that's too much in the one direction, and you must alter your fancy of her. See her as well with her brothers she loved dead at war or gone cold in British office, and no homage ever, from anyone, not even now and then. See her buying shoes with such hate for the shape of her feet that she fights with the girl who tries them on and shouts down the price of them. And see her as well drinking champagne and laughing until the tears run over her face and stain the silk gown on her bosom. And cursing the British intellects, the best that the little island can offer, outright to their noses. Or singing lullabies to Italian babies. See her wherever she is making the atmosphere her own.

She used to rock the dogs in her arms, said Hannah, and she used to revile me if I so much as slapped them to correct their habits in the house.

She had six of her own in Scotland, said Martin, and she's lived to herself with the death of the men of her family weighing heavy. A lot of things, like death and separation, he said, have happened to her and they have never happened to you and me.

Hannah listened to his tongue talking softly beside her, and so would he woo Eve with talk of her, she thought, after she was gone away. In one way or another would he turn the truth and wheedle and beguile them, and what could they do, the one or the other of them, except listen and wonder that the lies he spoke had such a sound of truth.

It was Eve, he said, who made McSweeney starve to death in prison. It was Eve, or some semblance of her, who sat outside the door and said to him when his courage was failing: You have no right to stop. And Eve it was who was offered a title at Court and what did she do but spit it back at them. I'll take your title, said she, when you've given me and the rest of the women the right to vote like men.

If a woman has led a strong and solitary life, said Martin. Then it's a strange thing to her to see other people acting in haste and flight as you and I have done.

Yes, said Hannah, that's true. But there's one thing I couldn't bear, Martin. I can't have you telling Eve a fairy-tale about me, and altering facts so that she'll condescend. If you must fix and explain, what will you do but destroy me? Don't speak my name to her, but let things happen as they will.

But at lunch the talk took another turn, and they walked out of the restaurant with their hands clasped together. They walked to the station, holding each other close, and this is the end, thought Hannah. This is the way ends come.

The thing Eve could not understand if you said it, said Hannah, is that this would never have happened to me if it had not been you. It never came into my head to be unfaithful, said the wine speaking wildly out in her. She knew she was old now forever, and settled in age. She was not twenty-four, but near it, and this is where love would end.

But Martin suddenly threw back his head and burst into laughter.

Look at the time! he said. It's three o'clock and the train left an hour ago!

CHAPTER XXIX

Children ran up and down, called out and fell for a moment on the gravel pathways. The flowers were lavender deepening to mauve and flourishing in a crown of rich red purple in the elaborate gardens. All the way from the avenue to the plot before the casino, the sod was up to lay the way for the miniature golf.

Martin stopped the car and they stepped out beside the glossy beds of flowers.

I'll meet you at six at the station, he said, and he took off his hat and put his arms about her. That will give us a half an hour together, he said, and he kissed her on the mouth. He held her close for a moment, despite the people. And then he kissed her again and suddenly his hands dropped down.

My God! he said, and his face collapsed before her. There's Eve sitting on that bench there, looking right at us!

Just walk away as if, said Martin. He put on his hat and smiled wanly at her. Just go without fuss and feathers, darling. I'll meet you at the station at six.

It was warm, it was April, and here it was the beginning of summer. Hannah walked down the wide gardens with the three dogs following behind. Her bag was in her hand and she swung it idly. Why didn't I wait in Monaco, she thought, as a woman of sense would have done? The dogs picked up their ears at the sound of her voice and hastened. As weak as water, she said in despise, and as full of error. I've a good mind to go off before he turns up at the station. She looked at the buses marked Marseilles and Toulon, but she knew that she was putrid and soft with weakness and that she would linger there, without pride, on the outskirts until Martin came to kiss her again and say good-bye.

And what has become of me? she cried out to herself. Where is the arrogance that took me out of my father's house and over the ocean? What has become of my courage? Is it this that idleness and subterfuge have done? And what a pretty thing is love, she thought, if it rots the bone in me! I should never have been a party to it. I should have left Martin content with the life he had.

She saw herself so well now that she could have turned back and given Martin and Eve the words they might not find to describe her. Eve, the strong woman who knew her way and had it, who sat there among the flower-beds and the children playing and took what it was she wanted: the sun, and the ease, and now Martin back in her life again, but not his passing fancy. What else was she or could be to them, thought

Hannah, but a weak and flavourless woman, a hesitant wife as frail as a thread who had left her husband overnight, and who was lingering now, on the outskirts, cringing, and waiting to be bid to go or come.

One thing she knew: they would never hear nor see of her again once she was rid of them. They had their bond of blood and spirit, and she would always be an outsider to them. They had their crooked Irish ways and their venom that would always be strange to her. They could hurl names at each other that no smaller love could swallow or forgive, and yet return in love to each other. Fiend and maniac, and jailbird and shrew, had flown bitterly between them, and now they could sit down side by side and talk of painting and poetry like Shanty Irish patching their patience together again after a family brawl.

There's no place for me in it, said Hannah, and she started down the stairs to the sea. All through the gardens had been people sitting: old people under sunshades, with their dresses of lace and their faces painted, old men wavering on their canes, and Hannah had passed them by as if they were frescoes peeling from the walls. Down she went to the water where the fine yachts were at anchor and where the sea was knocking in against the ramparts. It might have been Le Havre or Rouen for the little light and sun that came into her thoughts.

The dogs were free of their chains and went down like madmen, tearing at each other's coats and shouting out their joy. Hannah sat down on her bag at the edge and lit a cigarette and smoked it in quiet. The dogs went the length of the sea walk; she could see their tails splashing back and forth as they made the turn. She thought of the first days with Martin, and how they had come over at night and played at the Casino. High above her was the terrace, heavy with palms, where they had walked out in the moon in January. But she could not remember how his face looked then, free of his dual purpose, nor the guileless words he must then have said.

She remembered how Dilly and Eve had been set aside, like corpses with the earth cast down upon them. They had been the names of dead people spoken now and then with a little pretence at sorrow and regret. But nothing had come between, nor could, except Martin's ire when he thought she was looking at a sounder stronger man in passing. That was my youth, she thought, and this is my time of age. I can make a show of it, I can refuse to relinquish it. I can dye my hair and paint my face and do the way other women do.

But suddenly she flung her cigarette away on to the water, and lifted her head and looked from place to place all about. Here was the flock of elegant yachts browsing in the green salty pasture, and there the cropped field where they shot the pigeons down. On the other side of the bay stood the domes of the Prince's palace, and the slopes of the woodland speckled with staircases and stone. All these things were strange to her, as Martin now was strange, and only the thought of Eve seemed familiar to her, as if she and Eve were moved alike, and as though some singularity in them made them kin.

She thought of Eve as a young woman in Scotland with the brothers, the brave men of the family whose active talk had stirred her; and of the hardy dogs Eve had owned with their wet noses bright black in their stiff Aberdeen coats. And now Eve's life was solitary, for all these things were gone from her. The casino gardens and the tables were left, but Hannah felt no pity; only a hard pity and contempt for her own self who had no pride, as Eve had, to keep herself apart. Eve had walked across the country in the fogs or the heather with her dogs behind her, and Hannah too had done this and felt the same shy shrinking and scorn for strangers; and Hannah had spent time, in fair weather or foul, on her knees tending the earth so that things might come up in their season, and Eve in her own country had kneeled down and done likewise, and now they were pitted against each other as alien women might be.

Hannah sat there facing the sea, and she thought of her own ways and of Eve's ways, and she knew that they could have loved each other well had not Martin come between. She knew there was a bond between them, but that no speech could ever say it. I could have learned courage and pride from her, she thought, had not Martin tangled us so strangely.

The clock from the spire in Monaco was striking the half hour out over the water. Half-past five it was, and Hannah turned to make her way to the station. The dogs stood up from where they had fallen prone, and she snapped their leads in their collars. If Martin would be there at the station, or whether or not he would come at all, she did not know; and because of the dull grief in her heart she thought she could bear it very well if he came too late, or forgot the hour, and if she would never see him again. If he were not there, she could take the train and go with her sorrow undivided.

But when she stepped on to the platform, Martin came running out from among the many people. His cheeks were flushed from wine or fear and his eyes were soft and wild. He came running to her and took her arm and began speaking in haste to her.

Come, he said. This is the way out. Come quickly. You're not going away.

He dragged her off, with her bag in his hand, but at the door out Hannah stopped him and said: Believe me, Martin, believe me, we can't do this every day of our lives. This is the best way. I am going now. For once I'll act on my own wits, Martin. This is how it must be.

But you don't understand, said Martin. I've been looking two hours for you.

Hannah saw that his face was worn, and like a child's face, filled with fright.

Eve won't have me, he said. She's through with me. She wouldn't so much as let me open my mouth and explain to her. After seeing me kiss you like that she won't believe that I want you and me to be over. She never wants to set eye on me again. She made a terrible row in the garden. Just the sight of you like a red flag in her face.

We'll have a drink, what? he said. He looked tentatively, fearfully, into Hannah's eyes. Do you hate me too? he said softly. She had never before seen him so filled with fear and so broken. Have I lost you too through all the things I've said and let her say?

She called me this and that, he said. She made an awful scene in the garden. He could not stop speaking, repeating the words to her, pressing her fingers in shyness, as though she might speak and he feared what she might say.

PART III

CHAPTER XXX

The mountains were there behind, a rebuke to them for having stayed so long in crowded places. There were the mountains, whole and still, upright without effort, and without effort proclaiming that they could shape men in their image. If you lay down your arms here, weapons of spruce and pine will spring to life in your fingers. Martin turned to them, his hands thirsting, his eyes devouring the bold line of them wild as a mountain road leading uneven, broken, up under the ridge of snow. He would have them all for his own, contained within, consumed. He would have the mountains, big as a feast, volcanic or quaking within him, and then he would act. Everything would lie quiet in him for a day, no longer, and then he would go up into the mountains as if their stride were his own, go high as pleased his taste and settle. Or in another day, the word *settle* in itself might thwart him, and he would go up and on again in discovery, and look back on the way he had come as if it were the years of his life behind him.

But like a king in exile were his followers with him:

books that might break down the car, and papers piled to the roof of it. His people and his magazine he would have, as a lordly rebuke to anyone who said the contrary. In the end he would sell the car, if it came to that, to pay for it. Before he set out he wrote Mr. Alaric and the poet in Italy that the next number would come out in the fall.

They came to a place half-way up the lower alps one evening, and in the morning they hired a loft from a man who was going away. At night the window over their heads stood open and they lay there and watched the stars. Mr. Alaric and the poet were always on their tongues, and because Martin was far from them, or from any man, his faith in them grew firmer. He listened in comfort, lay still with his arms about Hannah harking when she sang; or they talked of the two writers whose work ran in his head, until Hannah thought she could have chosen them from any crowd of men.

At night the window was open in the beams and they could lie there and see the stars, or when the moon was up could face the milky veil of light that spread across the sky. They talked of the two young men, and of books they had read aloud, or of the French Revolution or of Russia, or Poe. I like the thought of the trees of liberty borne on with their roots out of the soil, said Martin in the dark. He had made a poem of it, saying: Or a glad day come with a procession crowned with foliage, pick-axe and spade, and a large tree borne forward on the shoulders of many men. Where have the days gone where slipped away when young men duelled drew blood perished for a play or motive behind it for a word or what shaped it? Where slipped the explanation of that unshaken glance into the eyes of nuns under their white crowns saying deeply: I am as pure as your souls sisters out and drying on the line like my wife's linen for I would do battle for a play or a line of poetry.

This became their life as the summer drew on. The dogs went through the fields all day or curbed their spirit to follow Hannah down the hill to market, and Martin sat typing at his table with the windows at both ends standing wide. One day passed like another, except for changes in the wind: the clouds passed like strong music over the sky, or the sun would shine, or the rain would pour over the pane in the thatches and drench the fields knee-deep with wet. This was their life: there was no need to squander their money when it came and Martin spoke of living simply so forever and bringing the magazine out with what they set aside. Every day there were manuscripts in the mail, and every day Hannah typed out his letters to strange people, drafted advertisements, pursued a list of yearly subscriptions. He was sure now, he knew that he would not falter. Every letter he opened set his foot surer on the strange mountain path.

There was one from an American writer, saying: You are better where you are, away from every aspect of writing except the pure functioning of it. If we are poets, then the issue is with form and content, an affair of the heart. Do you know that here literature is a matter of tea-parties! It is a matter of *where* you are printed, not *what* nor how you write. For a strange superstition has survived among most that editors or publishers are discriminating readers. Which is absurd. They carry their wares about in a suitcase, like salesmen for horse-medicine or cough-drops or something worse. Not good tough roistering salesmen with their own lingo, but an affected figure aped out of some London drawing-room. Keep to yourself, said the letter to Martin, keep to yourself and I think you'll do something for us nobody else has done.

I'll take that without a grain of salt, said Martin, smiling. I like the sound of it. 'Tis music in my ears. To be the one island visible at sea, the one shore on which men of genius may beach. To have many palms waving and coconuts hanging ripe and milky in reward. Stripped to essentials, though fully dressed, said Martin smiling as he danced, at a time when bread and butter would make traitors of us all.

On fine evenings Martin walked as far as the leaf-trees at the end of the orchard with Hannah, and they looked down on the needle and cone forests that blackened the slopes below. A burning pungent breath of strength rose thick as smoke from the dark boughs of pine and tar to them, and Martin walked with his arm around Hannah's waist, like a swain. Once he said:

I have Catholic blood in me that would run freer for repentance.

And from this she knew that the wound in his spirit was rankling and that his heart was heavy. And another time he said:

She's kept quiet three months now. She'd better not put her oar in at this late date.

But one morning there was a letter from Eve among the others. It was sent on from the bank in Cannes, for she did not know where Martin might be. It lay there with the others, and Martin picked it up and set it aside, looked close at the stamp, and then put it face down on the table. He read the letter from Italy, and the one from Mr. Alaric in Paris, and one from Lady Vanta which began breathlessly, saying: My darlings, what is happening about my stories? I feel so utterly adrift. I do want a word from you both. So many days have wheeled and dipped and gone swooping by. Tell me about you two lambs, and where is the magazine to be printed? What are you doing? she said. I am in a lovely place called St. Jean-les-Pins. It's noble with cliffs and pine trees and you both should come and see.

Then Martin picked up Eve's letter again and boldly ran his finger under the flap. He set his face aside from Hannah and pulled the sheet of linen out. Then he cleared his throat aloud and read to himself whatever Eve had written him, and Hannah filled her arms with their clothes to paddle clean in the brook below and started out the door. But Martin said Jesus Christ before she had closed it behind her.

Jesus Christ, he said. He held out the letter to her and said: Just read what she has to say.

Hannah took the letter from him and sat down where she was to read it. In her other arm were heaped the clothes she had been bearing away.

It began with no beginning, but: I have been thinking over all the things you said to me in Saint-Raphael and the things you wrote to me and *others*. I see the mistake now that I made in having to do with inferiors in taste as well as CLASS. That I exalted you, a felon, to the position of EDITOR will always be a regret to me.

Some of the words ran on in her fine British writing, and others were printed out black and wide so there would be no mistake.

I might have known by the other women you were entangled with how your choice in such matters ran, but I stupidly imagined that good contacts would alter things. Taking you at your word, I was gullible enough to think that each escapade would be the last. But now that you and your HARLOT are making a public show of yourselves with such as your drunken demonstration in the Monte Carlo gardens, I see no reason why I should be expected to stand by you EDITORIALLY. I shall probably go on with the magazine in my own right and I will publish a PUBLIC DENIAL of your having any further part in it, or ever having had any part for that matter except the flattering title of EDITOR which I was good enough to bestow on you.

You're both so CHEAP, she wrote, that you'd do anything for the few pennies I have. Thank God my eyes were opened in time to the trick you and your Billingsgate bride were trying to pull on me. I have heard from people in Paris that you now write of her as your WIFE, but I see no reason not to enlighten people and tell them exactly how things stand. I'm bored with your antics and with your companions who can make any kind of a cheap monkey of you. If literature can come out of lust and orgy, then I don't doubt that you'll be a great writer some day.

This was the way it ended, and when she had done Hannah folded the page over.

I've brought a lot of trouble on you, she said.

We must keep a sense of humour, said Martin, smiling wanly.

But suddenly he picked up his poems from the table and tore them across and across again in little pieces. Hannah cried out, but his face was white and set in anger.

God damn that woman, he said.

CHAPTER XXXI

In a fortnight they started up the hot valley to cooler places, and St. Jean, where Lady Vanta was, was to the north, but they kept off the road to it. Eve's fury had pursued them and changed the aspect of the country, but if they kept to themselves, they thought, they might again settle down in peace.

But the valley they climbed was like the throat of hell: nothing had survived the fire and lava save the singed grey flocks of sheep, and a bony goat or two that hobbled the edge above. From the side of the road fell a sheet of steel, engraved with the record of hard swift waters. The road before them was white with drifts of dust.

Up and around the spiral brink they drove, like a fly on the parched lips of a crater; up and on with the sun racing them like fire even into the gulfs of shade. Martin wiped his brow and looked up in weariness at the merciless flogging of the sun across the boulders. In the morning he said: we will drive a long way, as though he could outstrip some evil pursuit. And in the afternoon he said: we will stop at the first place we find.

The first place was Saint-André, flung suddenly wide on a plateau, sly and deceptive, with a long cool avenue of eucalyptus stalks designing its approach. Martin leaned back in relief and smiled as they drove down the dark fragrant lane of shadow to the outskirts of the village.

We'll have a drink on the terrace, what? And stop the night here, anyway, he said.

It was cool and promising, like a haven from the heat to them. In the narrow channel of shade that the trees cast, there was nothing to see but the green leaves rippling and running above, the smooth white barkless stems, and the dark weeping boughs concealing the sky beyond that gaped upon decay.

A young thing in spring-green slippers, sang Martin, stockings, silk vivid as lilac-time grass.

But he was weary, he was tired; it stood in his eyes like an omen. In the hotel he lay down on the clean new bed, for he had driven far. The place was small, but freshly done, with water leaping from the silver tap, and the clean walls painted grey. Hannah went to the bed and washed his face for him. When she washed back the dark wings of his brows, he looked up at her refreshed and smiled.

A young thing in spring-green slippers, he said. Do you suppose Eve ever thinks of the times they asked us to leave hotels in Italy because I coughed?

When the *bonne* knocked on the door and came in bearing towels to them, Martin sat up on the bed and lit a cigarette. He talked to her, smiling and moving his hands, with his eyes insisting that she understand his language. He wanted pigs' feet grilled in batter and breadcrumbs for his supper. He insisted, with his hands moving to convince her of the natural beauty of his hunger. A sick man would never ask for pigs' feet grilled, but she answered him shaking her head that they were not this time of year, as if they sprang up like seeds in the garden.

Get her out of here, said Martin suddenly. I'm going to cough. Take the cigarette, he said, and when I cough walk around the room and sing or something so they won't hear me.

The alps were closed like dry fists and the grass burned up to the window.

Do you suppose Eve, said Martin when he had done, remembers. You know sometimes I think, he said, that women can set years aside and forget them the way men can't.

The way I did with Dilly, said Hannah softly. She was taking the things from the bags and putting them here and there in the drawers and the cupboard.

That's not the same thing, said Martin. Suddenly he swung his legs off the bed, walked to the mirror and ran the dripping comb through his hair.

We'll get a place of our own, he said boldly. To hell with hotels. He looked at his face in the glass before him. Hannah, he said, maybe you could answer Eve's letter in some way or other. I'd just give her a piece of my mind if I sat down to it, and what would she do with that?

Hannah could see Eve very well sitting still on a bench in the sun, waiting for a letter from Martin, and watching the children play. She could picture the big dark halls of the Casino early in the day when few people were gambling, and Eve in her white clothes leaning over the table and tossing her coins out heedlessly long after other people had played. She saw how the wheel turned, for Eve did nothing else with her days but watched it turning. It was as though all her life depended on how the wheel would pause.

Or she imagined Eve sitting down next to the *croupier* at table, and when his arm stretched out beyond her to rake in the money, the colour would run up into Eve's face. For the sleeve of his coat might have brushed against her, and his black eyes or the sweep of his hair might have put her in mind of Martin. Hannah could picture the high smile of delight on her face when the young man took her money from her, or tossed out to her open hands the little round discs in exchange for the leaves of money she paid out. But if a woman should as much as step on her toe in error or jostle her, Eve would turn in fury and take off the creature's head with the arrogance of her insular tongue.

Eve sitting still on the bench she could see forever. Eve waiting there and watching the children play. Or Eve walking into her fine hotel, in solitary splendour, eyeing the key askance at the desk because there was no letter by its side. And where would her heart turn now in its sorrow, thought Hannah, if not to Mr. Alaric or to the poet ill in Italy?

In the morning the *bonne* came in to say that the washer-woman had so much work to do that she couldn't take in their laundry this summer.

What? said Martin with his dressing-gown on. What?

There must be some mistake, said Hannah.

It's an invitation to move on, said Martin. God, what a hole!

Don't be silly, said Hannah. In her mind the letter to Eve was forming, and her wits were turned crafty again shaping how she would bear Martin's gentlest thoughts to Eve in words that he himself might say. She sat at his typewriter, and he was shaving his face beside her. Slowly she wrote out the words that he disdained to peer at, struck out a phrase with X's as Martin did when he wrote, and typed in others above as was Martin's way. At that moment the *bonne* came back with Martin's shoes in her hand and said that the shoemaker had so much work this year that he couldn't touch their shoes for them. She stood on the edge of the room, as if in fear, and tossed down the shoes on the floor.

What in hell did she say? said Martin. One side of his face was feathered with lather.

She says you're a fine figure of a man, said Hannah,

but now it seemed certain to her that they were cast out again and must be on their way. Her tongue was dry and still in her mouth and when she struck at the words her hand was shaking.

Dear Eve, she wrote, dear Eve: I want things to be as they used to be between us—you painting your pictures, I writing my poems. How can you wipe out everything that has happened? Sometimes it seems true to me that women put years aside and forget all about them and men cannot do this way. I am lonely for you. I cannot bear you being alone.

She sat there, striking at the typewriter, and in a while the *bonne* returned to say that the proprietress, the lady buttoned in black from top to toe would have a word in the offing. Hannah folded up the letter and went out the door licking the stamp on the envelope addressed to Eve. Her thoughts were upon Eve who sat waiting in the Casino gardens, and even then she did not think what it might be the hotel woman had to say. The Frenchwoman stood in the stair-pit, looking up at Hannah with her cold canny eyes.

She heard the woman beginning to speak, but she was deaf with her thoughts and could not hear her. If I have written the wrong things, then it is done, and let it be, she was thinking.

Finish to enter, said the Frenchwoman. Come in here.

But other things were in Hannah's mind as she stepped into the woman's room and faced the sweet sorrow of the crucifix. Over their heads, Christ bled with artistry upon the cross. The carved rosary hung like a string of false teeth over the iron poster of the bedstead.

Madame, said the proprietress. You will have to go elsewhere. We are not prepared, she said without hesitation. Here we are not prepared for death.

Hannah stood with the letter to Eve in her hand, looking in bewilderment at the woman.

I don't know what you mean, she said.

Because we look shabby, she thought, they won't put up with us. Because my shoes are down at the heels and my skirt short now when I should be wearing long ones. And the cushions in the car frayed out and the fenders bent from bumping. For the ribbon faded on Martin's grey hat, maybe, and on account of the dogs, we have to go away.

I don't know what you mean, she said to the woman.

Your husband is very sick, said the Frenchwoman. You'll have to go away.

He's got a cold on the chest. He's got a touch of the grippe for the moment, said Hannah.

The woman shrugged her shoulders.

I'll have your bags carried down as soon as they're packed, she said.

A torrent of words came into Hannah's mouth, but she bit her lip fiercely and flung out into the hall. She fled from the sight of the woman, groping her way in haste down the dark of the corridor. When Martin heard her coming, he opened the door.

Where have you been, Hannah? Why did you leave me? he said.

I've been to the cabinay, said Hannah. I hate the woman that owns this place. Let's get out of here.

It's not so bad here, you know, said Martin. He went back to the mirror and patted the powder into his clean face.

Martin, said Hannah. She doesn't like the look of us.

Martin swung quickly around and stared at her. What? he said. What? An invitation?

An invitation ty-daidle-dee-dy to the waltz, said Hannah.

The bitch, the bastard, said Martin. He lit a cigarette in anger and strode across the room. God, what a dump! God, what a hole, Saint-André! He stood at the window, venting his spleen. We'll clear out all right, but I'll come back and haunt you! I'll eat your heart out, I'll curse and rot you!

The mountain trains were screaming like cats at the window, and suddenly the anger went out of Martin's face.

Anyway, think of the smoke and soot we'd have endured here all summer, he said. Anyway, said Martin, it would be like living on the tracks.

CHAPTER XXXII

The road led onward, up the valley, through wide ripe fields of grain. Up went the golden billowing slopes, rolled out smooth as honey to the edge of the dark blue heavens where a storm was threatening in the clouds. Now they were on their way again, and a great elation woke in them. They could see the peaks of stone ahead, seeming to horn upwards with intention to pierce and rip the evil scrolls of rain and wind.

Higher and higher they drove, singing aloud to each other, and the dark threats of the storm came in through the windows of the car in blasts of freshened air. Each thing that came seemed a promise of fairer things to come, and the wondrous storm gathering in the mountains made them cry aloud with joy.

God, what if we'd stuck in that hole and missed this! said Martin.

She saw him beside her, driving, and how any man could read illness in his face astounded her. His flesh was white, but his voice was lusty, and his shoulders broad and carried straight and swinging from his spine. Surely other men must cough at times as well as he, and other men often cleared their throats at table. Or was it the spark in his eye and his laughter sounding out that made them suspect when other men had sour lifeless faces? She could see nothing failing in him, and when he spoke of death it was another of his fancies that were so far from truth.

Higher they climbed, and out of the earth were the dizzy rows of stratæ flung, yellow and mole and prune and grey, spinning like tops on the emblazoned rock. Everything waiting, bent and bowed, for the rain that would split the day in two. And when they turned a curve in the side of the rock, without warning the rain smashed down upon them. It broke like a rocket on the windshield glass and went drenching down the road. Over their heads the shaley eaves were hung with swinging tassels of it; it fell like a cascade from the heights and went seething down beyond. The thunder had lowered on them and splintered into sound the very instant the stabs of lightning struck through the lashing ropes of rain. After each clap the echoes roared and dwindled and returned loud again, bumping away through the canyon, and muttering through the rain.

Ahead as they drove, the sheets of water seemed blown in four directions: first turned against them to force them down the narrow gorge, and a second mighty power sweeping them up and wiping out their tracks behind; and then over the canyon to the other summits swung flying white trapezes of blown rain which midway met fiercer trapezes flung, and joined and locked and fell to the iron depths of stone carved miles below.

They drove on through the fast falling rain, and the air came through in icy blasts upon their faces. On both sides writhed the whistling storm, caught on the shining antlers of the gorge, speared with blue light and unable to get free. And suddenly a pool of clarity swam in the air and on the peaks ahead; a bar of the sun had fallen, like a tree-trunk felled, and held the waters dammed as smooth as glass. And up the road they were driving to it, hastening, as though it might break or fade before they reached its brink. They could see they were coming forth and leaving the wild dark storm behind them. It was wedged down into the steep gorge and was murmuring there and tossing in complaint.

Now that they had passed through the storm, the deep widening pool of light seemed even a better thing to them. Hannah heard the last soft clamour of the thunder below with a sense of peace in her heart. The land they came through was fresh with mould and wet where the storm had drenched it; the earth was black as pitch and the moss turned spinach-green on the gleaming shale. Through the clear washed country they drove, and the pebbles and leaves were now like jewels shining out all about them, and the rocks and the quenched trees stood singly up in the light.

They were far from all things, from faces or habitation, and Martin talked boldly of the places they would go, up or down as they liked, for he held no rancour in him. All places seemed good to him for the work he had to do, and there was no more virtue in the east than in the west. In a little while they saw roofs beginning to unfold in the wilderness, and Martin stopped the car to look down over the opening plain. They saw the poor huts, and the towers of finer places, and the fields broken for cultivation, or the land smoothed out in idle estates. And the sight of it filled Martin with eagerness and unrest, as if he would willingly have been down amongst people, and as if he scarcely dared to be.

That must be Barcelonette beginning, he said. We might have tea there and think about it. If the people are nice, he said, you know what I mean. If the people seem gay.

The streets of it bore Spanish names, and the old faces in the doorways and on the balconies there had another texture. Here were there rings in the ears of the old women, and remnants of good lace pinned at their throats. Here something of another people survived in the broad hats and the fancy houses: something red and garish of the blood of the Counts of Barcelona, and another thing of prosperity and plunder from the wealth of the settlers come back rich from Mexico. They had chosen a fertile stronghold made fast by stone, in an eloquent valley where famine and drought remained without, in the length of a flourishing green pastureland that had not a word of good to say for the parching south. The Ubaye river, thick with cress, flowed through these foreigners' fields.

For its bustle and affluence Martin found this a place where he wanted to be. There were three hotels on the thriving square, and red tin tables and seats set out under the trees. It was a market day and the bartering done, the farmers of means were drinking together in their long black speckless coats, with their whips set aside upright against the trunks of the planes. Their full-brimmed black felt hats were back from their brows or laid carefully down on their knees.

Fine cars from other places stood all about, and side by side with their elegance were freshly-painted carts loaded with stout white sheep. The horses between the shafts were well groomed, handsome beasts, with coats as glossy as a chestnut's side. All of it seemed human and fair to Martin and Hannah, like a place where easy healthful people might be.

They chose the humblest hotel, because of the money they must put away, and although he said nothing of it, this was a wound to Martin's pride. He sat drinking his glass in the green leafy square and eyeing the smarter hotels across the way. He read his paper, and over the edge he watched the better cars in their splendour setting sail for Grenoble and Cuneo. For this was the great highway between the two places, the belt of travel that girded the mountains around. Martin watched the farmers drink, and rise, and pay out their sous from their embroidered purses.

Know ye the land where the cypress and myrtle, said Martin. To-morrow we'll ask about rooms outside on the hills. We could work very well here, he said. In the evening we could come down and look at all the people. To-morrow comes off the snow, like ice cream, he said.

In a minute he took out of his pocket the letter from the writer in America. He laid it out on the table between them and read it again in the evening light. The best of it he read aloud to Hannah, tasting the words slowly with the memory of the drink still lingering in his mouth: If we are poets, then the issue is with form and content not with ladies and gentlemen. And keep to yourself, said the letter, keep to yourself and you'll do something for us nobody else has done.

Martin lifted his chin, set his shoulders back, and buttoned his coat smartly over.

The trouble with me was, said Martin, that I laid down on the bed like a sick man when I got to Saint-André.

Before he stepped into the hotel dining-room for supper, he paused on the threshold with Hannah, settled his coat on his shoulders, and walked boldly in under the lights.

Know ye the land, he said gaily. If you step like a

man of health and wealth it's half the battle. He crossed the room with his reckless stride and pulled out the chair at Hannah's place. There were a great many people seated at the tables, and Martin sat down humming aloud, and looked strongly and brightly about the hall.

The mistake I made at Saint-André, he said, was to lean my head on my hand when I was tired. I remember doing it that first night there at table, and the woman looking in the door.

But just as he spoke his breath caught in his throat and he was seized with coughing. He covered his mouth with his hand, but his choking body was wrenched forward and back. Hannah gave him a glass of water, thinking: the dust when he drove, and out on the square, it's from nothing within him. The dust on the square, she thought, but her nails were deep in her palms, and he could not make his coughing cease. In a moment he stood up from his chair and in haste Hannah followed him out into the cool sinking twilight. He sat down at the tin table where the glasses remained, and drew his cloak about him.

Did you see the people, Hannah? he said. Every head in the dining-room turned to look when I coughed, ready to flay me. I can't go back, I can't stay here. Get the bags brought down from the room and the things together. Settle up with the hotel and I'll sit here and wait. There was something about this place I liked, he said, when she came back to him. But it's better that we go, for do you think it would suit me to be the poorest and meanest man in a prospering town? I'd need a new car and a patch or two on the seat of my constitution before I could feel equal to it. A hat on my head like the farmers had and I'd look like tommy-rot.

We'll find a simpler place, he said, where the rage of the vulture, the love of the turtle.

He put her into the car and they set off in the moonlight.

Where I can answer my letters and think my thoughts in peace, he said to her. They were travelling the cool white luminous path that washed clearly down the road.

Up soared the car again to the bitter harsh land of stone and desiccation, and on both sides stood the chastened mountains snowy-blue with light. The valley of wealth was white as flax behind them, and what was shadow or what was hill was indifferent to the eye. Each stood out as black and fathomless as the other, with the strong shining bands of the river weaving out and in.

Summit after summit built up ahead as though in ice: clear, and firm, and seamless. All about was the presence of the white unearthly night spread out like a cloak on the knotted ground. The tusks of the highest towers were strong as ivory-horn against the heavens, and for all the wondrous brilliance a few stars were shining, strangely golden in the bluish sky.

The promise that each thin valley proferred and withheld was so rare that they did not speak of where they might be going. Martin drove for a long time through the white glamorous land, and then he guided the car to the side of the road under the shelter of the hanging cliff. The ribs of the needle-trees cast a motionless shade on the whitened clay of the roadside. And there they sat speechless, harking to the sound of water falling below through the rocks, and to the warbling echo that returned up the steep alabaster wall.

In a little while Martin said: This is where we are going. We are safe here. His voice was hushed in peace and he sighed sweetly through his mouth. We are safe here, he said, and he put his arms around her. Side by side they lay down together, warm and close on the floor of the car. He was tired and he said: We are safe here, darling, and the dogs drew close to them for comfort. He was tired and Hannah was still awake, watching, when he fell asleep in her arms.

CHAPTER XXXIII

In a week they drove into St. Jean-les-Pins, and the first thing they saw was Lady Vanta in a lemon-yellow sweater on the other side of the square. Her head was bare and her red hair shone out in the sun. She was sitting reading a book on the hotel terrace, with her legs crossed over in her white skirt. When she heard the car she looked up from the page and saw them, and she uncrossed her bare legs and the high-heeled sandals that swung from her toes and ran heedlessly across the square.

My lambs, my lambs! she was crying out. My loves, my dearests!

They clasped her hands and kissed one another's faces, for it was strange and warming to be welcomed so by any human being.

Oh, and your beautiful dogs with you! cried Lady Vanta. What angels of you to really, really come!

She clasped their hands fondly in her broad white palms, and drew them over the square to the terrace of the hotel.

You must meet my old friend the *propriétaire*, said Lady Vanta. He's a perfect lamb. I've told him all about you—that you're an *homme de lettres distingué*, Martin darling. And all about Hannah, the sweet, who's still young enough to be eating peppermint sticks and rolling hoops. He'll be delighted to know you've come.

They both laughed aloud with Lady Vanta, for she pressed their arms close and cuddled their hands in her fingers. The more she talked the more they felt that they were grown young and spirited again. Only the thought of the *propriétaire* for a moment filled them with doubt and fear.

His name was Fleury, and his flesh flowered red; his eyes were flower blue and his hair milk-weed white. When Lady Vanta called out his name, he came through the door with his hawthorne smile in his teeth. He shook their hands and asked them to come and drink with him because they were Lady Vanta's friends, and because they had come at last. Lady Vanta had not been so gay, he said, since the other literary gentlemen went back to Paris a week ago.

Why weren't you here, my lambs? said Lady Vanta, sighing. Three of the bravest and dearest. They wanted to get back for the Cocteau rehearsals. I've been in mourning for them since they've gone.

The *propriétaire* poured out their drinks himself: brandy and port, and two fingers of vodka for Lady Vanta's spotless throat. He liked the look of painters and writing-men, he said, and their disregard for the time of night that sent other people to bed.

Sometimes, said he, Lady Vanta's friends sit here drinking until three and four in the morning. It gives a life to the place, it keeps things going. Last summer after Lady Vanta and her friends went away, the hotel was black at ten o'clock every night.

The drinking taste of the literary was a thing that pleased him very well. A Frenchman would take a pernod or two or a bottle of ordinary wine. But good vintages and dry champagne were in an artist's blood like a taste for pretty women. With this he nudged Martin in the side, and his face bloomed freshly into flower. He stroked his white moustaches out long and smooth, and his belly shook under his coat with zest.

They sat talking and laughing now, and all that had happened to them before seemed finished and left behind. We should have come here long ago, said Martin, and he looked with his bold merry eyes at Hannah.

And literary men are gay, said the *propriétaire*, and his own eye lit from the spark in Martin's eye. Can you dance and sing? he said to Martin.

I can! said Martin, and he jumped to his feet on the terrace. Tell him, Hannah, that I can do sleight-of-hand too.

Martin pulled up his cuffs from his wrists and began playing with bits of sugar and coins before them. His magical fingers thrust the sugar in one ear and drew it out from the other. He winged Lady Vanta's agate ring off into the air, and found it again in the knots of Mirette's shaggy coat. Mirette swung her tail in the sun and lifted her head to them, smiling. It was summer, the dust was deep, and the plane trees were in full leaf above them. And as Hannah laughed with the others, her heart suddenly halted as though every line and stroke of this were to be set down forever: Martin's lips were parted and he was laughing. He was wearing his loose grey suit and his chamois cape over his shoulders, and his hair had slipped over his temple. With his finger and thumb he was drawing forth two cubes of sugar from the paunch of the *pro-priétaire's* pocket, and the Frenchman himself was laughing, was shouting and shaking with laughter.

But in a moment, the pulse of life returned and Martin dropped his hand on Hannah's and said: We should have come here before, Hannah. We'll stay for a while and have our mail sent on.

Is Mr. Alaric really a bore or just so like that he seems a bore? said Lady Vanta after supper. I've known him a hundred years or so, and I've never heard him say one thing that could be set down in a book.

Nor do important people ever say things much worth repeating, said Martin.

Now take Eve Raeburn, said Lady Vanta, with a flicker of malice and curiosity in the match's halo thrown upon her puckered face. There's a person I can't picture in my mind at all. Is she old or young, for instance, and what kind of things does she say?

She's my aunt, on my father's side, said Martin in a moment. His voice had gone chill and far, because a stranger had spoken the name of someone who belonged to him. She's a very remarkable woman. If you had been in Monte Carlo recently you might have met her there.

Lady Vanta smoked her cigarette and shuddered in the evening air.

Monte Carlo! she said. I can't stand it. There's something breaks my heart about it. Probably the old women who never look in the glass, or who if they do are now too blind to see. If ever I go there for gaiety, then I sit at the tables with my mouth hanging wide at the yards of lace, turned yellow with tea, that swaddle them and piece them together. And their *point de Venise*. And their *point d'esprit*, she said, chortling at her humour. And the violets hand-painted on their brooches and on the backs of their gloves. My dear, when they put their glamour on in the morning, they must sit quite still to themselves like rats in a hole and refuse a glimmer of light. Here's my fard, and here's my patch, and here's my stick of grease paint. God strike me blind with terror if I cheat and peek into the glass.

And then the most violent of them, said Lady Vanta crooning her laughter, tie up the bit of face that remains in a white or a purple veil. Whether to hold what's left together, or to save the grace of the passersby, I know not. But once it's all mounted on stilts with lace-inset hose tied fast by faith and hope to the kneecaps castanetting, 'twould sink the fleet could it see its grandmothers in formation advancing on the h'Empire with their parasols in their hands.

Don't tell me Eve Raeburn looks like that, my lambs? said Lady Vanta with a gurgle of laughter. She wrote me such a nice letter about my tales I'd hate to have it so.

But now Martin's voice had gone chill as frost and he answered: She's the one unartificial Englishwoman I know.

The thing I like best of her, said Lady Vanta, is that she's committed murder the same as me.

Murder? said Martin.

Murder, said Lady Vanta. When she burned up the churches and public buildings, she must have done in a corpse or two by the way. There was a jolly old sexton done to a crisp in one church, I remember. Now why shouldn't it have been Eve Raeburn who set a match to his tail? The people I like, she said, have all done murder in one way or another. The King's English, or the French tongue, as Martin does, or me myself that did it in a peculiar way.

It was two years ago this month, she said, and she tossed her cigarette out to where it perished. And I was doing a bit of writing on the other side of the brook behind. Right in sight and sound of the hotel, mind you, watching the trout trip up and down the falls. And there was a French family blossomed forth on the rocks above me, summer had come and the French ladies set out in deepest mourning in celebration of it, balancing their picnic lunch on their hams, with their black crêpe canopies wagging on their heads.

And with them, said Lady Vanta, were a couple of brats disturbing my peace of mind for me. The one was a little girl with a mane of hair, and she was jumping about with this curtain of hair flapping down her back and crying out to the family, God love 'em! My hair's the most beautiful! It's full of reflections and everyone speaks of it! The mother drew herself up in black and said: *taes-toi*, beauty depends upon something else again. The church tells us that it depends upon the soul. Look at your little brother here for spiritual beauty! Her son was hung over her arm, thin with sick eyes, and puking the lunch they had packed into him, a child with his skin so pinched to his bones that it turned you queer in the pit to see him. Look at your little brother! said the French madame. He has a soul if nothing else to please you.

You must tell me, said Lady Vanta, how this seems to you as a story, for if you and Eve Raeburn want more of my work I could write it out proper you know. I've a bit of it down in my own way, and once sober I could decipher it for you. I've girt up my loins for so many literary crossings, she said, that I hope this one won't founder like the rest.

I'm bringing the magazine out myself in the fall,

said Martin. Go on, he said, go on. Have another drink and finish the story.

It was this ailing kid, said Lady Vanta. Now let me wet my whistle. It kept going nearer and nearer the water at the foot of the falls where I was hid away. I could see it with its spiny toes on the moss, stalking out like a stork with its sick belly swollen before it. The family was busy as weavers with cheese, and forgotten there was a child gone from their midst. No sooner had I written the opening lines of my poem than the bloody child fell in.

It fell in with a gulp, said Lady Vanta. I could hear it choking and gasping and I never looked up from the paper before me. The power for speech for once had left me and my pencil stood baulked where it had finished. Said I to myself, the kid is sick and look at its people. But you can't just leave it, said something else in my mind.

I could hear the cries of the child as it stifled, but weaker ones now for it had little enough health to begin with. Better leave it, said I to myself and once the decision was made, my pencil moved off of itself on the paper, composing a poem as clear and calm as a soul at anchor. It was printed on both sides of the Atlantic, nor did anyone know that its genius relied on its springing from death into being.

The family came scuttling down over the rocks just as I set down the last line to it, said Lady Vanta. They came sliding and gripping one after the other. And the little girl started in to cry at the sight of her brother lying there drowned in the shallow bed. I stayed long enough to see their faces, and to see the child out and hung drying, as blue and bloated, over the forearm, and then I went off through the woods unseen and home on the other side, and no one the wiser.

Lady Vanta sat grinning through the dark at Martin, and he drew his chamois cloak about him as if a breath of death had come his way.

Is there any truth in that? said Martin to her.

What is truth, my lad? said Lady Vanta. Some of us have no more than a nodding acquaintance with it.

She sat crooning her laughter in her white arms crossed over her bosom. Her square white face shone out like a mask in the dark with the black strokes of the mouth and eyes laid on to make it real.

Did I ever tell you, then, said Martin, of the voyage down I took in my aeroplane one evening? Its nose went six feet in the ground and the motor came out the other side. That was the night, said Martin smoking, that it took one of my lungs for a souvenir and kept my ribs for toothpicks.

Then that's what it is, said Lady Vanta chortling, that makes you haunt me like a piece of music.

There's nothing to me, said Martin. I'm not here at all. My boots were found on a tree-top, sticking up to scare the crows from their direction. My clothes, he said, and he touched his cloak, are now hung on a peg and stuffed with straw to make them human. Touch me, Lady Vanta, said Martin softly leaning forward. Touch me. That was the night I died.

Lady Vanta lifted her bleached broad hand and made as if to pass it through his substance. And then she faltered, as though fearing to find nothing there.

I think you're speaking the truth, she said. I don't need confirmation. This is the way to escape, she said, from the gall and the wormwood. If we talked all night we might manage, we might leave the worst bits of us behind.

CHAPTER XXXIV

The hotel was set off from the highway, as was the custom in these mountain places, by a yellow square with wide plane trees set all about its edge. And these trees, or others like them or even at times tall eucalyptus trees with bare white pungent trunks, marched off down the road itself, and up it, to form a clear avenue of shade for a mile without the two entries to the town. It was a place that was closed in winter because of the drifts of snow that submerged the road and put an end to anyone passing, but now it was a thoroughfare for travel and for flocks of sheep with their deep-tongued bells at their necks driven by.

Behind the hotel ran the stream with trout in its waters, and a bridge over it that led to the fir woods beyond on the hill. When Hannah and Martin came down from the creek side of the hotel one morning, they found the open square alive with sheep and cattle, and barriers set up, and gypsies' wagons halted, and the strong foul odour of all the beasts driven in for the summer fair. Flock after flock had come from far in the hills for the August market, had been driven down the road at night and folded, cramped and thirsting, into the temporary pens on the square. The cattle had bent their stiff legs under and settled down, lowing and complaining; and droves of swine with wisps of straw-white hair on their hocks and hind-quarters, too stout to walk but trundled there on carts, ran snorting and squealing from the thrust of a staff on their rumps or a hand that screwed their tails up fast behind them.

The three dogs ran sniffing in mad delight the net-work of stench and hide and bone. There were young mountain donkeys with mouths still sweet with milk who charged the great strange dogs and then took fright and scampered, soft as rabbits, back to their mother's side. There were calves with short stubborn brows and childish feet. There were sheepdogs who leapt up snarling if strangers drew too near.

Martin and Hannah sat down at a table at the other end, and a servant brought them their breakfast of coffee and bread. Down the length of the terrace they could see her come, bearing the tray and letters in her hand.

The mail, the mail, said Martin. The first that had come to them here. The mail, the mail. There were letters from Mr. Alaric and Dilly, and from the poet in Italy. A dozen long envelopes of manuscript were there, and when Martin saw the cheques he kissed their faces. And underneath everything else, there appeared a letter from Eve.

Martin picked it up, and then he said:

This must be in answer, Hannah, to your letter to Eve.

He took a drink of coffee quickly down as though to give himself courage for it, and then he ran the butter knife under the flap. He read it slowly, back and forth, the first page and the second; every word of the handwriting over the linen pages, and Hannah could see no alteration in his face. When he was done, he handed it over to Hannah.

Now what do you make of that, he said.

He lit a cigarette and sat watching her read the letter. He sat clearing his throat and drumming his fingers in concern on the cloth.

Dear Martin, said Eve. I feel very badly that you are so discouraged about everything. I'm afraid you've been drinking too much or you would not have such depression. It isn't natural to you! I don't remember you ever being depressed when you were with me. Perhaps you are not in a good altitude for you. Let me know where you are exactly and I'll get a bit of advice about whether or not it's a suitable place. I myself shall be off presently on a motor trip. It's become too hot to stay in Monte Carlo, and I've been having bad luck at the tables. I'm going to buy myself a little car, just big enough for two people and a chauffeur, and go north and see a few cool churches for a change. I've just met your friend Lady Vanta, by the way, who is here now. We get on very well together. I've never liked a woman so much in a long time. We have one great bond in common: a dislike of the new world casualness and of the American point of view. Your own remark about women forgetting years and men are not able is false, as you must have known when you wrote it. It's the man who goes lightly off without a hint of remorse, or else he regrets it when it is TOO LATE and that's a tragedy he has to face and no one can remedy it. I have every intention of going on with the magazine in the autumn, she ended. Do let me see some of your recent work, if your surroundings have permitted you to do any. I should like to consider it for my next number.

Now what do you think of that? said Martin when she handed the letter back to him.

And how could the two things piece together and make one woman, Hannah was thinking. How could the evil insinuating fury fit the sad lonely grief that invented a friend and friendship to take the edge off any pity they might feel? She had planned it well: a chauffeur, a new car, and the next number of the magazine to tempt him. If he argued well, he could have them all again. If he lied and damned, if he told her a story that would suit her needs, he could have all the things for which his heart was sore.

I'll write her a letter that will bring her down to earth, said Martin. He folded the letter up and put it away. She's never laid eye on Lady Vanta, and the other remarks are timed and placed to rile me. If she tries to bring out the magazine, I'll give her a piece of my mind. I'll have her up in court for the name of it's mine, and the idea, and the intention. She has nothing but money and spite to make me toe the line. I'll write her the magazine's mine, and I'll see her in hell before she gets it.

Hannah sat quiet, with her hands clasped. And every now and again Martin cleared his throat and rapped his fingers across the table top. The animals were crying out for thirst in the square behind them, and the sun was growing hot in the boughs. The speech and the stench and the hoofs and bleating rose in tumult from the dust, but the thought of Eve was clear and aloof in Hannah's mind.

Martin, you have so much of everything, she said to him. You have more than enough and to spare of everything, Martin. Of love, and beauty, and of genius, and belief. You have enough of everything to give part of it away.

He sat still for a moment, and then he said: You mean to Eve.

Hannah saw the other letters lying by his plate: the Italian poet's and Mr. Alaric's, and the manuscripts that would fill his dreams at night. They were no friends of hers, she knew, no matter how much she wanted them so. They were part of the time when Eve and Martin were together, and she did not belong. She could read their poems or their stories, but like a stranger buying and opening a book at any page whatsoever. They would never turn to her, because to her they had nothing to say. She had come between kin and turned blood black, and even Lady Vanta must know this. The friends he had knew, although they did not say it, that the magazine would come out when Eve and Martin were hand in glove again.

If you have no patience left, then let me write to Eve, said Hannah to him.

Then don't be too gentle with her, said Martin. For she might suspect it. She knows the kind of fury that I'd bring down on her head.

CHAPTER XXXV

Lady Vanta could not be alone, could not have silence. If there were hours of work to be done, Lady Vanta's beauty came to an end. She had a pale smiling mouth curved up like a bark for setting sail in conversation. When she sat on the terrace alone, rather than have it empty, she patted it full of yawns with the tip of her hand.

If I were a writer I'm sure that I'd write, she said to Martin. She had made herself a necklace and rings of the little green leaves of the box. But I'm peeled, I'm bare, every point in the room obstructs me. The end of the table there's like a dagger between my breasts.

She laughed drowsily at Martin and shook the stiff leaves of her bracelet.

Perhaps on moss, perhaps with a quill, perhaps if something swept me away. I'd be awfully brave about digging holes, said Lady Vanta wearily, if I thought there was anywhere a bait that words, like fish, would nibble. I've been vulgar, I've been mannerly, but I never see anything of them but their fins going the other way. If ever I get a few lines down on paper, she said, it's no more than the colour of their scales, when I seized them, left behind.

But writing here in the heat, she said, I forget which way I'm going. I bring out a fresh bunch of words every morning with my grapes, but once I've spat out the pips the silvery part is missing. I find they go down my gullet like magic with the skin. I've tried since ten to write, said Lady Vanta. With the tips of her fingers she pushed the pile of blank golden pages over to Martin's hand. I had such a pretty thought about the twinning of particles of frost the male and male, the doe with doe, the hind with hind. Now, fancy, she said, with this featherbed of heat upon me. I made Hannah a crown of laurel leaves instead, she said, to put upon her brow.

She set the wreath on Hannah's head, and put back the hair that was out of place.

I'm useless, like the season, she said. Only the season has a harvest and brings wine to the table. I can't even change a typewriter ribbon, she said. The sight of circles makes my head spin, and the point of a pencil is an arrow flying. Whenever I sit down to write, my mind gets in the way.

Or if ever she went to her room alone, the sound of the door closed was sufficient. The other woman, whoever she was, got up and shook her silky skin and came laughing across the floor. The chair was left rocking, and the book set down on its face to keep the page, so there could be no mistake for Lady Vanta.

When I sit down to write she puts her hand out on the page and wipes it clean, said Lady Vanta. She's always there saying two things in me when I should be saying one. If I look in the glass at any time of the day, she's there looking over my shoulder. She's neither fish nor fowl and her skin's a shade darker. It's when she trips me up in my Latin verbs, said Lady Vanta, that I come running down to your door. It's me that comes running quick on my toes and stops at your keyhole with my fingernail scratching. It's me saying, darlings, it's pore little Lady Vanta. It's Van with her curlers up wantin' in.

Lady Vanta called for her vodka, for now it was noon and time to begin. If you sat without drink the silence behind every tree crouched ready to spring. The words went out the back, could not be mustered without the clear white clarion-call of drink ringing out in the glasses. If you sat still and looked at one another's faces, the bottom fell out of the day.

Vodka, said Lady Vanta, makes a nice wire on which to string them. Trout, and flapping.

Down went the drink, and she looked into their eyes.

Hannah, Martin, some day I may ask you to bear a cross for me, and what'll you say to that? she said softly. Some day I may say to you, Martin, there was Greece, there was Troy, there's nobody else remembers. And how will you answer me, Martin? There were valiant men of might in their generations. There were Tola and Puah and Jashub and Shimrom.

She threw back her head on her white soft neck and tilted her yellow eyes at their faces.

And what if I should ask you, Martin, to be the greatest man of your time?

I died a hard death long ago, said Martin. You've forgotten.

Exactly, said Lady Vanta in a soft deep breath. She held up her second brimming glass of drink. That's why you're endowed, my darling. The field of endeavour before us all, like a green banner blowing. And you emblazoned on it: the gold harp of Ireland, sounding out for a wake, or a jig, or a comeallye.

Lady Vanta's hands laid hold of her green silk handkerchief. The skin drew tight on her knuckles and she tore the square in two.

Now take this half, said Lady Vanta, and keep it by you. If ever you're in trouble, then send it to me without a word and I'll come, said Lady Vanta. And if ever I'm in need, I'll send mine to you.

It was noon, and the heat of noon laid heavily on them. The gong for the lunch rang out on the terrace, and the Frenchwomen folded their knitting and rose. Lady Vanta held out her fair hands to Martin and Hannah.

Come, my darlings, she said. In to the feast, like Romans! She walked down the terrace, arm in arm with them, swaying a little amongst the wicker chairs.

In the morning there was another letter from Eve in Monte Carlo. When Martin had done reading, he handed the sheets of it to Hannah across the table on the terrace.

Dear Martin, it began, to show the bending of her temper. I'm glad you're pleased with the place you have found. A doctor here tells me that it is not at all what he would recommend to patients, but if the hotel people are content to have you, I suppose that must be your first consideration. Yes, Lady Vanta is still here and we are starting off to-morrow on a trip together. Write me care of the bank. I've found such a nice little car and we're planning an interesting trip. We'll keep to the mountains, stop in and see our old friend S. . . . at Hauteville (what a shame you can't be along!) and have a look at her latest work. I have had two letters from Jonathan and he is willing to send me twice as much as last time in the way of prose and perhaps a poem or two. But possibly this kind of talk no longer interests you?

Lady Vanta seems a lonely sort of person, the letter proceeded. I think being with me has cheered her up. She is a great admirer of your poetry and we have long talks about you. She regrets as much as I do that you are not FREE to come and go as you please. I know you so well, and know that an isolated life is not one of your own choosing. She spoke of having lunch with you at Vence in the spring, and says she found your COMPANION very colourless. I just mention this in passing. She said that she too found you depressed. I hope at least that your various excesses leave you some time for your own work, and think it too bad if you mistreat your energy.

I can't read any more, said Hannah. There were two more pages of it before her. It's between you and Eve, she said.

No, it isn't, said Martin. It's a reply to your letter. That should show you. If you humble yourself, she'll walk right over your body and soul.

She gave him the letter, folded over. If she said any more she thought that her voice would betray her and that the tears would come down her face.

But where does her pretence end and where begin? she suddenly cried out to Martin. Was she setting off in a smart new car that the talk of made Martin envy, or was this part of the subterfuge as well? or was she riding off in state alone behind a chauffeur, with her thoughts alive in fabrication of the presence on the empty seat beside her? Was she driving away alone with her lips moving of themselves as they did when she was agitated, conversing, with a faint smile on her mouth, with the fancy of Lady Vanta riding there? Was it: a cushion in the small of your back, Lady Vanta, or Vanta, or Van, by this time? And shall we stop here for a drink; ye like vodka, don't ye, and powder our faces and talk about me nephew again.

Don't despair, said Martin gently to her. Now everything will be clear and spoken. I'll write to her as I feel and you'll see how it will be.

If I went to see Eve, myself, said Hannah.

My God! cried Martin, and he burst into laughter. At least I can spare you that!

His face was so near that she took it against her own as if to comfort him, although he was strong and needed no comfort. She pressed his face close to her own, no matter who should see them, and suddenly, with her ear against his cheek, she heard the spring deep in the rock within him leap bubbling from its source and break. She sat as though frozen, with her cheek against him, harking as his own ears must hark, to the stream flowing underground, rippling and cascading. And then he took out his handkerchief and pressed it folded to his mouth, and stood up from his chair.

He offered his arm to Hannah, like an escort taking her in to dinner, and she rose on shaking knees and put her fingers through. Down the terrace they went arm in arm, down the length of people doing their fancy-work or reading their papers in the morning sun. Down the long row of faces lifted to watch them as they passed: the young man with his handkerchief folded to his lips, and the young woman smiling falsely at his side. At the far end, the hotel door seemed to retreat with every step they took. A comic couple walking with dignity towards the door that receded and jumped back, that retired as they came.

Their feet lagged, the sun rose, the faces of the women sewing lifted and turned away. And down the terrace Martin and Hannah went, pursuing the small black haven of the door which fled. Once on the threshold, the opening grinned wide, withdrew, shrank to a keyhole, and then roared open like a furnace and let them in. The hall was empty and they started the two flights of stairs. She put her arms about him and in bleak terrible strength, she bore him upwards against her heart. Don't breath, don't cough, don't speak, Martin. Don't open your mouth or I'll give you what for.

CHAPTER XXXVI

Before it was lunch time, Hannah went down to find Lady Vanta. She was sitting, cool and fresh on the terrace, drinking the aperitif with the *propriétaire* and a family of French people and smoothly speaking their tongue.

Now sit you down and have a drink like a lamb, she said to Hannah. I was just wondering where you two babes might be.

I have something to say to you, Lady Vanta, said Hannah. Not here, but over there.

Lady Vanta jumped up and walked out on the square under the plane trees, arm in arm with Hannah. The dust was dappled with shade and the motor cars of tourists were drawn up on the roadside for the mid-day meal. Faint sweet stirrings of hunger were drawing people out of their rooms and back from the hills to gather on the hotel terrace and wait the call to the dining-room.

Martin's had a hæmorrhage, Hannah said.

A hæmorrhage? said Lady Vanta, stopping short. My God, Hannah, what are you going to do?

I've done everything I can, said Hannah. He'll

have to lie quiet a long time now. He had a very bad one.

My God, said Lady Vanta. I suppose he ought to have nurses and things like that?

I can nurse him, said Hannah. I can do the things for him. But I'd like to have a very good doctor up from Nice.

I feel so helpless, said Lady Vanta. I'm not a practical person. I wouldn't know the first thing to do. Her hands were travelling, for all their calm blonde beauty, from skirt to blouse, from lip to bracelet in haste. If he's had them for years, she said, I suppose he takes them more or less for granted.

You can't take them that way, said Hannah. They don't come like that.

I know, said Lady Vanta. I know. It must be dreadful. Do you suppose, she said in a moment, do you suppose Monsieur Fleury will mind you staying on?

But we can't move away, said Hannah.

I feel terribly, really, about poor Martin, said Lady Vanta. She pressed Hannah close with her arm. I feel terribly. I feel so helpless. I brought you here and I feel responsible for everything. I'll speak to Monsieur Fleury myself, she said. I'll tell him I didn't know this was liable to happen. I feel so badly, she said in a moment to Hannah's silence. But I know I'd only hamper you if I went up in the room. I've never been faced with anything like this before, said Lady Vanta.

I'd just stand there, Hannah. I wouldn't know what to do.

And now the terrible greed and lust for the things other men had written or done were again like a wild hunger in Martin. The books that they had were the food and the drink he could not take in through his mouth. The manuscripts, and the photographs, and the books and reviews lay scattered on the covers, and when Hannah ceased reading aloud he reached out and touched their faces. There was one man who wrote of how beautiful horses seemed to him: the power of their hoofs, and the meat of their necks, and how they went over the country; and when Martin heard these words read out it set a fire of rapture burning in his eye.

The summer had given over to storming now, and all day in the room Hannah sat and read things aloud to him: Pound's poetry, and the letters of Poe to be the sustenance he could not take into his mouth. I wish Catterina the cat could see the food here, Poe's words ran on in delight. She would faint. Last night for supper we had the nicest tea you ever drank, strong and hot, wheat bread and rye bread, cheese, tea cakes (elegant) a great dish (2 dishes) of elegant ham, and 2 of cold veal piled up like a mountain and large slices—3 dishes of great cakes. I wish you could have seen the eggs and great dish of meat, he wrote. I wish Catterina the cat could see the food here.

Edgar Allan Poe, sick at heart for a square meal and a breath of fame in his nostrils, saying proudly: I haven't drunk a drop, so I hope to get out of trouble. I wish Catterina could see the food, with his arms out in love to her. She would faint. She would faint, and he would turn up her soft cat paws over her throbbing belly, he would bury his sorrowing face in her soft belly cat-fur and smother his love in Catterina-fur.

Hannah's voice read out Poe's words in the hotel room, and when she turned the page she came to the paragraph that said: Alas, my Magazine scheme has exploded—or, at least, I have been deprived, through the imbecility or idiocy of my partner, of all means of prosecuting it for the present. And at this Martin's eyes flashed open on the pillow and he smiled at Hannah.

Two of a kind, he whispered. Kindred obsessions, he said softly, to pick and choose. And quarrels you'd think there'd be no way of mending. I'd like to give Eve a piece of my mind, and he fingered the covers with his empty hands as though seeking something there. When I get well I'll answer her, he said.

His hand moved over the clothes until it came to the edge of Hannah's dress, and there it lay quiet. And suddenly some wondrous veil of sleep seemed to fall upon his features. He lay there with his hand touching her dress and his breath rising and falling. When Hannah looked at him sleeping there, she knew it would not be long now, that soon he would be sitting up and taking food. And soon he would be restored again and walking with her up the road at night.

She sat watching him asleep, with the book lying open, when a gentle knock sounded out on the door. And there stood the *propriétaire* in the doorway, looking in from the gloom of the hall with a letter in his hand. She saw his fresh ruddy face, and the blue eyes under his thick white brows, and the stiff cropped hair that stood upright over all his skull.

How is Mr. Sheehan? he said in a hushed voice, and this was the day he must have chosen, thought Hannah, this was the hour come to give her warning.

He's much better than yesterday, Hannah said.

Listen, Madame, he was saying, I had some grapefruit sent up from Nice to-day. I thought it might taste good to him.

Oh! said Hannah. She could think of nothing else to say. She clung fast to the doorknob and looked into his blooming face.

About the ice, he was saying softly to her, I have a sort of knife that was made particularly for that. I'll have the girl bring it up to you, when the train gets in from Nice.

I broke my scissors trying to break it this morning, said Hannah. The daylight from the room was shining on him, smoothing his moustaches long and fair, and silhouetting him against the dark.

If the dogs are a trouble to you, he said, speaking softly as if some secret were possessed between them,

I could fix them up in that place at the end where the goats used to be. You can't tend Mr. Sheehan with them under your feet.

His white cropped wig shone out like a light in the dusk of the hallway.

Here's a letter that Lady Vanta left when she went away, he said.

He put the envelope into her hand, and at the sound of him calling them, the three dogs jumped up from under the bed, stretched out their legs and shook their coats and went after him down the hall. Hannah walked over to the window and opened the letter by the window pane The wind was careening through the heavy top-knots of the trees, and the rain had begun to fall upon the glass.

My dearest lambs, said Lady Vanta's dauntless hand. Have just received word that one of my nearest and dearest is under the weather in Paris and must fly. I know we'll see each other *soon*. I feel so certain of this. It would be too cruel of fate to bring us together for such a brief moment if that's all there was to be to it. In the meantime, cherish each other, my darlings, for I love you both so well.

CHAPTER XXXVII

For two weeks he lay still on his back in bed, nourished on goat cheese and fruit juice, and suddenly in the black of night he sat up on his pillows. Don't bother about the ether, he said. Get the needle now. There isn't time.

She flashed on the light and ran to the cupboard. Bubble-rip, bubble-rip, bubble-rip, ran the tide of his blood behind her. She cracked off the end of an ampoule and slowly, patiently, without haste, drew the yellowish liquid in through the needle's gaping eye. She knew that the vessel was overflowing behind her, was streaming out over the covers and the bed. But all she could see in the room was his bare arm waiting, his white flesh riddled with holes where the steel had stabbed and stabbed him, waiting now for her to thrust the needle in. Yet every time she pierced him her own heart went sick and faint within her.

You're all right, Martin, you're all right, she said.

She stuffed the rubber bag full for his chest and laid it on him. The ends of her glassy fingers forced two white splinters of ice into his streaming mouth. You're all right, Martin. She knew there was a fountain of strength in him, and all this he could spare. In a moment he lay back and his hand clung strongly to her.

I'll have to have a shot in the veins, he whispered. He took his breath tremulously, tentatively, into his lungs and let it slowly out again. He tried the air warily, out and in, to see if it would stay. Even his voice had a perilous strange edge to Hannah, as though some edifice within him were ready to totter and perish. Already the awful tide lay thickening and drying on his mouth.

Have to get a man up from Nice, he said, and he smiled at her.

She saw it was two in the morning when she lifted her hand to ring the bell. The *propriétaire* had put his overcoat on and run down the hall to her.

Can we telephone for a doctor at Nice? she said.

He came into the room with his bare legs hanging out under his coat, and he kneeled down at the side of the bed by Martin. His white shirt was pressed down in the blood spilled out on the tiles, but he paid no heed.

I'll go now in my car, he said, whispering close to Martin. Bravo, Mr. Sheehan. He lifted his hand like a woman and put the hair back from Martin's face. The telephone is closed off now, my little friend, he whispered. But I'll drive down and get a fine man for you. Wait for me, you wait for me, darling, he said.

Martin smiled up at Hannah as Mr. Fleury sped out the door. His slipper flew off at the threshold but he did not pause.

Let's make it a party, said Martin. His voice was no

more than a breath in her ear, but his eyes were bold and merry. We'll send a telegram to Eve. Write it out before he goes, he said.

For a moment Hannah's heart went cold in apprehension, as though even Martin now knew some fatal thing that she had no knowledge of. She looked into his face beside her, and for the moment he must be beset with fear because they were alone in a cheap hotel amongst strangers where anything might befall them. For the moment his courage must be broken, and he was sending for Eve in fear.

You're all right, she said. You mustn't be frightened.

I'm not frightened, he whispered. I want a party, that's all. His mouth turned up and he smiled at her. We'll have champagne. Tell Mr. Fleury to bring caviare. He ought to be back by seven in the morning.

Hannah printed the telegram out, black and big for Mr. Fleury:

Martin ill. He wants you very much. Doctor coming from Nice. Hannah.

And now Eve will come, and we must find some language in common. We must find some tongue that the three of us can speak. The anger and lies will be set aside and we'll talk of ordinary things together: the cooking, the scenery, and Martin's diet. I'll be humble with Eve for all the wisdom she can give me. She's his blood and his kin to him, and I will stand aside.

In a little he seemed to be falling asleep, and Hannah put down a blanket on the floor beside him. She dressed herself in her short shabby suit and put her coat on and laid down by the bed. She lay there on the tiles of the floor by his side so that her movement would not stir the bed and start the blood again spilling from his body. And Martin lay quiet between the sheets, waiting, with his hand drooped over the edge to touch her hand, unmoving.

All night she lay quiet, turning the thought of Eve and Martin in her head. And so must Eve herself be lying, she thought, stark awake all night in her bed in Monte Carlo, or in another city, hugging the fancy of Lady Vanta to her to keep her warm. She had taken the magazine to make a disputed child of it. The half of it's mine must her black heart be saying in anguish. If you go gallivanting over the country with harlots, then leave the children to me. What's it to you if I bring them up Jews or Catholics? What's it to you if I don't bring them up at all?

All night Hannah lay still with the thought of her. Surely all of Eve's life had now become the deceit and the fancy written out to Martin, the sham and the subterfuge that would flay him to the quick. Never a manuscript had she touched, or opened the page of a book either, thought Hannah. All night she could hear the tough Scotch speech with an echo of deafness sounding in it; all night she could hear her git on with ye, or git out with ye, and the ring of Eve's laughter as if something funny had been said.

At six Mr. Fleury walked into the room with the doctor. He was a lean gentle man with a face as sharp as science. When Mr. Fleury slapped his back, he was near to being struck to the floor.

Champagne, whispered Martin strongly from the bed. Champagne. Champagne. Bring us a magnum.

Bravo! said Mr. Fleury, and he threw off his coat. I brought the caviare, he said. It will be a fine repast.

The doctor set down his little case and looked at Martin. He felt his pulse with his finger tips, and picked up the bottles one by one. Mr. Fleury was clearing a space on the corner of the table.

You can smoke a cigarette if you like, said the doctor to Martin, while this is being done.

He tightened the black rubber rope around Martin's arm above the elbow. Martin lifted his other hand and pointed at the sun. Just as the doctor put the needle's point in the vein, the swollen cork shot out of the champagne bottle and the sparkling golden juice streamed out over Mr. Fleury's hands. The creamy foam was slipping off like an edge of lace, and Mr. Fleury laughed aloud and tipped it over the glasses.

Ha, ha! he cried, and he held up the great bottle for them all to see the dripping petals of the flower that blossomed from it.

Martin lifted his eyes to look, and Hannah, he whispered. Without movement he inclined his head. Hannah, he said, seeing it fall into the glass stems. Hannah, have a glass of champagne.

CHAPTER XXXVIII

The hotel was quiet now, spacious and chill with gloom, for the end of the summer had sent the visitors back to Nice. The rain-swept terrace was stacked with empty chairs, tipped back against the dripping wall of the house. There were puddles and pools of rain caught and brimming in the packed soil of the square, and the boughs overhead were strung with beads of light. Over the roof were the thin clouds passing and melting, blown thin as silk and retiring before the wind's advance.

The rain was falling with less fury when Hannah went down to see if any mail had come. But great full drops of it fell splashing on her hands and face as she stood on the terrace and watched the weather lifting. Across the road at the Poste they were bearing the mail sacks out of the coach and into the little white house. The horses stood still in the shafts, with their heads lowered, waiting under the rain.

And Eve, will you write and put his heart at rest, she thought. Will you take up your pen and ease his mind. The same thing to all people you cannot be, nor can any woman. But if I have been foul to Dilly, then do not be the same to Martin. Eve, Eve, wherever you are, let your heart be honey the way it is for him.

She heard the dogs crying and clawing for her at the end of the terrace, but now she was hard and she paid no heed to them. The same thing to them all you cannot be, she said, but she saw them well crying for freedom. The whole wet luring world was wooing them and they could not bear to be closed away.

Eve, will you set your love to music? Will you plant it in the garden? Will you let it bear fruit for him and forget the sight of my face? Eve, be his south wind, for I have been the north wind of privation. What has my love done for him but sent him shaking through the alleys? Let my hair go grey and my face lean without him, but bring him a cargo of plenty. Let the young people who will soon be old people carry his name towards the sun.

She went up to the room, empty-handed. She sat down by the bed and opened the book and began reading to him where she had left off: The last time I saw Poe, she read, was in the afternoon of a dreary autumn day. A heavy shower had come up suddenly, and he was standing under an awning. I had an umbrella and my impulse was to share it with him on his way home. But something—certainly not unkindness—withheld me. I went on and left him there in the rain, pale, shivering, miserable. . . . There I shall always see him, poor, penniless, but proud, reliant, dominant. . . .

There was a sudden round knock on the door and Martin's eyes flashed wide.

That's Eve, he said.

It was the *bonne* with a telegram in her hand. Hannah took it from her and closed the door. It was sent from Eve, in Monte Carlo, and it said:

Telegram received yesterday. Can't possibly come. Dining with friends and Lady Vanta. Seeing printer to-morrow. Confident you are in good hands. Please address any further messages Miss Raeburn. Have never been called Eve Raeburn without prefix. Kindly sign own name and not that of intermediary. Also please return all manuscripts to me at once as may require them. Important.

Martin lifted his hand and made a gesture of dismissal.

Go on, go on reading about Poe, he said.

But there was the presence of Eve between them; in every word she had sent was the triumph of her glee. They who had treated her as light as the dust on their shoes, now that their spirit was broken they sent for her! And now that they were afraid, and turned to her like children, crying, she would show them the side and the might of the whip hand.

When they lay still in the dark, she was there between them. Hannah lay under the blanket and watched the stars from the floor. And Martin's hand remained apart, like a stranger absent from the country. Eve, be his south wind blowing him warmth and plenty. But the white stars were climbing in the north.

Hannah came into the room with a basket of fruit

one day, returned from the kitchen to him, and she saw a woman seated there with her back turned and talking to Martin by his bed.

Hullo, said Martin, and he looked up at her. Here's Eve, he said, and there was no change in his face.

A great new bottle of eau-de-Cologne stood on the table by the window, and the afternoon light came shining through its amber. There was a bunch of yellow roses scattered on the bed. Eve turned her head and said: Eh? When she saw Hannah, her faint queer smile wreathed round her mouth.

I didn't think you'd object, she said, if I just stopped in for a moment. I happened to be passing by.

She shook Hannah's hand, with her eyes averted and her face smiling blindly under her rosy turban. Then she turned back to Martin and the talk they had been having.

I've brought ye some books, Martin, she said. She looked at the one on the bed and gave a chuckle. You and your Edgar Allan Poe, she said. What kind of a country do ye come from, anyway? The men it turns out have no idea of taste.

Thank God, said Martin in his bold strong whisper from the depths of the bed. It gives the British a chance to vent their spleen.

Ye haven't changed a bit, said Eve, and she looked back over her shoulder and laughed to Hannah. I see he's learned no more wisdom than before, she said.

I was born with it, here, said Martin, and he lifted

his hand and tapped his heart. More than any Englishman would ever get wind of.

Behind them Hannah put out the fruit in the bowls, and Eve turned about with the great bunch of yellow flowers. The smile still hung on her lips, and she said: Maybe ye've nothing big enough here to put these in?

She had got to her feet, and in her long autumn-rosy coat and her close small hat, she halted beside Hannah. Her gloves were back, tucked in at the wrists, and there were jewels shining on her fingers. Under the smooth black rings of her hair, there were brilliants alight in her ears. She held the waxed white paper in her hands, and the heavy yellow heads and the fern came nodding over the edge. She was of a height with Hannah, and when she put the bouquet gently, as if it were a child, into Hannah's arms, her eyes returned from their absence and looked into Hannah's face.

They're beautiful, said Hannah. She bowed her head and drew her lips along their edges. And Eve stood motionless beside her, watching her whatever she did. In a moment she followed Hannah to the basin where she was unbinding the flowers' stems, and there she put her two fresh rosy finger tips on Hannah's cheek.

Ye've had a hard time, the two of you, she said. Her eyes were flooded with confusion. Ye're looking tired yourself.

The words were scarcely out of her mouth when her

eye lit on a bottle by the washstand. She seized it up in her fingers.

You're not giving that to Martin? she said.

Hannah shook off the drops of water from her fingers.

The doctor from Nice left that for when Martin can't go to sleep, she said.

That's opium, said Eve. You mustn't be doping Martin.

He's had two pills in three weeks' time, said Hannah. He can't sleep at night when there's something on his mind.

Eve looked straight at Hannah, and suddenly her eyes went small in fury: And who, may I ask you, young lady, is responsible for Martin having no peace of mind?

We're both of us at him like—like leeches! cried Hannah wildly. The single flowers she held fell from her quivering hands. Pull him apart, if that's what you want. I can't do it any longer. I want him whole, I want him Martin, whether he's yours or mine.

Eve rose up in her proud flesh and her clothing, spread mighty and high like a peacock in the room. There was something of delight in her face now that Hannah had cried out in despair.

So that's your plan now? said Eve. So that's how you think you'll get away? No, no! I've come, but I'm not going to stay, young lady. Ye've made your bed, the two of you, and it's not my affair.

She settled her coat on her shoulders and went humming across the room. And Martin's eyes flashed up as she approached him.

Climb down, Eve, he whispered loud with scorn. Climb down, climb down. Your high horse doesn't become you. Sit down and have some tea.

He shook his hand from the wrist, as if he had heard enough, and Eve sat down smiling in her faint malignant way.

I came for a word about the magazine, she said. You make yourself so inaccessible now, living in far places. The manuscripts I must have so I'll know what I can do.

I've had enough of your baronial rights, said Martin from his pillow. Hannah'll ring the bell for you, and like a fine lady you'll have your tea and your jam. But leave me what is mine, even if it perishes with me. Ahem, ahem, he cleared his throat and tossed upon the bed.

Ye talk as if you were daft, said Eve to him.

You talk like a fool, said he.

If Eve had come when he had called for her, things might have been other, thought Hannah. But she had come late when it pleased her to come, a high-handed woman disdaining beck or call. She had come of her own accord, when she liked, an arrogant woman that no ties could bind. If only the pride would break for once in her, thought Hannah; if only the vanity that lashed her would for once lie still. But no matter how Hannah turned in the room or sought for ways to halt their clamour, on and on like a madness went the terrible mating of their violence. Martin's voice was raised aloud so that Eve might hear the insults he flung into her face.

Your good King John, he sold your humanity and your freedom! He made ladies and gentlemen of you, with chains around your necks! He gave you handles before your names, and gold in your fist like a weapon!

Martin raised up on his elbow and swung his arm wide in the room.

There's not an Irishman dead or alive who would have put his name to the Magna Carta! If you've come here to lord it over me, he said, I'll tell you I don't give *that* for your height and your might!

He snapped his fingers under her nose, and Eve leaned forward with her face shaking close to his.

Ye talk like the ignorant fool you are, she said, with your kings and your barons! Ye don't know what breeding is or it wouldn't come so glib to your tongue!

Their furious speech was similar and like, thought Hannah, and out of their love for each other they spat their angry lies. Hannah saw how his rage had bleached and contorted him, and were I a brave woman, she thought in anguish, I would thrust Eve out from him. His face was washed white of everything but pain. But the thought shot through her hard and clear that it was Martin who had brooded and grieved, and who had called for Eve. It was Martin who said that the thought he held dearest was to see the three of them living at peace under the one roof. And if love there were, then this was love and she herself was the cause of strife between them.

Martin lay back upon his pillow and looked across the bed at Hannah. He might have read what was in her heart for the gentleness that was in his gaze.

Go out, Hannah, he said to her. Go out for a little while. There are things I must say to Eve that I can say better with you not here.

Hannah closed the door and went out from them, and down the long sightless hall. She could hear Martin's stricken voice ringing out from the room, either in irritation or anger, and she went down the corridor in shame that she had not the bravery or affront to remain by his side.

The dogs leapt up at the strange sight of her in the court, and she stood for a moment bewildered by the expanse of daylight and by the open sky that arched above her head. She put her hands on their necks and followed them in confusion, out through the covered gateway and over the road that bridged the stream. In all the time she and Martin had been in the place, she had never walked this way nor gone so far from him. On the other side she saw the land opening out in a meadow strewn with rocky paths. The soil was burdened and rich with the rains and the warmth of the summer that was dying; the cat-tails weighted the tubes of the grasses, the lavender was at its ripest, and the patches under the fir trees were richest loam. When she saw the dogs breasting the deep waves of grass and plunging hither and yon about her, she felt it might be that she was in the north again, and setting out alone for a walk with the dogs before anything had altered.

She was so little accustomed to walking now, that halfway up through the trees her heart beat warm and hard, and smote against her temples. She stopped still on the moss and waited, with her hands pressed back on the wounding bark, waiting for the breath to run quietly through her again. The trees were short, almost stunted here, as if the slope on which they stood brought them the worst of the avalanching snow in the spring; the ground was bevelled out where the rain must fall in such torrents that year after year the roots were washed clean of the soil. But the needles were dark and densely set, and the fir-apples, still crowned with a cap of raw green sap, hung thick throughout the boughs.

The dogs came back to touch her skirts with their noses, and Mirette lay down at her feet and waited there. And there as Hannah stood, watching the country all about her, the thought of Martin struck her like a blow. He had been a long time grieving for Eve's solitude, and now the two of them were together with their two voices in the room attacking each other as savage and sharp as wild birds of prey. If love had many sides, thought Hannah, then this was a portion of it. It had a furious face at times. It was a long steady pursuit that could not let the other be. There was no other life for Eve, except where Martin's interests were, and if she furthered or if she thwarted them, still it was love that drove her either way. And for Martin there was no rest nor peace, nor could be, if Eve were alone and sitting down alone at table, with his likeness framed in her room and her solitude speaking out to strangers saying: My nephew this, or my nephew that, for the chance of mentioning his name.

But when Hannah thought of him shouting his anger, her reason spun and swooned in her head, for what would become of him now? What would support him in the stead of health if he spat out his spirit and strength, like a spendthrift, on the air? She ran down the hillside to the hotel, ran up the stairs and down the sombre hallway. A wondrous urge of prayer and supplication was welling in her heart. She would fling the door open and fall down before Eve, and let the words that came crying out implore her. Eve, Eve, Eve, rang out within her, but her mouth was silent. She saw that Eve had opened the bedroom door, and come out, and closed it behind her, and stood quiet there in the hall.

Eve stood motionless on the threshold of Martin's room, and in some way she seemed altered, she seemed failing and diminished to Hannah. Her shoulders and her tall broad frame were bowed as though a weight of sorrow lay across her back. And now when she spoke there seemed a strange awed sweetness in her speech that Hannah had never heard there.

I don't know if ye can hear him, she said softly, and she put out her hand and drew Hannah forward. Listen now, Hannah, and tell me if you can hear him, she said, and Hannah stood hushed beside her. Behind the door she could hear the terrible hard sound of Martin sobbing, the awful gulp and shudder of his dry bitter sobs shaken out of his broken will.

Oh, my Martin! cried Hannah, and she sprang forward. What have you done to him? she said to Eve in fury. But Eve's strong womanly hand fell on her arm.

He's crying for you, Hannah, she said in sorrow. It's nothing I said to him. He had no ears for it after. He's crying because you were gone from him half an hour.

But Hannah had flung her aside and run into the room.

CHAPTER XXXIX

Eve came in dancing, came in skipping, she came in jigging with a Pernod in her hand. Have a drink, Hannah, a little drink, Hannah. It'll give ye a taste for the supper we're going to have. She would stay the night but she would stay no longer. My dark Rosaleen, she hummed high in her throat, my dark Rosaleen.

She would stay the night, but she'd be off in the morning. Her fancy of Lady Vanta was waiting her elsewhere with friends. We're going to drive far and wide. Have a little drink, Hannah, I didn't think your eyes were as Irish as they are. It's because your hair needs clipping and your face's gone thin.

She lifted Hannah's hair where it lay in her neck.

Have a little drink, Hannah, and come and see my dresses. She had taken a room on the other side of the hall. And there were her frocks shaking out on their hangers. Five pairs of elegant shoes were out of her bags already and set along the wall, waiting, with their toes turned in. Waiting for tangos, waiting for rhumbas, waiting till Martin could go stepping out again. I've been taking dancing lessons to fill in the time.

The time, said Eve, and the word gaped wide before them. The time, a chasm that would never fill. Fling seasons into it, one after the other, and they were carried off in the current.

All summer, said Eve, I've been dancing.

June, July, August, empty as corn-husks, flung on the waters and carried away.

Where'll you go with Martin when he's well? she said to Hannah. I'll look for places for you, back of Monte Carlo. There are places high up, ye know. Ye might like it there. Ye might have a little house, ye might come nearer.

Her boxes from China and her Indian bracelets were out on the bureau and on the tables round the room. She laid off her dress as she talked to Hannah, and out came her fair arms, full and bare.

An hotel room is no place for Martin. He needs a lot of space and a view that he can see. Your eyes look sick and tired, ye poor thing, she said to Hannah. Have a little drink and put some powder on your face.

She put on her Boxer coat, the richest one amongst them with embroidery so thick you could taste it on your tongue.

Eve, said Hannah softly, and she touched her sweeping by her. Eve, she said gently, but Eve did not hear.

Eh? she said. Eh? Will ye tie the sash up for me? I've ordered supper in his room and the best wines in the place.

She turned her head this way and that and laced the

buttons over. Her hair lay smooth and close in the glass, with curls around her face.

We'll have a drink in Martin's room, she said when she was ready. He could eat only toast and an egg, but she would have the best champagne. The best white wine and the best red wine and the roses she'd brought laid here and there on the cover. Her colour ran high and she laughed like a girl when she set the cloth to her liking. We're all of us hungry, she said as though it made them one. O my dark Rosaleen, she sang high, and she poured the wine into the glasses. Do not sigh do not weep! The priests are on the ocean green, they march along the deep. Now, Hannah, will you sit down and have your drink here? The white meat, the best meat, it was none of it too fair.

And Eve sang out: There's wine from the royal Pope, upon the ocean green! And Spanish ale shall give you hope, my dark Rosaleen!

Skipping and dancing and jigging she went in the room, laughing with the wine in her face, serving their plates out and carrying them hither and yon. Bird for Hannah, and the pure soul of a lobster out of his scarlet shell and into Martin's mouth.

Ha, ha, she said, ye didn't expect that, did ye, Martin? And git on with ye, and git out with ye, when he smiled into her face.

In the end she had the *propriétaire* in to drink the Château Yquem with them. She was all of a flutter and stir, and shaking with laughter because of his presence. She could not say his name fast enough, and hold it up clear as light in her glass to be toasted. Ye've been so good to my nephew, with a flutter and frenzy that filled her cup to overflowing.

You've been so good to my nephew, she said, and there they sat in his room with the golden bottles pouring. She must rouse their spirits and cheer them, and send them drunk to bed. You've been so good to the lamb I love, and her high gay voice ringing out in laughter. O wha will shoe my bonny foot? And wha will glove my hand? And wha will bind my middle jimp wi' a lang, lang linen band?

Monsieur Fleury shook with laughter, but he could not take his eyes from Martin. Whenever he drained his glass, he paused to stroke Martin's hand.

I've never seen anything like the literary, said Mr. Fleury, and Eve leaned over to fill his glass to the brim. She stood on her jigging feet, bubbling over with laughter.

Ah, the literary! she said. Git on with ye, Mr. Fleury! She could not stand still in her wild rejoicing.

Look at Mr. Sheehan laughing here, said the *propriétaire* as he lifted his glass. I like the literary the best of them all.

But Eve's eyes went suddenly close and small in her face. She filled up her own glass, but then she set the bottle down and looked around at Hannah.

I'm a literary woman myself, she said. Perhaps no one took the trouble to tell you.

Oh, it's easy to see you're a woman with a mind, said Mr. Fleury respectfully.

Oh, is it? said Eve with her smile stricken on her. Oh, is it really? She sat suddenly down in a chair, and You Frenchmen are all alike, she said. You like your women to be fools. The more whining and pathetic they seem, the more they suit your taste.

She broke into laughter again, but her hand was shaking. She could speak as she liked, for Martin knew little of French and saw naught but her quivering smile. He lay in his bed, contented, watching the faces around him. His countenance was filled with peace and grace.

If a woman with a mind I am, said Eve bitterly. Then I should have a doctor up here to tell me what to do for my nephew until he gets well. I should hear from his own lips what medicines he must have and what quantities to be given. A mistake might be made, for young people want their rest and their sleep, and if the patient is quiet, then they can get it. Needles, pills, drugs, in the hands of the young, are a madness. It's as easy to give an overdose as to put your lipstick on when you hear the doctor coming down the hall.

For Mrs. Sheehan here, said Eve, and her mouth turned sour on the name, has had so much on her mind for a gay young creature that she might fall into error. It's easy to give two pills instead of one when the patient's restless. They shake out so easy in your hand and they slide away so easy.

The doctor wrote everything out, said Mr. Fleury. He looked grievously into the drained depths of his glass.

Ah, but when you wake up tired at night, said Eve with her smile between them, you do it without knowing it. You tip up the bottle of stuff to congeal the blood three times instead of the once the doctor's written. It makes the heart beat slower. If you put in enough, the heart won't beat any more at all.

Then have another bottle on me! said Mr. Fleury, for his mind was on the drinking. Bottle in any shape or way meant taking the cool clear liquid down. We'll have one more on me, and Mr. Fleury stepped to the door, but Eve's humour had perished.

We'll do nothing of the kind, she said, we'll get to bed like honest people. I'll not have ye keeping my nephew awake all night with your drunken ways.

Hannah lay still on the floor with the blanket drawn over her. There was a breath of frost through the open window, and the night was black without. I am happy said Martin's voice above her, I am happy, and she heard him sigh for sleep. Under the one roof, the three of them. Under the one roof, with Eve behind her own door on the other side of the hall.

And *know that we by divine impulse,* Hannah was thinking as she lay watching the dark in the window, *for the salvation of Our soul, and of the souls of Our ancestors and of Our heirs, and for the honour of God, and the exaltation of Holy Church, and the amendment of Our kingdom, by advice of Our venerable fathers, Stephen, archbishop of Canterbury, primate of all England, and cardinal of the Holy Roman Church; the bishops William of London; Peter of Winchester; Jocelin of Bath and Glastonbury; Hugh of Lincoln; Walter of Worcester; William of Coventry; Benedict of Rochester, and Master Pandulph, sub-deacon and Counsellor, Alan of Galloway, constable of Scotland, and others Our Liegemen, have in the first place granted to God, and by this our present charter, confirmed on behalf of Ourselves and Our heirs for ever.*

But the door had opened silently in the dark, a presence had paused and Martin's breath ran softly in and out in sleep. Hannah saw the figure step and hark, saw Eve in slippers and gown feel her way across the room. She saw Eve pass the mirror in the cupboard door, and then the door swung back and the stars ran over its face. Eve was picking the bottles of medicine out, picking them out like flowers, one by one. Once her arms were burdened with the great bouquet, the mirror closed behind her: the stars ran back, the darkness fell complete, and Eve moved cautiously out into the hall.

CHAPTER XL

Um-um-um-um, said Martin, as though he were tasting something good. Look what Santa Claus is bringing!

Eve laughed gaily in her throat, chuckled and laid down the books beside him on the bed: Trollope, and Pickwick, and an anthology of poetry.

The morning was in as fresh and clear, as brilliant as though some veil had been torn from their sight. Outside were the yellow leaves of the boughs, and the changing foliage on the mountains.

I've been reading ballads, said Eve as she sat down in her dressing-robe and lit a cigarette beside him. I'm no' the Queen of Heaven hie come to pardon ye your sin. If Hannah would tie up the manuscripts in a parcel, she said smiling genially at them, I'll put them in my bag and take them off with me. And if ye've some of your own poems in duplicate, Martin, I'll take them along because I want your work to be in.

The light went out of Martin's face and he tossed back and forth in the covers.

What in hell are you talking about? he said.

I'm talking about the magazine, said Eve with a

chuckle of laughter. I haven't the time. They're expecting me. I have to be off to-day.

But Martin sat suddenly up in bed and tossed the covers from him. He swung his legs over the side, and he said: I'm not a sick man any more.

I'm not a sick man any more, he said. Put that in your pipe and smoke it. Don't think you can set me aside, he said. The magazine is mine.

His white hand lifted and tapped the core of his body.

It belongs to me, he said. Don't fool yourself. If you're going in one direction, then I'm going in the other. The one who gets to a printer first will send the magazine to press.

Where are my clothes? he said to Hannah. And ring the bell for the coiffeur. If you think you've got me down and out, you're making a big mistake. I'll have no one else's name on my magazine, he said, and he sat on the edge of the bed speaking clearly to Eve. I'm bringing it out next month and you might as well resign.

Eve sat on the chair in her dressing gown, and her smile was shaking around her mouth.

Ye talk like a millionaire, Martin, she said scornfully.

I've got money put aside, he said. Drag in your armada. I'll sweep the sea so clean, he said, that all I'll leave you is the brine. He pulled on his socks with his swift strong hands, and buttoned his shirt over. And when you go, Eve, he said bitterly, be sure you take your money with you! It might not be safe if you left any behind.

Give me my pants and my belt, Hannah, he said. But his belly had gone so lean that the belt could not hold no matter how fast he buckled it. When he stood up he lurched on his feet as though the room were falling apart.

Give me my sweater and coat, he said, and ring for the coiffeur.

Eve sat still on the chair, watching him with her small violent eyes while he put on his clothes. He walked boldly across the room to the basin to wash, but his hand reached out for the table and he suddenly sat down on a chair beside it.

I'll see you in hell before I give you my magazine, he said.

What are you mixing in the arts for? said Martin in a moment. What's your envy and gall got to do with doing great things? Your mind's one thing at night and another thing in the morning.

Mixing in art, ye call it? Eve cried out, and her laughter burst out of her wounded stricken heart. Mixing in art when it's me that's taught you everything! Have you ever had any honour or taste or education? Have you ever had anything but what I've put into your hands? You'll bring out the magazine without me, ye say! 'Twould be great sport to see ye do it! I've got ye out of this and that, my whole life's been wasted doing it. I've taken ye back twenty times after some other woman has sucked you dry! But this time I'll leave ye where you are, I've had enough of it! I've found someone of my own country, thank God, who's got breeding enough to be with me!

That's another lie, shouted Martin, and he brought his hand down on the table. But Eve leapt up and came fiercely forward:

America, she said in a sharp whisper, is overrun with the likes of you! Go back there with your maudlin bride, why don't you, and mingle with your kind! Your whole country's full of climbers climbing! You climbing up on me, or on Lady Vanta, or on anyone else who seems somebody to you, getting up on our shoulders because you're small yourself, scrambling up as best you can to see what you can see! And as for your companion, cried Eve, and she turned like a dervish on Hannah. Her furious lip curled back and her voice snarled with scorn. But Martin reached out his hand and seized the carafe of water from the table. It passed Eve's smooth oiled head as she ducked, and smashed upon the wall.

Get out of here! shouted Martin.

I'll not move a step, said Eve with her anger humming. I'll not move a step until I've had my say.

Don't say another word to Hannah, said Martin. His voice was strong and pure, but he sat clearing his throat in his chair.

Ah, to Hannah, to Hannah! mocked Eve. To Hannah, to Hannah! You're singing a different tune than you were six months ago! Hannah was this and Hannah was that, and you'd had enough of poverty. You were pulling at my skirts for love, and wouldn't I let you come back to me, and couldn't you live with me again? You were whining for a good word from me, and me fool enough to pay out money to you in Saint-Raphael and think there was any truth in what you were saying!

It was the coiffeur at the door that brought them to silence. With his little black case carried firm in his hand, he came into the room when Hannah opened the door. He was wearing his clean white barber's coat for he had only to step across the square to them.

Ah, Mr. Sheehan, I'm glad to see you up, he said. And he bowed to the ladies. Then he turned his back on them all and set to clearing a space for his implements on the table by Martin's side.

Seeing you in such good hands, said Eve with scorn, I'll be leaving.

Martin cleared his throat at her words but he did not turn his head.

I'll be going, said Eve. I hope your good health and your spirits continue. Good-bye, she said, and she did not look at Hannah.

Good-bye, said Martin, and he looked straight ahead into his own face in the glass.

The comb went rippling through his hair for a few

moments in silence, and then the bright snipping of the scissors encircled Martin's head.

I'm glad to see you up, said the coiffeur bending over. He parted the hair and laid it back and ran his scissors through. There's a superstition about cutting a man's hair in bed, he said, still smiling. The blades nipped near the temples and cut short the black silk hair. Sometimes we're called upon to do it. The steel ran through and laid the soft thick locks aside. After a man, he said, and he parted the hair on the other side and drew the comb through the depths of it. After a man has already passed on, he said.

CHAPTER XLI

When the man went out of the room, Martin walked to the bed and lay down upon it. He lay still with his eyes closed, resting his long white bones; and in a little while he said: What do you say Hannah. What do you say we pack up and go away.

His hand was lifted to shield his eyes from the room and he said: We might go almost anywhere. We might drive to Italy and see the poet there. He did not speak of Eve, but he lay there with his eyes shaded as if from some sight in the room. I believe in the Father and the Son and the Holy Ghost, he said. There's nothing can change it. I believe in men living like paupers and spending their substance elsewhere. Have a drink, Hannah, he said. I believe in you and me.

He did not cough, but a bright thread of blood ran suddenly from his mouth, went writhing like a living thing over the white of his shirt. Hannah saw his head go back, go back like a flower breaking from the stalk, and she flew crying into the hallway.

Eve, Eve, she heard her own voice shouting in the

door. Eve, bring me the medicines, bring back the medicines!

She ran to his side and ripped up the sleeve on his arm. She saw his skin riddled and bare, his waiting flesh like an island in a swimming sea; she saw her own hands seize the ice and force it down, and she saw Eve in chemise and stockings, dressing to go, come flying in through the door. Eve carried the bottles in her hands, but she cast them down when she saw what had become of Martin. She fell on her knees beside him and tore the shirt from his heart to lay her own hand there.

Hannah, Hannah, my darling, Eve cried out like a woman gone mad. Hannah, will you save him! Can you save him, Hannah, Hannah, my lamb?

His gleaming locks that the barber had cut were lying all about the floor. His breath was coming in little pieces, softly, softly, little by little was his breath coming in and going out. A little piece of it taken in, and then as if he had forgotten, a little piece of it let tattering out again. His eyes were open wide and looking at them, throwing out great dark ropes of appeal with which to bind them close.

For Christ's sake, he said in a minute, for the speech that had served him so well would not now forsake him. I'm dying, he said, and it seemed like an affront to him. I'm dying. That's what's happening to me, he said. It was a strange and a queer thing and he could not accustom himself to the thought of it.

You fool, said Eve. I never saw anyone look less like it.

Hannah stood close to the bed, and his fingers closed on her hand in strength as though his heart were in terror. She stood there staring into his face, helpless because there was no blood coming out of his mouth.

You'll be singing another tune to-morrow, said Eve with a chuckle. We'll get ye an ambulance up to-night and a doctor with trappings. We'll go back to civilization, she said. The three of us. We'll go back and begin all over again.

Some look of mischief came into Martin's face at that, and he said in his strong voice: After all, it's me that won.

Have it your own way, said Eve impatiently. You've worn me out. I'll argue no more with you.

And her hand with the rings on it went shaking like an old woman's hand over his shining hair.

All the leaves of the plane trees had fallen, and the square in the early dawn was cold with its quivering cloak laid low by the wet wind. The deep rushing tide of leaves murmured aloud as they bore him over, and the little alps all around were black with rain. They had put a tube for air in his teeth, and long deep shots of dreams into his veins.

The back of the ambulance fell open and the stretcher slid in on runners.

It's a hell of a day for flying, said Martin. He lay soft and white, like a dove fallen down in distress.

Hannah climbed up over the little step and sat down on the stool beside him.

Look at the pilot, he whispered. A beard like a bard, honey.

He put the tube back in his teeth and drew a great blast through it. When the motor started his mouth turned up and he smiled.

It may make you sick the first time going up, he said.

AFTERWORD

In 1977 I went to visit Kay Boyle in San Francisco, California. We had met once before, at a publication party for her novel, *Underground Woman*, in New York in 1974. But I had been reading her reports from Europe in *The New Yorker* since World War Two and admiring the clarity and fierce, antifascist passion of those pieces. On the evening of the party, I remember clearly my first sight of her seated on the sofa in the Doubleday suite talking to Nelson Algren (or was it Studs Terkel?), that noble, still beautiful head, her slim, elegant, almost fragile figure and the sparkle in her wise, ageing eyes when she greeted her friends and admirers and then me, a journalist who had reviewed her book well.

To the meeting in San Francisco, I brought copies of her early books for her to inscribe: *Year Before Last* was one of them. It was the Harrison Smith 1932 edition, dedicated to Emanuel Carnevali, the Italian poet she had respected and loved and who died a premature, horrendous death. It contained an author's note: "None of these characters here depicted have any connection with actual people, dead or living." At the time of that visit I knew little about her life.

I had not read *Being Geniuses Together 1920-1930*, in which her chapters alternate with Robert McAlmon's in an intriguing composite of memories by two Americans living in Europe in that decade, an autobiographical memoir she has described as a continuing conversation with McAlmon after his death.

Now I have read the Boyle-McAlmon volume and know how misleading the disclaimer was. It turns out that almost everything and everyone in *Year Before Last* is part and parcel of young Kay Boyle's life in France in the late Twenties. In the Afterword to *Being Geniuses Together*, which she wrote for a new edition in 1984, Kay Boyle says: "The pronoun 'I' is an awkward one to deal with, and I do so with impatience; for I have come to believe that autobiography to fulfil a worthy purpose should be primarily a defense of those who have been unjustly dealt with in one's own time, and whose lives and work ask for vindication." *Year Before Last* was written with that apostolic mission in mind, to record for all time the charmed but tragic life of the poet Ernest Walsh. But autobiographical accuracy is seldom the sole key to successful fiction. To know the history behind a novel is one way of increasing its texture and one's pleasure in reading it, but not the only one, and not the defining one or even the most important. It does not take into account the verbal skill of the novelist, the defining sense of form, the imaginative flights away from the "real", the known, all of which bring fact into fictional life.

First the fiction. Hannah, a twenty-three-year-old American girl from the middle west, has left her dull husband Dilly to go away with the beautiful, wild, doomed-to-die-in-five-years Irishman, Martin. Eve Raeburn, Martin's Scots aunt, is the angel for Martin's avant-garde quarterly. Eve's feelings towards the usurptive Hannah, as she regards her, are quite naturally hostile. Hannah leaves them alone and then, from a distance, threatens to take Martin's beloved magazine away from him and edit it herself. Martin has a sick friend, a poet in Italy with whom he is in deep, emotional communion. "For the poet in Italy ... is more my existence than mine", he says.

The history that produced Martin, Hannah, the magazine, the Scots aunt, the Italian poet, and the events of the tragic odyssey of Hannah and the dying Martin in a car laden with manuscripts, in search of a place for rest and recovery, is all put down by Kay Boyle in *Being Geniuses Together*, an account almost as moving as the novel itself. Ernest Walsh, an Irish-American former aviator, had obtained Kay Boyle's address from the Italian poet, Emanuel Carnevali. Walsh wrote to her of his plans to edit *This Quarter*, an avant-garde literary publication which would issue the work of many young writers living in Europe, as well as James Joyce and Ezra Pound. He would co-edit it with a Scots lady named Ethel Moorhead, and he was interested in Kay Boyle as a contributor. Kay Boyle was living in Normandy with her French husband, Richard Brault, whom she had met at the University of Cincinnati where he had been an engineering student.

They were both young when they married—Kay Boyle was nineteen and according to her account they were both impatient with convention and "committed to something called freedom". In 1924 she was threatened with what appeared to be tuberculosis; Walsh sent her a telegram from the South of France offering her the name of his own lung specialist. Her first meeting with Walsh at the Grasse railway station fixed her vision of the poet-editor that would be transformed into the character Martin: "The overcoat itself was a soft, light-coloured wool and he wore it like a supple cloak across his shoulders. He was tall and slender and ivory-skinned, with bold dark, long-lashed eyes, and his black eyebrows met savagely above his nose."

With him was his aunt, Ethel Moorhead, "between forty and fifty, I suppose ... and she had a Scottish clang to her voice ... She had short bobbed hair, with only a little grey in it, and the pince-nez she wore gave her an air of authority; but there was at the same time something like shyness, or wariness, in her small, uneasy brown eyes and her tense mouth." Living near their villa in a small hotel room, Kay Boyle learned of Moorhead's history. She was of a wealthy Scottish family, had money herself, and had been active in the English women's suffragist movement. She had come to Paris because of a small talent for painting and writing. There, at the elegant Claridge's Hotel, she met Ernest Walsh. He was without funds, she paid his hotel bill, they talked of founding a magazine and they rented the villa at which Kay Boyle visited them, and which she was to transform, in *Year Before Last*, into the picturesque place to which Martin first brings Hannah. It was the former home of the French shoe manufacturer who had put paper soles in the shoes he sold to soldiers in World War One.

In this villa Kay Boyle saw Ernest Walsh (he preferred to be called Michael, and she was to come close to this in the novel when she called him Martin) do his characteristic, joyful footwork to the sounds of the flushing of a toilet: "He stood up in his grey flannel pants and his brown suede shoes to do a little dance to the music of it." She learned that he had been born in Cuba to Irish parents and that he was one of those admirable and selfless writers who cared more about furthering the work of others than for his own success. He had a fine tenor voice, he was a merry man for whom "to be gay is one of those postures of courage".

Kay Boyle learned she was not tubercular. In her *pension* near the villa she continued to write her first novel, *Plagued by the Nightingale*, and she and Michael fell in love. Desperately concerned about the possibility that Ethel Moorhead would withdraw her support from *This Quarter*, still, they started off together: "For nothing mattered to me except Michael's beauty and his courage, and I wanted to pay homage to what he was for all my life." This is what she was doing, clearly, when she made him the hero and the subject, the cause and effect, of *Year Before Last* six years later.

Walsh and Kay Boyle set off together "on the run", as she writes in *Being Geniuses Together*. "We did not have a fixed abiding place, for once a hotel-keeper had heard Michael clear his throat or cough there would be no room available ... or we would be asked to move on the next day." Too soon, after many moves, in September of 1928, "the terrible process of dying by haemorrhaging began for Michael". The beautiful pages given over to Martin's dying in the novel are condensed into a few painful lines in *Being Geniuses Together*. Kay Boyle was carrying Walsh's child when he died in October, convinced that the magazine he so loved would continue to appear. The child, Sharon, was born early in the next year. Kay Boyle's husband spent Christmas with her, and then sent her money to keep her and her child. Ethel Moorhead, all forgiven for the moment between them, assisted the young mother and her child: "Out of the greatness of her heart and in her contempt for all official authority ... she registered Sharon at the Mairie de Nice as Michael's legitimate child."

None of this resolution to the tensions of their life together appears in the book. Martin is in an ambulance, he makes a last gallant gesture under the influence of heavy sedation, he thinks they are going up in a plane, and the novel ends. It is as though the still heart-broken author wanted to leave us with the still-living Walsh, as he continued to be alive in her memory. To Kay Boyle-Hannah, Ernest Walsh's fiery and unselfish integrity deserved this immortality.

Even as he was dying she saw him as healthy, finding it hard to understand "how any man could read illness in his face ... His flesh was white, but his voice was lusty, and his shoulders broad and carried straight and swinging from his spine ... She could see nothing failing in him, and when he spoke of death it was another of his fancies that were so far from the truth." This is at once the sentiment of the autobiography, and the words of the novel. Again and again, Hannah testifies to Kay Boyle's view of the man she loved in the last year of his life: "Martin, you have so much of everything ... You have more than enough and to spare of everything, Martin. Of love, and beauty, and of genius, and belief. You have enough of everything to give part of it away."

There is much more than certifiable autobiographical echoes in this delicate, elegant novel. There is the portrait of Lady Vanta, the fraudulent, selfish, cowardly and pretentious lover of literature who flees before the spectacle of Martin's dying. There is Kay Boyle's stylistic accomplishment of creating in Hannah a self-effacing presence in the novel, in the face of bigger, or domineering, or verbose, or monied or cruel women who are attracted to Martin or to his friends, all of them eventually dissolved before Hannah's single-minded, youthfully determined will to keep her beloved alive.

Once before, in her first novel, *Plagued by the Nightingale* (preceded only by a collection in 1929, *Wedding Day and Other Stories*), Kay Boyle dealt with her early life in France. Chronologically it precedes *Year Before Last* and was written two years before the novel at hand. It is a record of her experiences as a young American girl (Boyle here becomes Bridget who is later to become Hannah) brought to France by her husband Nicholas to live with his wealthy, numerous, stingy family. Kay Boyle's re-creation of the family, in gentle, sensitive, almost poetic prose, is the novel's main achievement. Bridget at first encounters the family uncritically, eagerly, and then slowly grows aware of their narrow, bigoted ways. Still, her view is full of unusual understanding, even compassion for one so young. She is, in character and sensibility, Hannah's precursor, for, since the girl Bridget, the woman Hannah has grown in understanding and undaunted devotion. She has learned to seize what she wants and loves, to defend with passion the man she believes in. She has become a deeply loving woman whose every utterance reveals an extraordinary awareness. She understands expatriation and its costs: "It was a terrible thing, thought Hannah, the sun that drew people from their own lands and set them off in isolation. In this part of the country every foreign ear was cocked for the sound of English, and when strangers found others who spoke their tongue they did what they could to move closer together." To Martin, she defines love: "I knew that love is narrow as a coffin. It is not wide and warm, she said, like—like Whitman's love. It casts everyone else out. It is sharp and pointed, like a thorn." And Kay Boyle, looking at her self-heroine and Walsh-Martin, writes memorably of their kiss: "Their mouths fell upon each other in famine."

The texture of the novel is the texture of Hannah's sensibility. She watches Martin, smiling and dancing, without money yet courageous and gay, "at a time when bread and butter would make traitors of us all". She admires Martin and loves life, her dogs, even the food she so lovingly prepares for them to share: "In the roasting pan on the timber, the bones of the pigeons sizzled and snapped as she carved them in two."

In 1932, when she was thirty, and six years after Walsh died, Kay Boyle published this novel of her younger self. We are lucky to have it available to us again after so long, to relish its gentle passions, its extraordinary example of selfless devotion, its youthful hymn of praise to the pure, selfless literary life that Martin exemplifies. Most of all, it is fine that, after more than fifty years of quiescence, *Year Before Last* rises again to fulfil what Kay Boyle has reminded us is the true purpose of autobiography, "a defense of those who have been unjustly dealt with in one's own time, and whose life and work ask for vindication". *Year Before Last* is Kay Boyle's vindication for herself and Ernest Walsh, the doomed young poet and editor who the world and fortune stepped upon, like, in her image, the great feathers of the peacock which are trod into the dust.

Doris Grumbach
Copenhagen, 1985

The first Virago Modern Classic was published in London in 1978, launching a list dedicated to the celebration of women writers and to the rediscovery and reprinting of their works. While the series is called "Modern Classics" it is not true that these works of fiction are universally and equally considered "great," although that is often the case. Published with new critical and biographical introductions, books appear in the series for different reasons: sometimes for their importance in literary history; sometimes because they illuminate particular aspects of women's lives, both personal and public. They may be classics of comedy or storytelling; their interest can be historical, feminist, political, or literary. In any case, in their variety and richness they promise to confuse forever the question of what women's fiction is all about, while at the same time affirming a true female tradition in literature.

Initially, the Virago Modern Classics concentrated on English novels and short stories published in the early decades of the century. As the series has grown, it has broadened to include works of fiction from different centuries and from different countries, cultures, and literary traditions; there are books written by black women, by Catholic and Jewish women, by women of almost every English-speaking country, and there are several relevant novels by men.

Nearly 200 Virago Modern Classics will have been published in England by the end of 1985. During that same year, Penguin Books began to publish Virago Modern Classics in the United States, with the expectation of having some 40 titles from the series available by the end of 1986. Some of the earlier books in the series were published in the United States by The Dial Press.

Other PENGUIN/VIRAGO MODERN CLASSICS

FANNY BURNEY
Cecilia

CATHERINE CARSWELL
Open the Door!

MARY CHOLMONDELEY
Red Pottage

DOROTHY EDWARDS
Rhapsody
Winter Sonata

GEORGE ELIOT
The Lifted Veil

M. J. FARRELL
Devoted Ladies
Mad Puppetstown
The Rising Tide
Two Days in Aragon

SUSAN FERRIER
Marriage

MARY AND JANE FINDLATER
Crossriggs

MARTHA GELLHORN
A Stricken Field

RADCLYFFE HALL
Adam's Breed

WINIFRED HOLTBY
Poor Caroline

STORM JAMESON
Company Parade
Women Against Men

MARGARET KENNEDY
Troy Chimneys

BETTY MILLER
On the Side of the Angels

KATE O'BRIEN
Mary Lavelle
That Lady

MRS. OLIPHANT
Hester

MOLLIE PANTER-DOWNES
One Fine Day

VITA SACKVILLE-WEST
No Signposts in the Sea

SARAH SCOTT & BARBARA MONTAGU
Millenium Hall

LAURA TALBOT
The Gentlewomen

ELIZABETH TAYLOR
The Devastating Boys
A Game of Hide and Seek
Palladian
The Wedding Group

ELSA TRIOLET
A Fine of 200 Francs

E. H. YOUNG
The Curate's Wife
Jenny Wren

MRS. HUMPHRY WARD
Marcella